DON'T Remind ME

LACEY BURKE

Print ISBN: 978-1-964973-00-5

Cover Designer: Kari March
Editor: Jessica, HEA Author Services
Copyeditor: Editing4Indies

*For every struggling perfectionist who's told their
imposter syndrome to go fuck itself.*

Content Note

While *Don't Remind Me* is a light contemporary romance, it does contain mention of topics that may be sensitive for some readers, including discussion of abortion policy and mention of online and written harassment, including death threats and the threat of sexual violence. Please take care of yourself while reading.

Chapter One
Dani

The profile picture stared back at me from my work computer's screen. Stephanie Beauford's shining smile, shinier hair, and glowing skin practically blinded me as her hands cradled her delicately round and unmistakable baby bump.

She's pregnant.

Something about the fact had shut down my brain, and I needed it to pull itself together so I could get back to being a functioning human. One whose life was in no way impacted by Alec and Stephanie Beauford, no matter how many babies they had.

Let it be as many as they wanted. They could pop out an entire Little League team for all it mattered to me. If the photo was anything to go by, Stephanie was thrilled to be pregnant, and I was thrilled for her.

I was.

Thrilled for both of them. They were good people who deserved good things, and I wanted them to be happy.

At this moment, it just also felt as though my stomach had been shoved into the wringer of a mop bucket and squeezed to the consistency of a limp rag.

"Hey, did word come through about the sponsorship yet?" Robin asked over the wall of my cubicle.

"Meeting's in ten minutes," I mumbled. My gaze snagged on Stephanie's wedding band, and my thumb grazed along my empty ring finger as I tried not to imagine the weight of the cool metal against my skin.

"Who's the hot mama?"

Robin's voice in my ear jerked me away from the screen to find her peering over my shoulder, the bright cherry red of her hair snapping my attention back to the present.

"No one." I closed the profile picture and clicked back to the home screen, but Robin caught the name on the profile first.

"Beauford…wait." Her voice dropped to a whisper as she leaned closer. "Is that *you-know-whose* wife?"

"Yup." I forced my voice even. Stephanie's pregnancy was no big deal, just like my staring at her pregnant photo was no big deal.

Nothing about this was in any way a big deal.

I pulled my blazer off the back of my chair, avoiding Robin's assessing gaze, and shrugged it on before gathering my things for the meeting.

It's not like I wished I was the pregnant one. I didn't even know if I wanted kids, period. Definitely not now. The vise grip around my stomach was only there because—

Robin gave a short gasp, her perfectly lined eyes widening

as her mouth dropped into an O, her whole modern pinup aesthetic only emphasizing the drama. "You had another dream about him last night, didn't you?"

My shoulders dropped with a sigh.

Robin's red pout spread into a devious grin. "You totally did. Was it hot?"

"Hot?" Kelly's head popped up from the cubicle on the other side of mine. "Who's hot?"

"Dani's married ex she keeps dreaming about whose wife is now pregnant," Robin said.

Kelly leaned her arms along the top of the cubicle wall. "Hell yes, what kind of dreams are we talking about? Steam level one to ten. Go."

I narrowed my eyes at Robin. "Why do I tell you things?"

She smirked, entirely too pleased. "Because I'm still the best friend you've made since moving here, and your loneliness overrides your better judgment."

I rolled my eyes but couldn't argue.

"Oh, come on, don't be embarrassed," Kelly said. "We all stalk our exes' new partners on social media from time to time."

"I wasn't stalking her." Which was true. I'd hidden her and Alec's posts from my feed years ago to avoid this very thing. "A mutual friend from college posted a photo with her, and I just…got curious."

The fact that the photo showed up on my feed the morning after I'd had another dream about Alec was just the universe being cruel.

But this was the pattern. Whenever I managed to push aside thoughts of Alec and what might have been long enough to feel like I'd truly moved on—*finally*—my subconscious decided to throw him back in my face while I was asleep, dredging up every ounce of longing, desire, and heartbreak I'd once had for him.

It didn't matter that it was only a dream, or that we'd broken up years ago, or that, from the little I knew about her from college friends and social media, I actually *liked* Stephanie for Alec. Every time I woke up from a dream that featured him —even if all we did was wave to each other across a disjointed dreamscape—those feelings were as fresh as if we'd been together yesterday.

It was like my body remembered what it was like to love him, and no matter how much my brain tried to let go, my body wasn't ready to.

Worst of all was that as much as it hurt to be reminded of it all again, it also felt *good*. Better than anything I'd felt with another person. And a part of me wondered if maybe Alec was my one chance to experience it, and I'd let him go.

"I'm curious if you ever plan to go on an actual date," Robin said. "You've lived in Philly for six months, and so far, your dreams are the only place you've seen any action. Maybe if you stepped up your real-world game, your brain would cool it on the ex porn."

I snorted. "My dreams aren't remotely porn-like." I'd almost prefer if they were. At least then I might get an orgasm once in a while instead of just angst.

"My point stands. We need to get you a himbo to bone. Or at the very least a hot bartender. In my experience, they've got skills—the female ones anyway. I assume the skill set crosses genders."

"It does," Kelly said, inspecting her nails.

Robin snapped her fingers and pointed at Kelly.

"Noted." I stood from my chair, writing pad in hand. "But boning will have to wait until after my meeting. And probably until after the symposium is over, seeing as once the last of the funding comes through, the only things I'll be dreaming about are panelist speakers and venue decor."

Robin flashed her brows. "Kinky."

In her dreams, they probably would be.

I swatted her ass with my notepad and headed for the conference room.

I was the first one there, which gave me time to scan my notes again before my boss and the board member we were meeting with arrived. I could already recite the details of this event better than my own life story, down to the last cent of the budget and minute of the schedule, but being too prepared was the only thing that made me feel prepared enough. Especially when it came to the symposium.

It wasn't the first event of this kind I'd ever planned—I'd helped put together a few multiday conference/fundraisers in the past and knew what needed to be done—I'd just never been the one in charge. The one making the decisions instead of simply executing them. Top that off with the fact that this was HBC's first time hosting an event of this scale *and* the first event I was organizing since getting hired, and I wanted to make sure it was as close to perfect as possible. Not just to prove my boss was right to hire me but because this event mattered.

It wasn't some pointless golf tournament dressed up as charity or a corporate retreat that was just an excuse to get drunk on the company dime. I'd planned enough of those that if I'd been the one playing golf, I'd be goddamn Tiger Woods by now. And I'd rather trust fall with a hornet's nest than coordinate another team-building exercise.

This event wasn't for show. It was a three-day symposium bringing together nationwide experts to speak on reducing pregnancy-related mortality and a fundraiser for HBC's first-ever prenatal health clinic and birthing center.

As a nonprofit, HBC's mission had always been to help low-income people carry out healthy pregnancies, but this was the first time they were going about it in such a direct way. The clinic they aimed to build—*we* aimed to build—would provide comprehensive care to those who couldn't otherwise afford it. And the project couldn't move forward if this symposium didn't raise enough cash.

As the new marketing and events manager, it was my job to ensure it did. And that couldn't happen if we didn't secure this final sponsor.

Laughter came from the hallway, and through the glass walls of the conference room, I spotted Talia and another woman approaching.

"Oh, Dani, wonderful," Talia said as they walked through the door. Her smile shone as brightly as her yellow blazer against the deep brown of her complexion. It was a genuine smile too. One I was still sometimes surprised to see from HBC's chief communications officer and my boss. Affection hadn't exactly been a quality of many of my former supervisors.

I stood as they rounded to my side of the long table, and Talia gestured to the shorter white woman beside her. She looked older than Talia by a decade or so, in her fifties maybe, and carried the confidence every one of those years afforded her. "This is Jillian Matice, a member of our board whom I don't believe you've met."

I extended my hand to Jillian. "A pleasure to meet you."

Jillian offered a warm smile as her manicured hand gripped mine in a firm shake. "The pleasure's all mine. Talia has been raving about you," she said with a wink.

My chest tightened, nerves overwhelming any pride the praise might have brought. I tried to hide them with my own smile. "We're so grateful for your help with the symposium."

"You haven't heard the half of it," Talia said, crossing her arms with the triumphant look of a negotiator who'd just closed a deal. "Jillian's committed Matice Enterprises as a full sponsor for the event *and* has generously offered up her new restaurant to cater the whole thing."

The relief rising in my chest took a hard left and crash-landed somewhere around my spleen. "That's…" No words came. My brain was too busy cataloging what a change in caterer meant for my production schedule.

The menus would need to be updated, for starters. Which would require adjusting the dinnerware order, redesigning the place cards, and probably adding the restaurant's branding. That had the potential to be a whole thing in itself, depending on the branding style. The website would need to be updated, along with the invitations and email correspondence…and at least a dozen other things.

"Wow. Thank you so much," I finally managed, hoping my voice didn't sound as tense as every one of my muscles felt.

It wasn't that I was ungrateful. The offer *was* generous, and we'd been waiting for this sponsorship. But the catering detail was unexpected, and with my stress about this event already wrapped around my neck like a choker, the only thing I wanted to do now was turn back to my notepad and write out a dozen new lists.

I tightened the grip on my pen.

"I'm thrilled to do it," Jillian said. "My chef is too good not to show off, and this clinic is too important to not get built. We'll swing by the restaurant after lunch so you can meet him."

"Lunch?" I looked at Talia.

She nodded toward the door. "Come on. I'm buying. We deserve to celebrate." She raised her eyebrows knowingly at my hesitation, and I forced in a deep breath.

I rarely left the office for lunch, usually opting to eat at my desk to get more work done. Once a week or so, Robin managed to drag me away from my computer to eat with her and Kelly in the courtyard, but never for more than twenty minutes.

I knew how it sounded, but I didn't think of myself as uptight or compulsive, and I'd never been this rigid at any of my corporate jobs. I just also hadn't cared about those jobs. Not like I did this one, where I had a boss who both valued and believed in me, a reason to raise money other than lining already rich pockets, and a place I could finally see myself settling into for the long term.

A place I could belong.

If I failed, I might lose it all. And who knew if I'd ever find something as good again.

Jillian led the way out of the conference room, looking like she owned the building in her tailored dress. Talia waited for me by the door as I gathered my things, the stillness of her presence a stark contrast to the tornado in my chest.

Her hand landed on my forearm as I passed, and she gave a light squeeze. "You got this," she whispered.

The confidence in her tone bolstered me enough that my shoulders eased down an inch. I gave a firm nod. I'd been here long enough to know Talia didn't believe in things blindly. She believed in what she had cause to, and right now, she believed in me.

I was determined to prove her right.

———

Jillian insisted on paying for lunch. I had a feeling she insisted on a lot of things and that she usually got her way. I admired that about her. She knew what she wanted and what it took to get it, so that was what she did.

She and Talia did most of the talking throughout the meal, catching up like old friends, laughing loud enough to turn heads across the café's patio. Their easygoing dynamic eased the tension from my muscles, and before long, I was laughing along with them.

By the time we strolled up to the sleek stone exterior of Jillian's restaurant in Rittenhouse Square, my body was loose in the way that came after a cocktail or two despite drinking only water at lunch. I'd even released any apprehension about the change in catering plans. Hell, it might make my job easier. I'd have direct access to the chef in a way I wouldn't have with the hotel's catering operation, and Jillian would ensure we got everything we needed.

This would be good.

My skin cooled slightly as we stepped under the shade of the restaurant's black awning. Its starkness was softened by the green plants hanging off the second-story balcony, balancing the whole look in a classic yet feminine way.

"Welcome to Ardena," Jillian said as she held open the door for us.

My breath caught as we walked into a carefully crafted wash of color. "This is lovely," I said.

The dining room was surprisingly large for this area of the city, made to feel even bigger by the high floor-to-ceiling windows. Rich earth-toned fabrics warmed the space, while eclectic lighting, colorful paintings, and hanging plants made it feel almost cozy. Adding to that vibe was the lounge area that divided the dining room from the bar. Two decadent-looking blue velvet couches faced each other in the center, inviting people to sink into them. The whole thing was distinctly Jillian —tailored and sophisticated while managing to be uniquely grounded.

"Thank you. I'm really quite proud," she said, taking in the space as if seeing it for the first time. Her eyes lit up when they reached the bar. "And this…" She waved her hands toward the far end of the sleek white countertop where a man in loose black pants and a white tee was bent over a notepad. "This here is the real gem," she said as she guided us toward him.

I couldn't make out much of him aside from him being white with short brown hair, broad shoulders, and a faint scruff of beard lining his jaw. Still, it was enough to send a flutter of nerves through my stomach that was nothing like the anxiety I'd felt at the office.

Robin wasn't wrong about me needing to date, and I was suddenly painfully aware of how long it'd been since I'd interacted with a man I found attractive.

"I'd like to introduce you to the man behind the magic," Jillian said.

He straightened from the bar, revealing his tall frame, his T-shirt pulling tight across his chest. Sharp blue eyes collided with mine, and I held my breath.

He was *very* attractive. And painfully my type. Brown hair, blue eyes, and just a hint of gruffness. Like Alec.

A lot like Alec, actually.

Something tugged beneath the fluttering in my stomach. A tickle like déjà vu but not quite.

"Jase," Jillian said. "Meet Dani Mills, your new partner in crime."

My stomach dropped at his name as recognition slammed into me with the force of a speeding car.

No.

"Dani, meet my executive chef…"

This is not happening.

"Jase Beauford."

All the air fled my lungs as I held his startling blue gaze, and for a second, I was looking into the eyes of my past.

Beauford.

As in Alec Beauford.

As in my ex-boyfriend Alec Beauford.

My ex-boyfriend who I could not stop dreaming about and who happened to have an older brother named—you guessed it —Jase.

This is not happening.

But it was. Because looking back at me was none other than Alec's brother.

Alec, who I wanted nothing more than to shove to the furthest recesses of my mind and forget all about so I could stop being haunted by his smile and his handsome face and the perfect cut of his jaw. A jaw that was apparently some sort of arousal trigger for my brain because here I was, staring at the very same and equally handsome jawline of his brother, imagining running my hand along its edge.

If I could have smacked myself in the face without raising alarm bells for the other three people here, I would have. There could be no imagining. No anything.

This was Alec's brother. *His brother*, who I now had to work closely with for the next three months if I had any shot of pulling this event off.

How is this happening?

Any semblance of ease I'd managed to find over lunch disintegrated as my anxiety roared back to life more violently than a hurricane.

Three months of Alec's brother.

Shit.

Chapter Two
Jase

A BEAUTIFUL WOMAN was staring at me, and I couldn't tell if she was pissed off or terrified.

At first, I thought maybe she was checking me out, but then her whole body went tense, her fair skin growing paler as her blue-green eyes went huge, and…was she shaking?

"Nice to meet you," I said with a nod to her and the other woman beside Jillian, trying to come across as both professional and nonthreatening. Not a balance I usually had to achieve, but then again, I couldn't remember a woman ever looking at me like I'd kidnapped her beloved pet goldfish, filleted it in front of her, then served it to her as sushi.

Maybe the women were unsatisfied customers Jillian was trying to win over. My shoulders tightened at the thought. If someone's experience here had been terrible enough to warrant the owner make it up to them, I'd failed at my job.

Dani lifted her mouth into what could only be classified as a smile in the broadest sense of the term and gritted out, "You too," before dropping her eyes to the barstool in front of her.

I swung my gaze to Jillian for an assist. Or a clue as to what the hell was going on. "Partner in crime for what?" I asked.

My boss lifted her chin a fraction, a glint in her eye, and I knew right then I would hate whatever came out of her mouth next.

"Talia and Dani work for the Healthy Birth Coalition of Philadelphia, and they're putting together a fundraiser. I've volunteered us to cater it."

My brows shot up, and I fought to keep my voice neutral. "Did you?"

Dani glanced at me from beneath dark lashes.

"And when is this happening?" I asked.

"September," Jillian replied.

My jaw flexed. "This September?"

Jillian raised her chin higher, nose practically aimed at the fucking ceiling as if daring me to challenge her. "That's right."

I nodded, forcing my grimace into a smile as fake as Dani's had been. "I see."

Tension clung to the silence between us like static about to crack. Finally, the other woman cut in.

"You know, Dani and I should probably get back to the office," she said, laying a hand on Jillian's arm. Jillian's combative posture melted as she turned to the woman. "We can't thank you enough for all you're doing for the symposium." Then she nodded to me. "You too, Chef."

Her smile seemed genuine, and it was almost enough to pierce through the frustration simmering beneath my skin. Frustration I think she saw, because she wasted no time giving Jillian a hug and turning for the door.

Dani was right behind her, but Jillian stopped her before she could make her escape.

"Oh, Dani! Why don't you swing by on Monday? Jase will be here, and you two can start planning out the menu. I know there's no time to waste."

I muffled a snort. The moment we lost our audience, I'd be addressing a thing or two with my boss.

Dani gave a tight smile, looking almost pained. "Sounds good," she mumbled as she tucked a long strand of dark hair behind her ear. Her gaze lifted to mine for a second before dropping to the floor, and she hurried after her colleague.

I waited until the door swung closed behind her, then pinned my full attention on Jillian and crossed my arms over my chest.

She flashed me a look of innocence, then spun on her heel and headed for the stairs to her office, shoes clacking on the hardwood with each step. I rounded the bar and weaved through the tables after her.

"Jillian."

She waved her hand over her shoulder as she climbed the stairs. "No need to thank me, Jase. Your enthusiasm is thanks enough."

I took the stairs two at a time. For someone so small, she was alarmingly quick. "This isn't what we agreed, Jillian."

"And what did we agree?"

I crested the top step and followed her into the office across from the staff room, my hands landing on my hips as she took a seat at her desk.

"We agreed that as long as we turned a profit, I'd have the final say in how we run things. We've been in the green for five months."

"And you did an impressive job getting us there so quickly," she said as she neatened a stack of papers that were already neat.

"I also never signed on for a catering gig."

"Which is why you're so fortunate to work for a brilliant woman like me who did it for you. You're welcome."

I squeezed my eyes shut, pinching the bridge of my nose to fight off the headache slowly but surely piercing my brain and shredding the last of my sanity with it.

"I thought you'd be thrilled about it," Jillian added lightly, "seeing as we also agreed I would fund your restaurant concept of choice once we hit our goals here. The word of mouth this kind of event can generate could be the boost we need to get us there."

"It could also sink us." My hand dropped to my side. "Do you have any idea how hard it is to pull off a catering gig of this scale? And do well? With a crew our size?"

"Then it's good I have such an excellent chef to do it."

I brushed off the attempt at flattery. "Are they even paying for this, or is it all out of pocket for us?"

"They have an allotted food budget for the event, and anything beyond that I'll cover personally. Ardena's accounts won't be touched."

Oh good, so it was just her *personal* finances I had to worry about. I took a step forward. "Jillian—"

"Jase." I came up short as she turned in her chair to face me, the lightness gone from her voice. "It's a fundraiser for an organization I believe in, doing work that matters. This is important to me. I want them to have the best, and that's you."

My shoulders sank, chest collapsing on a sigh.

I didn't want to do this. It felt last minute and impulsive, and it deviated from the focus I'd set for the restaurant for this year. A focus I *knew* would get us where we wanted to be.

Was this possible? Yes. Assuming that Dani girl knew what she was doing, which, based on our meeting, I was far from convinced of.

But Jillian had already given me a lot she hadn't needed to —the kind of freedom and control over her restaurant that most people would never let go of, no matter how good the chef. Plus, she was promising more. A restaurant of my own. A promise she'd shown every indication of keeping.

And when it came down to it, she *was* the boss, and no matter how patient her words, she wasn't asking.

"Fine," I grumbled.

A smile lit up her face.

"But," I said, holding up a finger, "I get final say on the menu. If we're doing this, we're doing it right. Nothing bacon wrapped." I counted off on my hand. "Nothing stuffed. Absolutely no 'puffs' of any kind."

Jillian nodded along earnestly. "Agreed. I trust your judgment wholeheartedly. I won't get involved." I raised a brow, and a corner of her mouth quirked. "Any *more* involved."

I gave it a week until she was whispering appetizer suggestions in Dani's ear.

"I'm going to get your restaurant ready for a successful dinner service now," I said, turning for the door. "I'd appreciate it if you didn't commit us to cater any other high-profile events in the meantime. No royal weddings, please."

"So just regular ones, then?"

I shook my head, lips tugging up despite myself, and headed for the stairs. One thing I'd never have to worry about while working for Jillian was things getting too predictable.

Halfway down the hall, my phone buzzed in my pocket. I paused and stared at the name on the screen.

This was the second time my mom had called today. If I ignored her again, she'd either give up until tomorrow or call another four times, probably in the middle of service. Either option would mean having to listen to her go on about how I never make time to talk to her, which would either spiral into her heavily implying I had a drug problem (based on nothing whatsoever) or insisting my life was falling apart without Gabby in it. Sometimes she managed to do both in one go.

Most of the time, I was glad to be back living in the US, but a six-hour time difference and international calling fees sounded like heaven right now.

I ducked into the staff room and closed the door behind me before leaning against one of the lockers and answering. "Hey, Mom."

"Oh, there you are. I thought I was going to have to keep calling. You hardly ever answer."

"Yeah, sorry. Just working a lot."

"Your brother works a lot and still manages to answer my calls."

I let my head fall back against the locker, welcoming the dull thud against my skull. I doubted she called Alec in the middle of his workday at whatever insurance company he was at, but sure. "Yeah. Sorry."

"I just worry about you. You haven't been home in a while, and Alec said he's hardly heard from you. We just wonder what you've been up to—"

"I know, Mom," I said, forcing my voice even as I reeled in my patience. She wasn't wrong that I hadn't been home in a while, and I tried to remind myself this was coming from a place of love. "I'll try to find a time to visit, but I have to get back to prepping for service, so—"

"Actually, that's why I called. Stephanie's baby shower is in a couple of months, and I wanted to make sure you'd be here for it."

No.

I barely bit back the response in time. It was frustrating enough being compared to Alec over the phone. The last thing I wanted was to be face-to-face with his perfect life so my parents could see all the ways I'd failed them that much clearer.

"Do guys even go to baby showers?" I asked lamely instead.

She scoffed. "That doesn't matter. It's a family event, and you should be there. Your father and I expect it. And you could bring Gabby."

Here we go.

"Mom, Gabby and I haven't talked since we broke up. Almost a year ago." Which was exactly what I'd told my mom the last time she asked about Gabby.

"Oh, I know, but you two were so good together, and she got along with Stephanie so well. I just thought it would be nice."

I was pretty sure Gabby had met my brother's wife a grand total of two times in the two and a half years we'd dated. I'd be surprised if they'd said more than five sentences to each other.

"Plus, you never know when a second chance could come about. I bet if you asked, she'd be thrilled."

"I'm pretty sure she moved back to Boston, so I don't see that happening."

There came a knock on the door. It cracked open to reveal Aubrey's small frame, an inquisitive look on her face. My absence had officially been noticed by my sous chef.

I pointed at the phone at my ear, then held up a finger to let her know I'd be down in a minute. She nodded and closed the door behind her.

"Look, Mom, I really have to go. We'll talk more about the baby shower later, okay?"

"But—"

"I love you, bye."

I hung up and tossed the phone onto the nearest bench, leaning my hands on the cool wood as I let my breath drain out of me. My heart pounded as though I'd just completed a circuit at the gym, and for a second, I forgot I wasn't still an angry eighteen-year-old refusing to go to college.

I wasn't sure my parents ever remembered.

Jillian did, though. So did my staff downstairs, and that was where I needed to focus.

On good food. Good service. Building this place up to the potential I knew it had. Potential I was determined to reach.

I took one last cleansing breath and pocketed my phone, the version of myself I felt good about finding its way back to me as I headed down to the kitchen to do the one thing I knew best.

Chapter Three
Dani

"That's your suggestion? Sleep with him?"

I glared at the smudge in the window's top corner that I couldn't quite reach with my rag and lifted higher on my toes, my balance on the windowsill growing more precarious.

"What?" Robin's voice floated out of my phone's speaker from where it sat on the small wooden coffee table behind me. "You said he was hot, right?"

"Of course, he's hot. He's Alec's older brother. He's like Alec one-point-oh." A slightly taller, slightly broader, more mysterious, and no less disarming Alec. The icy blue of Jase's eyes flashed to the front of my mind for about the hundredth time since I'd bolted from Ardena earlier that afternoon, bringing a shiver with it and a lick of heat close behind.

I wished I could say I couldn't remember the last time I'd felt this visceral attraction to someone, but I could. I remembered far too often in my dreams. The way Alec's own blue gaze pulled me in and made it impossible to turn away. How his smile made my stomach flutter and my skin burn. How his touch—

No.

I would not think about his touch.

"Well then, what's the problem?" Robin asked.

"The problem," I growled, swatting the rag against the window in a last-ditch effort to reach the smudge. It didn't work. "Is that I'm trying to *forget* Alec. It's been almost ten years, goddammit. I should not still be thinking about him. And now I have to look at what is practically his genetic clone for the next three months?" A more attractive clone, if that was even possible.

I hopped down from the window ledge and tossed the dust rag into the bucket of cleaning supplies before rummaging around for a toothbrush. I'd already cleared off, dusted, and reorganized my bookshelf; swept and mopped the floors; and polished the windows of my studio apartment. The baseboards were next.

"I'm sorry, but how is this not your perfect solution?" Robin argued. "Your body has basically been begging for one last ride on the Alec-go-round, and now here's a carbon copy, all rugged and brooding, for you to scratch that itch with one last time and boot it out of your subconscious. Buh-bye Dream Alec."

I knelt in front of the baseboard below the window by my bed, a toothbrush in one hand and a spray bottle of cleaning solution in the other. "I can't just sleep with him," I said as I scrubbed out my frustration. "I have to work with him. And how would that go over with his family? He's Alec's *brother.*"

Robin chuckled. "Yes, I heard. I'm not suggesting you marry the guy. And didn't you say he didn't even recognize you? His family would never know."

I paused my scrubbing. "I'm not sure. It didn't seem like he did."

The look of confusion he'd worn as I stood there, hardly able to speak, certainly gave the impression he had no clue who I was besides the strange woman he was being forced to work with. And he *was* being forced, of that I was sure. He'd been as blindsided to learn about the symposium as I'd been to see him.

"We only met once while Alec and I were together," I explained. At a family Christmas party Alec's parents had thrown over winter break my junior year of college.

Now that I thought about it, I wasn't sure Jase and I had even been formally introduced. There was just an image of him in my mind, standing in front of a wooden staircase across a room full of Alec's aunts and uncles, his arms crossed and eyes listless. His hair had been longer then, falling across his forehead in careless waves instead of the sharp cut it had now, just long enough on top to grip with your fingers.

Not that I'd be doing that.

"Do you think I should tell him?" I asked Robin as I shuffled on my knees to the next section of the baseboard.

"Why would you?"

"To explain why I was the most awkward a person could possibly be today?"

"Or you could just ignore it and move on. For all you know, telling him might make things *more* awkward."

A solid point. And I could totally act normal around him from here on out. It was just the surprise of seeing anyone tied to Alec that threw me off today. I'd be fine now.

One hundred percent fine.

I glanced up to see how much of the baseboards I had left,

then took stock of the anxious buzz still churning its way through my ribs like a chainsaw.

Maybe I'd clean the oven next.

ON MONDAY AFTERNOON, I walked through the doors of Ardena determined to ignore the fact that Jase was Alec's brother. It held no relevance to me. Alec was in my past, and Jase was just one of the many people whose help I needed to pull off what would hopefully be a wildly successful event.

The fact that my apartment was the cleanest it had been in the six months I'd lived there also held no relevance to the situation.

Goose bumps broke out over my legs as the cool air from the AC hit the skin below my shorts. I rolled down the sleeves of my blazer as I approached the bar, searching the room for Jase.

A young woman in a white chef jacket emerged from the doorway at the far end of the bar that I assumed led to the kitchen. Her blond hair was pulled back in a ponytail and tucked under a white cap, and bright tattoos decorated the cool-beige skin of her forearms to where they disappeared beneath her short sleeves. The moment she spotted me, she paused, eyes widening before she turned and hurried back the way she'd come.

Before I could make sense of it, Jase strode through the same doorway, shrinking the room to nothing with his commanding presence. I clasped the pendant of one of my necklaces and tugged it along its chain as he headed my way, ignoring the pounding of my heart.

The smile that formed on his lips was more relaxed than the one he'd given on Friday. It softened his whole face with an approachable ease that caught my breath in my throat.

He resembled Alec in so many ways.

Yet I caught subtle differences in how he moved, in the hardness of his jaw, in the definition of his forearms. It was all too much, too confusing for my mind and body to process.

"Hey, welcome back."

His voice was deeper than Alec's. Fuller. For whatever reason, my brain found that worth noting.

"Come in and sit down. You want a drink?" he asked, hand hovering over the cooler behind the bar.

I snapped out of my daze and slid onto the stool closest to the door, looping my bag over the hook beneath the counter and pulling out my event binder.

"Sparkling water, if you have it? Or tap is fine." Look at me go, almost a complete sentence. And spoken at a normal register too.

Jase ducked down and grabbed a carafe from a shelf beside the cooler, then brought it over to a fancy-looking fountain with two nozzles. He filled the carafe from the nozzle on the left and headed back to where I sat, grabbing a water glass on the way, his every movement fluid. He set the glass in front of me and filled it from the carafe, which he then placed on the bar beside me. Bubbles rose in the clear liquid, quickly condensing the surface of the glass.

"You guys have sparkling water on *tap*?" I asked.

He nodded as he opened the cooler and pulled out a lemon along with a small knife and cutting board. "It's just regular tap water that our system filters, chills, and carbonates," he said, slicing the lemon in half, then into smaller wedges with the ease and speed of someone clearly comfortable with a blade. "Saves us money on bottled products, and it's better for the environment."

He put two wedges on a saucer and placed it in front of me, then slid the rest into a plastic container and marked it with tape.

"Thanks."

His mouth tilted up, and I found my eyes glued to his lips.

Stop it.

I tore my gaze away, snatching a lemon slice and squeezing it into my glass before he could notice the heat rising in my cheeks. Not great, but nothing I couldn't recover from.

"So your fundraiser," he said, setting aside the cutting board and leaning his forearms on the bar. "I thought we should start by reviewing your food budget."

I nodded, lowering the water glass from my lips as I finished my sip. "I was thinking that too." I flipped open my binder and pulled out the budget, along with the menu I'd selected from the hotel caterer, my muscles relaxing a bit as I settled into the familiarity of my job. This I knew how to do.

I placed the papers in front of him. "I know it's a tight budget for four meals, but I was able to make it work with the hotel's menu. I thought we could keep the same food items to make it easier since we know the ingredients are cheap enough."

"We could," he said as he studied both pages. His face stayed neutral, making it too difficult for me to read his thoughts on the idea. "What are the four meals?"

"The first night is a cocktail hour with hors d'oeuvres. Day two includes breakfast and lunch during the speaking panels. Then, the last day is the fundraiser gala dinner."

He nodded along, then studied the pages another minute. "This is actually more to work with than I expected. We can definitely plan out something nice." He flashed me a smile that deepened the lines around his mouth. "Should be fun."

The corner of my mouth rose at the boyish look on his face, something in my chest lifting with it. "Fun? You mean you won't be bored by the lack of scallops or caviar or whatever other expensive products chefs love these days?"

He straightened and folded his arms, a quirk creasing his brow. "Are you implying all chefs are snobbish? Or are you too good for caviar?"

I wrinkled my nose. "Not too good for, just baffled by. I mean, fish eggs? Really?"

Laughter rolled through his chest, full and deep. It set off an explosion of giddiness that settled low in my core.

"But seriously," I continued, my body easing into the conversation. "I don't blame chefs for wanting to play with expensive ingredients. I just can't offer you that luxury here."

He lowered his folded arms to the bar and peered at the menu. "I really don't mind. I like the challenge. Plus, it's similar to a concept I'm working on for a new restaurant, so this gives me a chance to fine-tune it."

I leaned in, mirroring his pose. "What concept is that?"

"I'm aiming for accessible fine dining. I want to serve average people elevated food that doesn't cost three-hundred dollars a plate."

"Isn't that what you do here?" I asked, glancing around the dining room. "Ardena's prices aren't that high, are they?"

"No, but they aren't cheap. Still too high for most of our staff if we didn't give them a discount. And this is more casual fine dining. I want a place where college students who have never experienced more than an Olive Garden can try something new. For the mom working two jobs to be able to bring her kids out for a special meal at a fancy restaurant without having to worry about making rent late. I want to expose as many people as possible to the kind of food that changed my life. Food that I never would have been able to experience if I hadn't stumbled into the back of a kitchen and started washing pots."

Passion spilled from his every word and made it impossible to look away. It called to the echo of longing rattling around inside me that had spent the last nine years searching for a passion as strong within myself, a purpose for what I was doing. It was only now that I was working at HBC that I'd started to find it.

When he realized I hadn't responded, he dropped his gaze, almost bashful. "Anyway. I don't even know if I'll be able to pull it off. It'll take impeccable budgeting and management to keep that sort of operation in business, but…yeah."

"I think that sounds amazing," I said honestly.

He glanced up, his sharp blue eyes catching mine as his lips lifted. "Thanks."

I thought back to that boy at the Christmas party and the listlessness in his eyes. Not a trace of it stared back at me now. Our gazes held, and I didn't feel a chainsaw in my chest or cold clamminess in my palms. My body was loose, my mind quiet for the first time all weekend.

Did I ever feel like this around Alec?

The moment I thought it, my stomach turned.

"I used to date Alec," I blurted, the words spilling from me without conscious thought. "In college. We were together. Used to be, I mean. We're not anymore. Obviously."

Stop fucking talking.

Jase's shoulders jerked back, his spine going rigid as his face went blank. "What?"

I swallowed, my mouth suddenly lined with sandpaper. "Alec. Your brother."

"I know who he is," he snapped, then clenched his mouth shut. A muscle ticked in his jaw.

"Right." I gripped the edges of my binder. "Well, we dated."

He threw his gaze to the side with a sharp exhale of what might have been disbelief, as if he had no clue what to do with this information. I didn't really know either, except that it suddenly felt wrong to sit here talking with him, for him to share these parts of himself with me, and for him to not know the history, however far removed it was, between us.

"Okay," he finally said.

"I just thought you should know," I attempted by way of explanation. "I mean, it's not like it matters. We haven't spoken in years, and he's married and…everything." Stephanie's pregnant belly flashed through my mind. "I guess I just didn't want it to be weird if you talked to him and it came up or—"

"Can we get back to the menu?" he asked, avoiding my gaze. The words were stiff. As cold and detached as the rest of him had gone. Like a door had slammed shut on the warmth and laid-back ease he'd embodied a moment before. I wanted to pound my fists against it until it opened again.

"Of course." I tucked my hair behind my ear, my face heating to about a thousand degrees.

I never should have said anything. Not only was it completely unprofessional for me to bring up my dating history at all, much less in the context of his brother, but now he probably thought I was some crazy ex stalking his family with the hopes of wedging my way back into Alec's life. And at this point, anything I said to convince him otherwise would only make it worse.

"I'm not cooking this."

It took a second for my mind to reel itself in and realize he meant the existing catering menu. "What? Why?"

He slid the paper back my way. "Besides the whole thing being boring and lazy, it's totally unoriginal." I guess that answered my question on what he thought of the idea. His opinion wasn't a shock so much as his standoffish delivery of it.

"Does it have to be original if it tastes good?" It wasn't like I was asking for frozen pizza bites. The menu came from one of the top-rated caterers in the city.

"If my and Ardena's names are going to be on it, then yeah," he said plainly.

I searched his face for some hint of the excitement he'd shown earlier, but all I found was a wall of indifference.

I pulled the old menu onto my binder and skimmed it again, running through a timeline for workshopping a whole new menu. It wasn't like I had much of a choice. Thanks to Jillian, I was stuck with Jase, and I couldn't force him to cook something he refused. "I guess come up with your own, then."

"Any food restrictions?"

"No."

"Good. I can have a tasting ready for you in a week. Anything else for today?"

I whipped up my head to find him two steps back from the bar, his body angled toward the kitchen. "I…no."

He walked away without another word.

I sat frozen as I watched him disappear into the back, struggling to process what had happened. With each second that passed, more humiliation flooded me. In the span of two minutes, things had gone from surprisingly great to Jase practically running away from me.

Whatever hope I'd had of things going at all smoothly between us was clearly scorched to shit, thanks to my big mouth. And now I'd have to relive the humiliation whenever I saw him.

I'd thought being reminded of Alec every time I looked at Jase for the next three months would be torture enough, but this was worse. This was having to see Jase's judgment every time he looked at *me*.

I had to get out of here. Now.

I sprang from my stool and hurried to gather my stuff, refusing to be here when he walked back out. My bag caught on the hook, and I wrestled it free, then shoved my binder inside as fast as my shaking hands could manage.

Fuck, why were my hands shaking? Why did I care this much about what Jase thought?

Alec's brother or not, at the end of the day, he was a means to an end, and I didn't need him to like me or think highly of me to pull this event off. I just needed him to cook good food.

I threw the strap of my bag over my shoulder and lowered my head as I strode for the front door, trying to forget the fullness of his smile as we'd talked and the glowing sort of heat it had blossomed inside me. Or how quickly it had all been wiped away by his blank stare.

If I walked fast enough, maybe I could leave behind the sting of it still lingering in my chest.

Chapter Four
Jase

BAXTER PURRED IN MY LAP, his gray fluffy body stretched out so his head hung off the edge of my thigh, oblivious to the waves of disappointment pouring through my computer screen. Dr. Ohara studied me with the same careful attention he always did during our sessions, and the sensation of being stripped naked and shoved under a microscope had yet to grow any more comfortable. I shifted in my seat on my couch.

"And then?" Dr. Ohara asked. "What happened next?"

"I walked away."

"That's it? You didn't say anything else?"

I shook my head and winced. I didn't need a psychology degree to recognize I'd fucked up. I could even list all the ways how: withdrawing, avoidance, defensiveness. Generally being a dick. It hadn't even felt like me doing it. More like some adolescent asshole had taken over my brain the second Dani told me she'd dated Alec.

What were the chances that she of all people would be tied to him?

And why did it have to be her?

My work was the one place my brother was never supposed to be able to touch me, the one piece of my life I could live out from under the crushing weight of his perfection.

Until now.

"What's coming up for you as you think back on this?" Dr. Ohara asked.

"Anger," I said right away.

"Good. Anger at what?"

I opened my mouth to answer, then realized I didn't know. Despite how I'd reacted to Dani, it wasn't her I was mad at. She didn't do anything wrong, and this situation had to be just as awkward for her. It definitely explained her bizarre behavior when we'd first met.

She probably still has feelings for him.

It wasn't the first time I'd thought it. You didn't act that way about someone who meant nothing to you.

Alec *would* keep a girl loving him years after they broke up. I wasn't even sure any of my girlfriends had really loved me while we were together.

And there I'd been yesterday, thinking maybe there was something between Dani and me. The whole time we talked, she probably compared me to *him*, tallying up all the ways I didn't live up.

I wanted to be mad at Alec, but that wasn't fair either. He hadn't done any of this on purpose. It wasn't his fault he was naturally good at everything. Just like it wasn't his fault that I was a fuckup.

If anything, I was angry with myself.

"I'm mad I still feel this way," I admitted.

"What way is that?"

He knew. We'd been in this place many times before, which was why I knew he would make me say it. "Like I'm not good enough."

The words hurt as they came out, yanking at something raw deep within my chest. I clenched my jaw and took a long inhale through my nose to try and relieve the pressure behind my eyes. Focusing on Baxter helped, my hand drawing steady strokes over his fur. His purrs grew louder, easing some of the sting.

Dr. Ohara's next words were gentle but firm. "You're not a failure for feeling this way, Jase. In fact, the more you catch yourself when you are feeling it, the easier it will be to start changing the thought pattern that has you believing it. But in the meantime, it's important you learn not to take that feeling out on other people."

I nodded, watching Baxter's belly rise and fall, the tips of his fur lighter where it caught the sun. "I know."

I pictured the hurt that had flashed through Dani's face when I'd insulted her menu and dismissed all her hard work. Dismissed her. She hadn't deserved it. Especially not when she'd been brave enough to be honest in the first place.

"So what do I do?" I asked, finally meeting Dr. Ohara's gaze through the screen.

"Well," he said, adjusting his narrow glasses, "you've got two options. The first is you can keep existing within these rigid boxes you've drawn around yourself as Alec's brother, and around Dani as his ex, and keep your interactions defined by those roles."

So basically what happened yesterday, but on repeat for the

next three months. I'd rather shuck oysters all day, every day from now until the symposium.

"Or you can try loosening the lines a bit. Be open to the possibility that more than one thing can be true. That Dani can both have once loved your brother *and* value and respect you for your work now. That one doesn't lessen the other or even have anything to do with the other."

I nodded, liking the sound of that a lot. I just wasn't sure I could do it.

"An apology might be nice too," he added.

A weak smile pulled at my lips. "Yeah."

That was probably a good idea.

"*Ow*, FUCK." I snapped my hand back from the pan sitting on the stove and grabbed a rag, ignoring the throbbing in my finger.

"You good, Chef?" Zach asked.

"Yeah." I hadn't burned myself that carelessly in years, which made it pretty fucking clear where my head was at. My staff noticed.

"He's just nervous because he fucked up last week, and now Jillian's on his ass to play nice," Luis said, getting a snicker from Zach.

The two young guys were across the small kitchen from me with their cutting boards. Zach's tall, thin pale frame, pierced and tatted from head to toe, made Luis's light brown baby face and smaller stature look practically angelic in comparison.

It was true that Jillian had been especially frosty toward me since the Dani debacle last week. The guys had heard bits of the tense conversation from the kitchen and gossiped about it like a bunch of teenagers until word reached Jillian. She didn't know what the root of the issue had been, and I had no intention of telling her. All she cared about was that I fixed it.

It's just an apology. Simple.

Except I had no clue how to go about it. Just say I'm sorry? Was that enough? Somehow, I'd managed to have three different long-term relationships over the course of my adult life and had never once been in the position of making a formal apology.

I was well aware that wasn't in fact a good sign regarding the quality of those relationships.

"What happened with the nonprofit girl anyway?" Luis asked.

"She probably demanded Chef serve raw cherry tomatoes. You know how much he hates those," Zach said.

Aubrey snorted from the prep bench beside me, the bright colors of her tattoos visible in my periphery.

"It's the texture," I said in defense. "I don't like things exploding in my mouth when I bite into them."

"Guess we should warn Chef's next girlfriend not to expect him to go down on her, then," Luis joked. Zach chuckled, and I shook my head.

"Little tip for you, Luis," Aubrey cut in. "If you're biting something down there hard enough that it explodes, the only thing she should expect is a trip to the hospital."

Luis turned to Zach as if searching for confirmation.

"What are you looking at him for?" Aubrey teased. "He only goes down on dudes."

"Yeah," Zach said. "I like things exploding in my mouth."

Luis howled with laughter as I fought my own grin.

"All right, let's reel it back in, please," I said. "Where are you two at with your prep?"

The laughter cut out immediately as the two young cooks lowered their heads back to their tasks.

"Yes, Chef."

"Almost done, Chef."

I had a good crew here even though our kitchen culture was much looser than most of the places I'd worked when I was coming up. That had been intentional on my part, wanting to let my staff still feel like people when they walked through these doors instead of cogs in a machine to be ground down. But there had to be a balance to it, and my guys knew that when service began and tickets rolled in, their only focus was the food.

Aubrey eyed me as the other two set to work, her own cutting board covered with perfectly julienned bell peppers. "Really, though, you good?"

"Huh? Yeah, of course. Just want to make sure this menu is right."

It wasn't about the menu. The menu rocked.

Call me conceited, but the one thing I'd ever been able to feel fully confident in was my ability to cook good food, and I believed in the food I'd planned out for this event. The problem was the woman who'd be tasting it today.

"She's pretty," Aubrey said.

"Who?"

She tilted her head to the side like *oh, please.*

I gave my sauce in the pan a swirl. "What does that matter?"

She shrugged. "Just an observation. One that perhaps you've made too. That's all." She had a sly smile on her face as if she'd figured out some grand secret. Sometimes I wished I hadn't hired such an observant sous chef.

"You can go ahead and shut this line of thinking down right now," I said. "It's not happening. She's a client." And was probably still in love with my brother.

"Well, she's here, so whatever the deal is, it's time to make it happen."

My gaze swung through the door to the dining room as Dani walked past the host stand. She wore another loose blazer, this time with a dress under it that stopped above her knees, showing off the long lines of her legs. Her hair was pulled up, a few loose strands falling around her neck to frame her soft face, her full lips pursed like she was ready for battle, and her eyes— they were anything but soft.

The terrified creature from the day we'd first met was nowhere in sight, and a powerhouse stood in its place.

My pulse quickened as I watched her take the seat at the end of the bar. Nerves tightened my stomach, bracing me, though for what, I couldn't say. Just that whatever it was, I wasn't sure I'd survive it.

Chapter Five
Dani

WHEN I WALKED into Ardena this time, I didn't wait for an invite. I marched straight to the bar and took a seat. I was here to sample some dishes, give my feedback so the menus could be finalized, and get out. If Jase wasn't the one who served me, all the better.

Just his name had my stomach churning with a nauseating mix of embarrassment and frustration, and only partly because of what had happened last week.

So he was weirded out that I'd dated his brother. Or maybe just that I'd brought it up nine years later in the most awkward way possible. My honesty wasn't something I was going to let myself be ashamed of. Neither was my history with Alec.

Yes, the dreams were annoying as hell, and super fucking inconvenient when they dredged up feelings I would rather remained in the past.

But I wasn't delusional. I didn't think Alec and I were soulmates. I didn't believe for a second that if his marriage suddenly ended with no baby in the picture (which, to be clear, I was *not* hoping for), and he magically appeared in front of me that we would be each other's happily ever after.

I didn't *know* Alec anymore. People changed a lot in nine years—I had. And there was no reason to believe the person I was now would in any way be right for the person Alec had become or vice versa.

Dream Alec was a fantasy to me, the personification of my unmet hopes and desires, which was where the real problem came in…because apparently, now so was Jase.

A very physical, sweaty, toe-curling fantasy that had you waking up rubbing your legs together, breath short, just like I had this morning, pulse pounding in places that made you wish you'd stayed asleep even thirty seconds longer to draw it out. I shifted in my seat, neck heating as the images replayed in my mind.

A throat cleared.

I snapped out of my haze, breaths a little shallow, to find Jase standing in all his tall, rugged glory, holding a plate of something that smelled un*believably* good, his white chef coat tight across his chest, sleeves rolled up to reveal his toned forearms. I couldn't even blame my brain for dreaming of him last night. A hot guy who cooked? That was the fantasy of every straight girl I knew.

If only that made it easier to look him in the eye.

Thankfully, he seemed to be avoiding my gaze, which gave the warmth in my face and the heat between my legs time to cool while he set the plate in front of me and placed a roll of silverware beside it.

"Is that a carrot?" I asked, staring at the swirls of color

arranged on my plate into what was truly a work of art, a long orange shape sitting in the center.

"Yes," he said gruffly.

I met his stare, brows drawn. "You want to put carrots on the menu?"

His jaw tightened. "What's wrong with carrots?"

"Nothing. Just when you were going off about only cooking mind-blowing food I didn't envision carrots."

He crossed his arms and lifted his chin. "Try it."

I glared at his smug confidence but rolled out the silverware and cut a piece of carrot, pausing to breathe in the aromas floating up from the dish. It really did smell incredible.

Then the glazed bite landed on my tongue, and a moan practically exploded from my chest. "Holy shit," I breathed, too caught off guard by what was happening in my mouth to process my own words. "This is really good."

I may have heard a huff of laughter, but I couldn't be sure because my eyes had fallen shut, the savory goodness coating my tongue and the subtlest hint of sweetness that lay beneath it the only things I cared about anymore. When the flavor started to fade, I went back for another bite, making sure to get some of every component on my fork. I managed to hold in my next moan, but barely.

"What the hell did you do to this carrot to make it taste so good?" I asked. I wasn't trying to flatter him, but he seemed to soften at the words all the same, his shoulders lowering an inch.

"They're roasted carrots with almond and pine nut praline, arugula chimichurri, and golden raisins," he said. "I thought it could be the first course for the gala."

"Done." This was a thousand times better than the coconut shrimp from the hotel's menu.

He nodded once, then turned for the kitchen and left me to my love affair with my new favorite vegetable.

The rest of the tasting went pretty much the same way. He came out with a dish that looked like it belonged in a museum rather than on a dining table, and I lost upper brain function from how good it tasted. Then he revealed it was made with something mundane like a potato or broccoli stalk, and I lost my mind all over again.

We didn't speak much outside of discussing the dishes. I wasn't sure what to say. He'd made it clear he had no interest in being buddies, and given my mind's unconscious after-dark activities, it was probably best I limited my interactions with the Beauford boys.

I was scraping the last traces of grilled nectarine and burnt sugar ice cream from my plate, only barely restraining myself from throwing aside my fork and straight up licking off what was left, when Jase cleared his throat again. He'd stayed behind the bar while I ate this course instead of heading back to the kitchen like he had all the others, which I took to mean this was the last dish of the afternoon. I tried not to let my disappointment show.

He had one hand resting on his hip while the other rubbed his jaw, strong fingers scraping over his brown scruff. "Look," he started. I braced myself for a blunt remark.

"Oh good, Dani, you're still here," Jillian said from behind me.

She scurried across the dining room in a chic red dress that emphasized the auburn tone of her dark hair and the rose color on her cheeks. With her heels, her eyes were level with mine when she reached my stool.

"Hi, Jillian," I said as I placed my spoon on the officially empty plate. I sighed as I pushed it away. *Goodbye, sweet, sweet heaven.*

"How was the menu tasting? I trust Jase has been on his best behavior." Her tone held a subtle scolding as she flashed him a look. He grunted in response, and I could make out the monumental effort he used to hold back an eye roll. It was impressive, actually.

"It was amazing," I answered, focusing on Jillian. "You were right about Jase. He's incredibly talented."

I kept my gaze locked on her as I said it, avoiding Jase so I wouldn't have to acknowledge the statement as the compliment it was, even though a part of me was glad he was there to hear it. In a way, it wasn't even a compliment; it was a fact. He'd cooked the best food I'd ever eaten, and he deserved to hear me say it once. I didn't plan on doing it again. His ego didn't need the assist.

Jillian gave a pleased smile, pride rising in her cheeks. "Excellent. We'll make sure this is the best damn fundraiser this city has ever seen."

A small knot formed beneath my ribs that hoped she was right. There was no reason she shouldn't be, as long as no one messed up too completely.

As long as *I* didn't.

The food in my stomach no longer sat quite so well.

"Speaking of which," she continued. "I just got off the phone with Talia, and we thought it would be good to reach out to a few of the local media outlets I have connections with to generate some buzz for the event. It would be a boost for both HBC and Ardena, and maybe it could even bring in a few more donations. We wrote a quick press release, but Talia wanted you to review it before I send it out. What do you think?"

"Oh, uh, yeah, that sounds great. You're right; the more people we get talking about the event and the clinic, the better."

Jillian clapped her hands in a flurry. "Perfect. You stay right there, and I'll go forward you the draft." She scuttled toward the stairs, and I couldn't help but grin.

"She's like a kid," Jase said with fondness in his voice.

Our gazes caught, our smiles matching, and for a second, it was like it had been last week before I'd said anything about Alec and taken a sledgehammer to the gentle comradery forming between us.

I broke our stare, turning my attention to my bag to pull out my laptop. "If you could get me the details for the finalized cocktail menu by next week, that'll give me time to start designing its layout while you move on to finalizing the other three."

"Sure, no problem. I—"

"I just sent it. Did it go through?"

Jase let out a heavy sigh as Jillian reemerged, marching over with determined strides.

I refreshed my email. "Got it."

She pulled out the barstool next to mine and shimmied onto the seat as I opened the attachment. I stole a glimpse at Jase, who pressed his lips together and gave a slow nod as if accepting his dismissal before picking up my empty dessert plate and withdrawing to the kitchen.

I watched him go, struck by the odd sense that not all of him wanted to leave.

Even odder was how not all of me wanted him to either.

Chapter Six
Jase

"You planning on doing any cooking today, or have you switched careers to bartending?" Aubrey asked as she walked up to where I leaned against the counter behind the bar. She grabbed the ice scoop and filled the plastic deli container she used as a drinking cup with ice.

I'd been here for the last hour, one ankle hooked over the other, arms crossed over my chest, watching the scene play out in the dining room. I hadn't even changed out of my street clothes yet, still wearing jeans and a T-shirt. It wasn't unusual for me to arrive early to work, but me not doing anything once I got here was.

I shot her a smirk. "Like you don't have it covered in there."

I'd first worked with Aubrey at my last job before coming to Ardena. I'd been the executive chef, and she'd been one of two sous chefs, the only woman in a kitchen of ten cooks. That ratio was still fairly common in professional kitchens, but that kitchen in particular made being a woman ten times more difficult, thanks to the owner of the restaurant being a grade A prick.

Every day, I'd watched the other sous chef—a guy named Christian who thought the snot in his nose deserved a Michelin star—pass off the most difficult and time-consuming tasks to Aubrey, then turn to the owner and whisper in his ear that she was slow and sloppy. He'd mock her for thinking she would ever make executive chef, knowing she would never complain. To complain was to be seen as weak, and no woman could afford that in this industry. Anything I said to the owner about firing the asshole was ignored, along with every attempt at higher wages for the line cooks and more reasonable hours all around.

When Jillian offered me the job to run her new restaurant, it had been a no-brainer. So had asking Aubrey to come with me as my sous chef.

Best two decisions I ever made.

She scoffed as she topped off her cup with water. "Of course, I do. Just don't want you to get rusty. I'm not sure Zach or Luis could handle sous chef just yet if Jillian was forced to kick you to the curb."

I chuckled, but my attention slid back to the couches in the center of the room.

"How's it going?" Aubrey asked, following my gaze.

"Good, I think. Been pretty standard questions."

Jillian's press release from a few days ago managed to land Dani three interviews at the restaurant. She currently sat on one of the blue velvet couches, finishing up with reporter number two. I had no idea whether she'd done this before or was just a natural, but watching her, you'd assume talking to the press was her full-time job.

Her body was at ease, her legs crossed in a way that came off as laid-back while at the same time in total control, and she'd lean in ever so slightly as the reporters spoke, communicating they were in the driver's seat, when really she was the one to plant the seed for the next question with her every response.

I'd watched her strike the same balance with Jillian as they'd worked out the final draft of the press release. How she'd smoothly sneak in and take command without the other person realizing it. A good number of my former bosses had strived for that same skill and fallen short. Something told me Dani didn't realize she possessed it at all.

To top it off, she clearly knew her stuff. Answers rolled off her tongue without hesitation about HBC's mission and the clinic they were trying to build, even touching on Jillian's contributions and Ardena. And none of it sounded stiff or like regurgitated talking points.

Jillian had only been here for the first interview before needing to run. She'd sat behind the reporter and looked on with the same sharp smile she wore whenever she sensed victory.

As for me, I didn't have a real reason for being here. None other than that this restaurant meant as much to me as it did Jillian, and I cared about the kind of press it got. I was just keeping an eye on things.

I nearly had myself convinced.

As the third reporter settled on the couch across from Dani, I started to feel like maybe I had a reason to.

"He looks cutthroat," Aubrey mumbled.

I'd witnessed the other sous chef at our last restaurant outwardly grin as the owner towered over Aubrey and screamed in her face about a misplaced box of rags she'd had nothing to do with. Her baseline for cutthroat was scaling the roof of the Comcast building.

The hairs on the back of my neck rose.

The reporter was a white guy at least my age, maybe older, though a frat-boy aura still clung to the lapels of his pin-striped blazer. His mouth quirked in a way that, combined with his narrowed eyes, seemed almost competitive. As if he was after something he knew Dani wouldn't give up willingly, and it was his job to pry it out of her. A viper sensing its prey with a smug certainty that might have been intimidating if it weren't for Dani's easy confidence.

I hadn't seen that confidence in her the first day we met, but the second she got in her element, it infused her like a vanilla bean did bourbon, and not even this reporter seemed to shake it.

He leaned back on the couch and crossed one leg over the other, resting his notepad on his knee. "Bill Sewick, the *Citizen Daily*. Miss Mills," he began, false charm in his tone. "How do you justify using the money of well-meaning donors to throw an extravagant party in order to gain notoriety?"

My shoulders stiffened.

Dani just gave an easy smile. "The symposium is an educational event as much as a fundraiser. Some of the most notable experts in their fields are joining us to discuss possible solutions to the maternal health crisis we face in this country. With the money we hope to raise at the gala, we'll be able to put some of those solutions into practice right here in our very own city. I believe that's exactly the sort of impact our donors hope to make with their contributions."

"By solutions, you mean this proposed health clinic the Healthy Birth Coalition intends to build in Colwyn? How exactly is a free clinic going to make more of an impact on maternal health than the numerous hospitals already in the area?"

Aubrey leaned in and murmured, "Jeez, what's this guy got against health clinics?"

Beat me, but I wasn't interested in finding out. A sour feeling wound its way around my gut.

"While hospitals provide crucial care for this city, not all have dedicated labor and delivery departments, and many are out of network or simply too far away for a large percentage of the population to access, especially those in lower-income areas," Dani explained. "The HBC Prenatal Health Clinic and Birth Center will be dedicated to offering low- and no-cost prenatal, birthing, and infant care to an area currently lacking those services, so those who might not normally be able to afford access can have it."

"Will abortions be one of those *services*?" He dug into the last word like it was something he'd fished out of the trash.

Aubrey sucked a breath through her teeth, seeing as clearly as I did where this was headed.

The slightest tension pulled at Dani's shoulders, but she kept her face composed as she answered. "Abortion is a medical intervention legal in the state of Pennsylvania. HBC believes all medical decisions should be left to a patient and their physician."

"But will the physicians at your clinic be offering them?" the reporter asked. The snark in his tone grated my ears, and I was about two seconds from marching across the dining room and kindly inviting him to get the fuck out of my restaurant.

Why would Jillian agree to this interview? It wasn't like it served some secret agenda of hers. She outwardly, loudly supported the right to choose.

"The entire licensed and certified medical staff of this clinic will provide our patients with the highest level of care," Dani answered simply.

The reporter gritted his teeth, mouth twisting into a sneer. He either held genuine anger around the issue or wasn't getting the response he was aiming for. My bet was on the latter. "The people funding your clinic deserve to know whether their money will be used to slaughter innocent babies. Will abortions be performed, yes or no?"

That was it.

I made it two steps toward the dining room before Dani's voice stopped me in my tracks. The patient veneer she'd maintained until now shattered like glass, her new tone sharp enough to kill.

"Mr. Sewick, this clinic will be a full-service birthing center providing the same services as any labor and delivery department in this city. Go ask Philadelphia Memorial Hospital if they perform abortions, and you'll have your answer. While you're there, ask them how many pregnant patients they lose to heart conditions each year and how many complications they see from preeclampsia that went untreated due to lack of prenatal care. Ask them how many children in the state were born preterm due to iron deficiency anemia and how many mothers would still be alive if their depression had been diagnosed. And since I doubt you will, allow me to enlighten you.

"More than eighty percent of pregnancy-related deaths in

the United States are preventable, with over half of those deaths happening up to one year after delivery. The prenatal and follow-up care that can prevent these deaths are exactly the kinds of services this clinic plans to provide. The mission—the *only* mission—of this clinic is to *save* lives, both the lives of those who are pregnant and of their babies, unborn or otherwise. And you and anyone who disagrees with our cause are welcome to not donate."

Dani held herself straight in her seat, shoulders down and head high, like a fucking queen on her throne, calmly meeting the glare the reporter was trying to burn through her skull. I was ready to march over and kneel at her feet. Or maybe give her a high five and then shove my finger in the reporter's face before tossing him out on his ass.

I didn't get the chance. With one quirk of Dani's brow, the reporter curled his lip with a huff, grumbling something as he gathered his things and stalked out.

Aubrey chuckled under her breath. "Right, so don't mess with Dani. Noted." She slapped me on the shoulder and headed back to the kitchen.

I couldn't stop my smirk. I was smug and *proud* and impressed as hell.

Dani closed her eyes and took a deep breath, then stood from the couch and made her way to the bar. I pulled two pint glasses from the glass fridge and filled one with beer and one with the cider I'd seen her drinking the other night with Jillian.

When she reached the bar, she plopped into her usual end stool and slumped forward as if all the energy had drained out of her. She straightened as I approached, that defensive edge she sometimes had sharpening in her eye. It morphed to confusion as I placed the cider in front of her, then amusement as I tapped my glass against hers and raised it in cheers.

I paused with the glass halfway to my mouth, watching her. Waiting.

She eyed the cider, then me, the corners of her mouth lifting slightly as she grabbed the drink and brought it to her lips.

I did the same with mine, not bothering to hide my grin.

Chapter Seven
Dani

I HIT SAVE on the changes to the panel descriptions Talia and I had decided on this morning, then sent them to her for final approval before pulling up the panelists' bios so I could start cutting them to size. We were a little over two months out from the symposium, and things were going surprisingly well.

Entertainment for the cocktail party and gala had been booked, along with travel and housing accommodations for the out-of-town speakers. The invitations had been designed, the cocktail, breakfast, and lunch menus finalized, and so far, we were on track to stay under budget.

Why that was all surprising, I didn't know. I'd created a production schedule breaking down each step that needed to be completed and by when, along with detailed checklists for tasks and reminders on my work calendar. I was *meticulous* in the planning of this event, more so than any I'd planned before, but it never quite managed to shake free the worry burrowed deep beneath my ribs that waited for something to explode.

Or collapse.

Or face general destruction of any kind.

I could admit Jase was largely to thank for the budget and menu successes. He'd crafted a vision for the food I hadn't thought possible for the cost he was sticking to, and he'd been the picture of professionalism since that first tasting, meeting every deadline we agreed to with total preparedness and putting me at ease with his simple confidence that nothing he put forth would be anything less than excellent.

It was nice having that steadying force to brush up against, even if our interactions had stayed strictly polite since our shared drink after the press interviews.

That had been nice too. An interaction I stopped my brain from focusing on for longer than a second, or else that weird fluttering beneath my sternum would start up again. That was…not something I needed to deal with right now.

The wall of my cubicle shook with a smack, and I looked up to see Robin walk past, her finger gun shooting back at me. "Save you a seat?"

"Yeah, I'll be there in a sec."

She nodded and turned the corner to the large break room, a few other people following on their way to the staff meeting.

I saved what I was working on and grabbed my notepad, then made my way into the room, scanning the mostly full round tables until I spotted Robin's short red pinup curls and gemstone barrette. I squeezed through and dropped into the empty seat beside her.

"Do we know what this is for?" I asked. We typically had one all-staff meeting a month, and our most recent had been just last week. The calendar pop-up this morning scheduling this meeting had sent intrigue rippling through the office.

"No one I've talked to knows," Robin said.

Kelly lowered the nails she was biting. "What if they're firing a bunch of us?" she asked, switching to the nails on her other hand.

That had been my first thought too, but it didn't make sense. As far as I knew, we were on track for donations, and it wasn't like we had to worry about stocks dropping.

The murmur of others discussing the same possibility grew as the rest of the staff filed in, some taking up spots along the walls as the tables filled, the minutes dragging on as we waited in uncertainty.

Finally, Executive Director Gardner walked through the door, and the room quieted. Talia was with her, along with a tall Black man I'd never seen before. He looked around Talia's age—mid-forties if I had to guess—and despite his impressive height, it was the gun holstered at his waist that caught my eye.

"Thank you for rearranging your schedules for this meeting," Director Gardner said from the front of the room lined with cabinets. She was a petite Black woman with shortly cropped gray hair, who appeared almost comically small standing beside the mystery man. He towered over her by a good foot.

"We'll make it quick," she continued, then gestured to the man who had what I could now clearly make out as a security badge insignia on the sleeve of his shirt. "This is Geffery Fisher. He'll be providing security for the building for the next few weeks. There's no reason to be alarmed." She raised her hands as whispers erupted. "We're just putting a few routine precautions in place due to the recent attention we've been getting online."

The article.

My gaze flew to Talia, who met my eye with a quick shake of her head. *Don't worry about it,* she was saying, but my breathing had already gone shallow.

Just over a week had passed since my interview with Bill Sewick of the *Citizen Daily* was published, along with the two other interviews Jillian had set up at Ardena. The first two had been the nice boost in press we'd wanted for the symposium.

The third one, not so much.

Despite Jase's congratulatory drink, he'd been livid at the *Citizen Daily* reporter, and Jillian had apologized to me profusely for three days after Jase told her what happened. If I didn't know better, I'd almost think he'd been enraged for *me*, but his restaurant's reputation made much more sense.

And while Ardena's mention in the article hadn't been flattering, it was far from the defamatory ire the reporter had spat about HBC, much of which—as HBC's spokesperson—had fallen directly on me.

Maybe the reporter felt I humiliated him at the interview. If the "*fucking bitch*" he'd ground out as he left was anything to go on, he didn't appreciate being challenged by a woman. One younger than him, no less.

Or maybe he really did believe abortion was this evil, hate-fueled thing and I was the epitome of immorality for defending it. Whatever the reason, he hadn't held back, making me as much the villain of his story as HBC. A story that conveniently brushed over every other goal, service, and mission the clinic aimed to provide.

When Jillian had called her contact at the website to demand an explanation, she was told the original reporter set to do the interview had gone into labor and was out on maternity leave, and Mr. Sewick had volunteered to fill in. Apparently, it hadn't been the outlet's idea to go with the abortion angle…but they wouldn't be taking down the article either. Not when it was generating such a strong response.

I hadn't thought it needed to be taken down. Even if it wasn't the message we wanted surrounding the symposium, it was true that all press really was good. Our buzz on social media had exploded in the past week, and most of our supporters seemed more fired up than anything, their enthusiasm for the clinic rising.

Sure, there were incensed people and the expected amount of trolls, but that was the internet. Nothing that warranted security. Definitely not enough to explain the armed guard standing at the front of the break room.

Director Gardner continued in her calm tone. "Feel free to introduce yourself to Mr. Fisher as you see him around. Let's make him feel welcome. And if you have any questions or concerns, you can bring them to me or Talia." Talia nodded at the room with her signature warm smile, looking no more bothered than if Director Gardner had said we should go to her to discuss new designs for staff T-shirts. "That'll be all for today. Thanks, everyone."

I was out of my chair and beelining for Talia before the director had finished her sentence. Before I could speak, Talia said, "Come with me."

She led the way along the edge of the room, slipping past our colleagues still engaged in conversation as they shuffled toward the exit. When we reached her office, she motioned me inside and shut the door behind us, then faced me with hands raised as if to calm a wild animal.

"There's nothing to worry about," she said confidently. "Just a little hate mail we've been getting at the office." My stomach hit the floor, smattering across the beige carpet. My face must have dropped, too, because she hurried to add, "Nothing extreme. But these things can sometimes get worse before they get better, so we want to be safe. That's all."

"But it *is* the article, right? It's because of what I said?" I lowered myself into the chair in front of her desk and gripped my necklace. "I'm so sorry, Talia. I should have handled it completely differently. Not said anything and just ended the interview after his first question. I knew what he was doing, but I didn't want my silence to be twisted into some sort of shame for our work. I had no idea it would get this kind of attention. I—"

"Dani, *breathe*," Talia said as she circled her desk to sit in her chair.

I forced out a shaky breath.

"It's *okay*. I promise. I wouldn't have had you do a single thing differently. In fact, I probably would have said a lot worse myself. I'm proud of the way you represented this organization."

"But hate mail? Talia, that's—"

"To be expected."

My doubt must have shown on my face.

"No, really. We always knew it was a possibility with this project. That's why we included a security guard in the budget for this year. Nothing about this surprised or upset me, Director Gardner, or the board. If it wasn't this article, it would have been something else. It just comes with the territory. It'll die down within a few weeks."

"And if it doesn't?"

Talia leaned across her desk, brows lifting in assurance. "*It will.* You just keep doing what you're doing. Because you're doing a great job."

I chewed my bottom lip, pendant tugging along its chain as I tried to let the words sink in. They didn't get far. Not through the rock-solid worry that had formed a fortress of doubt just beneath my skin.

I'd been waiting for something to go wrong with this event, and here it was. Maybe Talia and the board didn't care, but my actions had led to this.

My only comfort was that the worst of the article had mostly been pointed at me. If things got worse, I could always resign and take the harshest of the criticism with me. Go back to Chicago or Tampa or Baltimore and plan team retreats and annual conferences in the corporate world again. My mother would be thrilled.

Or I could start all over in a new city.

Again.

Just the thought had my eyes burning. I cleared the lump from my throat. "I'll go say hi to Mr. Fisher and get back to work." I rose from the chair, keeping my gaze low so my composure didn't crack.

"Chin up, Mills," Talia said as I turned for the door.

I gave a quick nod and hurried from her office, retreating to the relative privacy of my cubicle, where I sank into my chair and gasped for breath.

I wanted to crawl under my desk and curl into a ball until the loop of worst-case scenarios blasting on repeat in my head dimmed back to its usual volume, low enough to ignore.

The irony was that the one time it had been silent was during that interview. I hadn't analyzed my every response or spent any time doubting myself. I'd just let my instincts take over.

For a moment, I'd thought I could trust them. Even more so when Jase offered me that drink.

Here was my reminder that instincts weren't always sensible. Feelings could lie. I couldn't let them get the better of me again.

This was the first crack in the glass this symposium sat on.

One more and the whole thing might shatter.

Chapter Eight
Jase

Me: At work. I'll call you tomorrow.

I SHOT off the text as I reached the bottom of the office stairs and shut off my phone before slipping it into my pocket. It probably made me a horrible son, but in all fairness, I had already talked to my mom once this week. Any more than that felt like overkill.

Alec probably didn't go more than two days between check-ins. Then again, he also didn't get lectured on what an awful disappointment he was during every conversation with her. Even Dr. Ohara agreed it was okay for me to take some space from my family when I needed it, and I'd taken a hell of a lot more than a week between phone calls in the past. She could survive one more day.

"Jase."

I paused at the door to the kitchen and turned to where Dani sat at the middle of the bar with a paper and pen in hand. She hopped off her stool and rounded the counter, drawing my eyes to her long legs. The skirt she wore hugged her hips perfectly, ending just below her knee, a flash of thigh peeking out through the short slit with her every step.

My blood warmed as images I'd fought for weeks assaulted my mind. Running my hand up that leg and brushing my fingers over the sensitive skin behind her knee. The soft gasp that would escape her lips and turn to a sigh as I inched up her skirt to trail my touch along her inner thigh, see if her skin there was even softer than it looked everywhere else. How her hips would seek me out, begging me to go higher.

My cock stirred, and I forced my thoughts to the ten pounds of raw shrimp waiting to be deveined in the kitchen. Chef pants did almost nothing to hide an erection, and the last thing I needed was for my little brother's ex-girlfriend to see that. Especially when she was the cause.

She stopped in front of me and held out the paper, her blue-green eyes intense with concentration. It did nothing to ease the stiffness in my pants.

"I need you to look over the rental form to confirm the plateware order is correct. I'll be placing it this afternoon, so if we miss anything, you're stuck with what the hotel has on hand, and they may not have enough."

"I already checked it over," I said. "Twice."

We'd finalized the last of the menus earlier in the week, making plateware the last major catering task that needed to be handled until much closer to the actual event. It also meant Dani wouldn't have a reason to be here anymore. I tried not to think about how that made my stomach twist.

"Okay, well, can you do it again?" She shook the paper at me.

I crossed my arms over my chest. "Three times is a bit excessive, isn't it? Or more like six since you've probably triple-checked it yourself. Am I right?"

The blush in her cheeks as she narrowed her eyes told me I was. And while I was all for being thorough, I got the sense something more was going on here.

"I just want to be sure there are no mistakes."

"There aren't. I know because I already double-checked."

Her eyes fell closed on an exhale before she opened them to glare at me. "Can you just check again, please?"

"Exactly what kind of catastrophic mistake do you think could come from a plateware order form?" I asked instead. "I mean, having to use salad bowls instead of soup bowls wouldn't be ideal, but it isn't the end of the world."

She finally dropped her arm and stormed her way back to her seat. "Yeah, well, some mistakes can't be so easily fixed."

I followed on my side of the bar. "What do you mean?"

"Exactly what I said." She slammed the order form onto the counter and slid back onto the stool.

"Is this about the article?" I asked. "Because that wasn't your mistake."

I knew there'd been some uproar online over the health clinic. Jillian felt awful, especially since Ardena's mention had been a blip compared to the pummeling Dani received, but I didn't see that as Jillian's fault either. As far as I was concerned, the only one responsible was that asshole reporter who'd set out to stir up outrage from the start.

I'd never been so tempted to spit in someone's food. Not that he'd ever be welcome in one of my restaurants again, as long as I had a say.

"It doesn't matter. There's still no taking it back." She turned to her laptop and mumbled, "Among other things."

I studied her for a long moment as she willfully ignored me. Then I uncrossed my arms and braced my hands on the counter behind me. "So what happened between you and my brother, anyway?"

Her head whipped up so fast she nearly fell out of her seat. "What?"

I gave a casual shrug. "Why'd you break up? It seems like you two would have been good together."

The words burned my tongue, mostly because they were true. I *could* see them together, taking on the corporate world, living the power couple dream. It was never a dream I'd had for myself, never one I'd even thought about until recently. Even in those passing thoughts, I knew it wasn't right for me.

Not the way Alec lived it, at least.

She rolled her shoulders and returned her gaze to her screen. "I don't see how that matters."

"That's what you were talking about, right? A mistake that couldn't be fixed? I mean, I just assumed, seeing how you're still in love with him and all."

"Hold on," she said, face appalled. "I'm not still in love with him."

"I'm not judging you for it—"

She threw her hands in the air. "I'm not still in love with him! It's been almost *a decade*."

I lifted my own hands in concession. "If you say so."

"I do," she said firmly, eyes blazing.

I had to bite my cheek to keep from smiling. Don't ask me why. Just that seeing her fired up like this sparked something within me that wanted to poke deeper, tear that carefully constructed appearance of hers wide open to reveal whatever burned underneath.

Even that first day we'd met to go over the menu, the time I'd been a complete dick to her after she'd told me about Alec, a part of me had wanted to see more.

I had been a dick, though, mostly because of my own issues, and I wasn't trying to do that again. I sobered my expression. "But really," I asked softly. "Why'd you guys split?" And then, because I liked to make myself suffer, tacked on, "He suck in bed?"

She narrowed her eyes. "No. That wasn't a problem."

Damn.

Her face relaxed, shoulders dropping on an exhale. "I don't fully know what happened. Things were good. *Really* good."

I ignored the twinge in my gut and focused on her.

"And then…" She looked at the shelves of liquor behind me, her gaze far away. "I don't know. He was graduating, and he had all these plans while I still had my senior year to go, and suddenly, it all felt like a lot. I was overwhelmed and unsure of what I wanted, which was the exact opposite of how he felt. I didn't know how to handle it." She shrugged. "So I ended it. I thought I needed space to figure it out. Meanwhile, he moved on, married Stephanie, has a baby on the way, and here I am nine years later still trying."

My chest burned as I listened, and not with the jealousy I'd expected. That I'd been prepared for.

This was recognition.

Her voice held the same insecurity I'd carried most of my life. The self-doubt that was so easy to drown in when faced with the tsunami of unflinching certainty that was my brother.

And I knew what it was like to live with that self-doubt and not be able to shake it.

"I don't know," I said. "Sounds to me like you did what you felt was best for you at the time, the best you knew how. I wouldn't call that a mistake."

Her gaze finally shifted, locking with mine.

And there she was, the burning heart of her on full display, open and honest and *real*. Full of passion and curiosity and a little bit of fear, but too determined to let that stop her.

I swallowed hard. "I'm sorry. For what I said that day. How I acted when you told me about you and Alec. It wasn't okay."

Her brows lifted for a moment before her eyes softened, the corners of her mouth tipping up ever so slightly. My eyes lingered on her lips.

"Apology accepted."

I stepped to the bar and slid the order form my way. Her smile grew as I picked it up and read it over for the third time.

I ignored the way my heart pounded in my chest.

Chapter Nine
Dani

Monday morning rolled around, and as I made my way through the office, it occurred to me what the jolts of energy shooting up my legs and sticking in my chest were. I was *nervous*, which was ridiculous. I was just going to Ardena to drop off some symposium invitations for Jillian, who'd wanted to personalize a few before they were mailed. I'd sent out the rest with the office's mail this morning.

The invitations going out made everything more real. The turning of a corner with no going back. This event was happening now, whether I got the signage, name tags, guest welcome packages, and a hundred other details finished or not. It was just a matter of what kind of experience the guests would have when they arrived.

That wasn't why I was nervous, though.

He might not even be there, I reminded myself as I pushed through the main door of the building into the thick July heat. It washed over my air-conditioned skin with cozy warmth that quickly turned blistering. Hot waves radiated off the asphalt parking lot beneath my feet. The flutter in my stomach only grew with each step.

He probably wouldn't be there. I was pretty sure Mondays had been one of Jase's days off before Jillian roped him into catering the symposium, and now that the menus were finalized, I doubted he'd have a reason to be there an extra day.

But he might.

And that possibility alone was enough to send me over the edge.

The edge of what, I wasn't sure. Just that after our conversation last week, I hadn't been able to stop picturing his eyes as he said, "I wouldn't call that a mistake," or the way the muscles in his arms flexed as he crossed them over his chest. Or his lips —those fucking lips—as he'd smirked at my demands.

I'd imagined those lips on a dozen different places along my body since, from my throat to my toes with some notable stops in between. Just the thought had my stomach clenching and my body growing warm in a way that had nothing to do with the weather. I couldn't remember the last time I'd been this horny.

And okay, not all of me loved that it was Alec's older brother I was lusting over, but it'd been so long since I'd felt this kind of attraction to anyone that a bigger part of me desperately wanted to enjoy it. It wasn't like I was going to tackle him and start humping his leg. I just wanted another glimpse of his chiseled jaw and to see his hands glide across a cutting board.

His hands were…yeah.

I was so caught up dreaming about them that I almost missed the scrap of paper on my windshield. At first glance, it looked like a ticket, but this was HBC's lot, and my car was where I always parked it.

I snatched the folded white paper from under the wiper. Nothing on the outside.

I flipped it open and read the words scratched inside.

My blood froze, my skin going cold. All of me went still except for my heart pounding in my ears as I read the note again.

Then I spun from my car and ran back inside.

THE DEATH THREAT lay open on Talia's desk, the words glaring up at me, tracking my movements as I paced back and forth across her office. Nausea churned my stomach, climbing its way up my throat. Mr. Fisher—Geffery, he'd told me to call him—was here too, discussing the best course of action with Talia.

I couldn't breathe.

It wasn't just the note. It was that it had been left on my car. That whoever left it knew which car was mine in the first place. That they had been bold enough to do this in broad daylight.

Did they know where I lived? Would they follow me home? Try to hurt me?

What about the office? I'd read articles about nonprofits like ours across the country being attacked. Gasoline poured under their doors and ignited with people inside. Stink bombs set off in the ventilation systems.

Shootings.

Was this how those had all started? With hate mail and a note on a windshield?

I shook out my hands to try to get them to steady, but they wouldn't. Instead, I clenched them into fists, pulling in short breaths as I attempted to take in what Geffery was saying.

"There were no other notes on anyone else's car. It does appear as though they targeted Dani specifically."

"Can we take it to the police?" Talia asked, the two of them standing around her desk, hovering over the note.

"We can, but it's not much for them to go on. Even with the rest of the hate mail coming to the office, I wouldn't expect the cops to be able to do anything."

Talia nodded firmly. She was as steady as the brick building we stood in, eyes narrowed in concentration, perfectly in control. I was pretty sure her calmness was the only reason I hadn't passed out.

"Then we prioritize Dani's safety until things cool off." She trained her gaze on me, where I continued to pace in the corner of the room. "How would you feel about working from home until after the symposium? You'll come into the office for certain meetings, and we'll have Geffery escort you to and from your car, but you don't need to be here the rest of the time."

My eyes jumped from her to Geffery and back. "You think it's safe there? My apartment?" I didn't even try to hide the tremor in my voice.

"The fact that you haven't gotten any hate mail there makes me think whoever did this is only focused on the office," Geffery said. "They probably were here this morning planning to do something like graffiti the side of the building and saw you get out of your car. I'm guessing they made a last-minute call to leave the note, then ran. That said, you should stay on alert for a week or two. Let me know if you see anything strange around your place. I'll file a report with the police to be on the safe side, and we can update them if you notice anything suspicious."

I nodded, more from reflex than from comprehension, as

my body went numb. Something landed on my upper arms, and I jumped.

"Dani. *Dani.*" Talia was in front of me, gripping my biceps to hold me steady. I hadn't even noticed her move. "You don't have to do this. We can cancel the symposium. It's not worth your safety."

That shook me a little from my panicked haze. I furrowed my brow. "We can't cancel. We need the money from the symposium to open the clinic." And the invitations had already gone out.

"We'll get it next year. Let things calm down fully and try again."

She was serious. Her gaze was as steady as the rest of her, expression resolved.

A fuse of rage lit its way down my spine. "*No,*" I said forcefully. "You can't cancel because of this. I won't let us be bullied into giving up on the good this clinic can do just because people like Bill Sewick would rather spout ignorance."

Talia released my arms and straightened, studying me. "Are you sure? Because the board would understand."

I shook my head, my body settling somewhat back into itself. "Don't go to the board. I'm sure. I'll work from home. I was just freaked out, but if Geffery thinks it's okay, then I'll do it." I pushed every ounce of confidence I could muster into my voice, my determination enough to suppress my fear, at least for the time being.

It must have worked because Talia's shoulders lowered. "All right. We'll move forward with it. But only as long as you're sure."

I almost laughed. There wasn't a single thing about my life I was sure of. Not my career choices or the number of times I'd moved because of them. Not my decision to break up with Alec and not reach out to him again in the months after. Not my college major, or quitting drama club in high school, or picking clarinet over the flute in the fourth grade. Hell, not even my nail polish selection.

I didn't know if I was sure about this. It was possible I didn't know *how* to be sure about anything.

But that same reckless confidence that had unraveled in me during the interview was mounting within me again, silencing all the voices in my head that were throwing out doubts. Maybe it was my gut, or maybe it was just bad judgment, but if it was what I needed to grab hold of in order to see this event through, then that was what I'd do.

This symposium was happening.

No matter what.

Chapter Ten
Jase

MONDAYS WERE OFFICIALLY my day off. At least according to the schedule hanging on the wall beside where I sat at Jillian's desk.

Then again, I made the schedule, which meant I could have off any day I wanted. I chose Mondays because our hours were shorter and it tended to be the slowest night of the week. But slow for us was usually still pretty steady, so I liked to stop in during the afternoon to ensure the staff were set. If nothing else, I spent an hour or two in the office handling food orders and brainstorming new menu ideas for the coming week.

My mom would call me a workaholic—or she would if she believed I worked as much as I said I did. I was pretty sure she thought I was lying half the time to avoid talking to her and was actually out getting wasted every night.

I could admit I was guilty of using work to avoid talking to her, but I never lied. If I said I was working, I was working.

And yeah, there was a time when I'd partied more, but nothing she would have heard about. It wasn't like I'd ever ended up in jail. She had no reason to doubt me other than the fact that I wasn't the golden one of her two sons. I was the one who chose to quit baseball in the third grade while Alec went on to be varsity captain. Obviously, I was a monster who couldn't be trusted.

I tried to brush off the stinging in my chest and return my attention to the earnings report in my hand.

We'd had another good month. A new high. I was tempted to take a picture and send it to my parents. *See? I'm not a fuckup.*

It probably wouldn't make a difference. Not to mention, I was supposed to be learning to validate my own worth regardless of my parents' opinions. Not exactly easy after thirty-three years, but fuck if I wasn't trying.

I finished with the report, emailed next week's schedule to the staff, then tidied up Jillian's desk and headed downstairs. When I reached the dining room, my body stilled, the space swelling with electricity that tingled along my skin.

I hadn't expected to see her today.

Dani stood inside the door a few feet past the host stand, somehow looking regal in a tank top and pants. Her dark hair was up in a way that looked effortless and flawless all at once, and I had the sudden urge to drive my hands into the strands and muss them up, see how beautiful she looked disheveled.

Until I caught the way her hands were clutched to her chest.

Her legs were close together, elbows tucked in at her sides, everything about her trying to appear small. Everything except her eyes, which were almost as wide as the orb lanterns along the walls as she stared aimlessly behind the bar.

"Dani?"

She blinked as if coming out of a daze. "Hey," she said as I approached, her voice tight. A strained smile pulled at her lips. She was the girl from the first day we met all over again—only, this time, there was no question she was terrified. She uncrossed her arms to reveal a handful of dark purple envelopes. "I just came to drop these off for Jillian." Her hand trembled as she passed them to me.

I placed them on the bar, my eyes never leaving her face. "What's going on?"

She shook her head like she didn't know what I was talking about, but she also wouldn't meet my gaze. "I, um, left a Post-it on the top one with my cell number," she said, pointing at the envelopes. "I'll be working from home for a bit, so if Jillian needs to reach me, she can call me directly instead of at the office."

A slick feeling worked its way up my spine. "Why are you working from home?"

She shook her head again and swallowed. "It's nothing," she said, forcing brightness into her voice. It sounded high and squeaky and fake, and the wrongness of it clashed in my head like a smoke alarm, making my stomach curl. I never wanted her to be fake with me. Especially not when it was obvious something serious was going on. "There was just a note on my car, and Talia and the security guard thought it might be safer for me to stay home for the time being, but they're sure it's nothing to worry about."

My brain cut out at *safer*, my muscles pulling tight as my instincts went on high alert. "What kind of note? Are you okay?"

She clearly wasn't. Her chin quivered and her nostrils flared as she blinked back tears.

Everything in me ached to reach out and pull her to me. I

would have if I was sure it wouldn't freak her out more. The need to comfort her, to shield her, gripped me so suddenly I didn't know what to do with it.

"I, um…" She dropped her gaze to the floor. "I'd rather not talk about it. It's no big deal, honestly. Just let Jillian know for me, yeah?" Her reddened eyes flashed to mine for the briefest of seconds before she turned for the door.

"Wait." My mind raced as she paused, my pulse chasing close behind.

The light from the floor-to-ceiling windows framed her with its glow as she looked over her shoulder.

"You could work here if you want."

Her eyes widened.

"It's quiet during the day," I said. Which was the exact moment someone dropped what sounded like a steel pot on the floor, the crash blaring through the restaurant. "Most of the time," I added, one corner of my mouth lifting. "Quieter than a coffee shop, and you won't have to pay seven fifty for a latte to use the Wi-Fi. You could use Jillian's office if you wanted. She wouldn't mind, plus then she'd know exactly where to find you if she had any last-minute ideas for the symposium."

I wasn't sure why I was pushing the idea so hard. Only that I couldn't watch her leave and do nothing. I didn't know where she lived—if she had roommates or a doorman or any sort of security. And I had no clue what the note said or who the fucker was who'd left it on her car.

But I did know what it was like to need a safe space. And this restaurant was mine.

I'd built it that way. I'd hired the staff, trained them to work as a team, and cultivated an environment where we actually cared about one another. Not just for me, but so this could be a safe space for anyone who worked here. The kind of space I'd been lucky enough to find at eighteen.

And more than anything, I wanted Dani to feel safe.

"And you wouldn't be alone," I said finally.

She stood quiet for several long beats, chest heaving with short breaths as she fought to stay composed. Then it was like the walls around her crumbled, her face falling and shoulders dropping as she took three giant steps forward and crushed herself to me.

My arms were around her in an instant, pulling her tighter against my chest as if I could block out anything that could possibly hurt her. I'd sure as hell try.

She let out a long, shaky breath, burying her face in the crook of my neck, her hands squeezing around my waist. Eventually, the pounding of her heart against my ribs calmed, and the trembling of her body eased. I rubbed small circles against her lower back, in no rush to release her.

After another moment, she loosened her grip and leaned back enough to meet my gaze. "Thank you," she said. Her eyes were a little puffy, but they'd softened, the tension and fear from before replaced with a warmth that had my muscles unwinding and emotion burning in my chest.

"Any time," I replied, voice thick.

We stayed like that, arms loose around each other as our gazes lingered. Light green flecks dotted her irises, swimming in the crystal-blue waters of her eyes.

Her gaze flicked to my lips, and my pulse hammered against my skin as my eyes dropped to her mouth, my every thought evaporating except for how soft her lips must feel.

Then she pulled away, breaking the spell as a shock of cool air rushed between us.

"Um…okay." A flustered smile touched her lips as a blush crept up her throat. "I guess I'll see you tomorrow, then." A lightness in her voice hinted at relief, and she tucked a nonexistent strand of hair behind her ear, glancing at me one last time before turning for the door.

I stuck my hands in my pockets, staring after her until she disappeared around the corner and my sense of equilibrium returned.

I knew exactly where I'd be every Monday from now on.

Chapter Eleven
Dani

THE INTERNET WAS AN INCREDIBLE THING—NEARLY unlimited information available with the click of a button. Yet as I clicked to the tenth page of my latest search results, I wondered if I'd hit a limit. Chances were, if I hadn't found what I was looking for on pages one through nine, I wouldn't find it on ten, eleven, or twelve, but I skimmed the page and clicked to the next one anyway. My brain was blanking hard on ideas, and doing this at least felt productive.

My gaze fell to the clock in the bottom corner of my screen. Ardena opened in six minutes, and the clinking of silverware being polished and tables being set floated up the stairs to where I sat in Jillian's office.

I'd worked at the bar most of the day, the kitchen staff flowing around me in a well-practiced routine that was equal parts fascinating and relaxing to observe. It was like a tightly choreographed dance; everyone knew exactly what to do and where to go, moving in sync through a thousand complicated steps made to look simple from how well practiced they were.

When the serving staff arrived at four, I'd moved up to the office, though I could have called it a day. Probably should have, seeing as my brain felt like a chewing gum bubble that had been blown to its limit and would burst across my face if I attempted to fill it with another thought. What I needed was to go home, eat an early dinner, and get a full night's sleep.

Except I didn't want to go home yet. Didn't want to eat dinner on my couch by myself and give my mind a chance to think about all the things I didn't have to worry about within the safety of these walls. Things like nasty words, hateful comments, and violent people.

I hated that they'd gotten to me. That they'd hooked themselves into my mind and made it impossible for me to let them go. I wanted so badly to be the type of person who wasn't bothered, who could simply brush them aside or be strong enough not to care, but I wasn't.

I was just afraid.

Afraid to go home to the stillness and quiet of my apartment. Afraid to be there alone.

Yesterday, when I agreed to work from home, I hadn't realized how afraid of it I was until Jase offered me a different option. That note on my car made me feel exposed, like I'd been locked in a glass box that anyone could see into at any time, and his invitation to work here was like pulling a curtain shut. At least for part of the day.

I knew my brain would eventually stop randomly producing worst-case scenarios. I'd stop tensing at random noises in my studio, and the tiny apartment would go back to feeling like the home I'd started to create. But right now, it just felt like another place where I might be exposed without anyone to turn to for help.

That was a downside to moving around so much: not having people. No boyfriend to come stay with me, no neighbor to keep an eye out, no friend's couch to crash on. I'd never minded before. I had yet to meet a jar I couldn't eventually open myself, and if I needed a cup of sugar, I went to the store.

But now? Being *not alone* sounded really nice.

I could probably stay with Robin if I asked, but would that be weird? We were friends, but maybe not to the level of "crash on your couch because of a potential stalker" friends. That seemed like it should come after "get sloppy drunk and black out on your couch" friends, which we hadn't yet achieved, though that one at least felt close.

Then again, this probably wasn't that big a deal. Last night had been fine. This morning too. There'd been no sign of anyone following me, no creepers lingering outside my apartment. Even my social media had cooled off. Now, I just needed my keyed-up anxiety to follow suit.

Five more fruitless pages down the search-result rabbit hole, and I finally gave up. I closed the browser and leaned back in Jillian's absurdly comfortable office chair. That, along with the antique-style wooden desk, was the extent of the furniture in the small space. Unlike the dining room, she'd kept her office simple.

I stared at my spreadsheet. "This should not be that difficult," I said to myself.

"What's that?"

I startled, smacking my hands on the desk to stop from tipping over the chair. "Jesus," I said as I took in where Jase leaned against the doorframe. Even relaxed, his tall body filled the space, claiming all my attention. It really wasn't fair someone could look so good while scaring the shit out of you.

He smirked. "Sorry. I was just coming to check if you were still here." He nodded at my laptop. "Problem?"

I sighed. "Just trying to come up with a few more silent auction ideas for the gala. We've already got a bunch of smaller items, like a massage package at a local spa and a weekend getaway at the hotel where the dinner's being held. Plus a date night here, courtesy of Jillian."

He nodded at that, his icy-blue eyes smoldering—yes, smoldering—as he paid attention to my every word.

He had a way of doing that—listening so fully his body went still, his every focus on the person speaking to him. I'd seen him do it with Jillian before. His staff too. I was still growing used to it, so accustomed to fighting not to be spoken over in the corporate world. Or by my mother, who pretty much lived in the corporate world, so I guess that made sense.

"But I'd like to find at least one or two bigger items to help us reach our fundraising goal," I continued, looking back at my incomplete spreadsheet. "So far, none of our board members have found someone to donate a boat."

"Does it have to be a boat?" he asked.

"A new car would work too," I said, only half serious.

"Motor vehicles. Got it."

I sent him a sidelong glance. "You know someone with a hookup?"

He flashed his brow. "That's me. I exclusively hang out with luxury car dealers and yacht owners. I just choose to walk everywhere for the exercise."

My gaze swept over his broad chest and shoulders, traveling down his torso to what I was sure were incredible abs. They were hidden beneath his chef jacket, but I remembered how firm they'd been against me the day before, how strong his arms had felt wrapped around me. Only his forearms were visible now, but the sight of those along with his hands were enough to make me shiver.

I dropped my gaze, swallowing my *Seems to be working* comment. That would officially be flirting, and while I was willing to let myself fantasize about his stupidly hot body—because, come on, there was no stopping that—flirting felt like taking it too far.

My phone rang, saving me from myself.

"Sorry," I said as I dug through my bag. I found my phone on the third ring, catching sight of Robin's name before I silenced it.

"No worries, I should get back down." He grabbed the side of the doorframe as he turned to leave, a muscle in his forearm flexing in a way that shouldn't have made me want to rub my legs together. And yet...

"Right," I said, dragging my attention to shutting down my laptop. "I'll get out of here."

"Oh no, that's not…" He held up a hand. "You can stay as long as you want. You're not in the way."

My phone buzzed with a text.

Robin: Drinks tonight. Nonnegotiable.

I flashed him the phone. "I'm being summoned anyway. You know of any good bars around here?"

Robin had a favorite spot—or jawn, as she called it—a few blocks north of the office, a trendy sort of dive bar decorated with an eclectic variety of lamps that featured live music, but it

was on the opposite side of the city from my apartment, and I
didn't have my car with me. It had been nice enough weather,
and Ardena was close enough to my place that I'd decided to
walk. Public transit was an option, but I wasn't super familiar
with it yet, and right now, the idea of taking it at night had me
more anxious than going home. There was always a ride app.
The weekday fares might even be low enough for me to justify
using it for a single drink.

Jase's brow furrowed. "You realize there's a bar downstairs,
right? You sat at it for eight hours today?"

I gave a dry laugh, shaking my head. "I'm not drinking
here. That'd be…"

His eyes narrowed as he crossed his arms, shifting his
weight to lean against the doorframe. "Go on. That'd be what?
You got something against my restaurant?"

"No," I said quickly. "Of course not. I just…don't want to
be in the way. During the day is one thing, but I'd feel like I was
overstepping by being here while you were open."

He tipped his head back slightly, studying me.

I met his gaze for a moment but shifted away, my chest
growing warm under his scrutiny. Not with shame, but something similar to that exposed sensation I had with the note. Like
he could see right through me. Only this wasn't scary. At least
not in the same way.

Before I could overthink things, my phone rang again.
Robin.

Jase stepped into the hallway and pointed at my phone.
"You should stay for a drink. Dinner too. I'll give you the
employee discount, seeing as you work here now."

I rolled my eyes, ready to argue, but he was already gone,

his footsteps heavy on the stairs. I looked at my phone for one more ring, then answered.

"Hey," I said. "You interested in getting dinner too?"

"THIS IS the only place I'm ever getting drinks from now on," Robin said as our server, Neela, set down our second round.

I smiled in thanks as Robin took a sip of her fancy cocktail and moaned loud enough that the older gentleman at the table beside ours looked over. Neela suppressed a grin as she turned away, and I brought my own fancy drink to my lips.

I couldn't remember what was in it, but tart sweetness exploded on my tongue with the first sip, dissipating into a tingly warmth that burned just enough to be alcohol but also might have been magic. It turned out the right bartender could do as much with tequila and pomegranate juice as Jase could with a carrot. And he could do *a lot* with a carrot.

Why did that sound so dirty?

"I think I'm drunk," I said as I pulled another crostini onto my plate. It was topped with something creamy that was too delicate to be cheese, bits of artichoke that practically melted on my tongue, and something else that gave it a zing and left my mouth watering for more. We hadn't ordered anything yet, but Neela had brought them out to us "courtesy of the chef, " and they were the only thing keeping me from crossing over into truly drunk territory.

I hadn't had hard liquor in months, and two rounds on an empty stomach was asking for trouble. Based on the flush in Robin's cheeks, she was in the same boat. Maybe this would be our "get sloppy drunk and black out on your couch" night.

That seemed like a horrible idea for a Tuesday.

"Drunk enough to spill all the delicious details about a certain ex's older brother?" Robin asked. "You tap that yet?"

I almost choked on crostini. "No," I coughed out before managing to swallow. "There's nothing to tap."

Robin snorted. "There's a whole damn maple tree just waiting for you to climb him."

I chuckled at the visual, but the thing my mind clung to was how little I'd thought of Jase in terms of being Alec's brother these past few weeks. At the start of working together, I'd assumed every little thing he did would remind me of Alec, yet aside from some similar physical characteristics, they had almost nothing in common. And even the things they *did* have in common, they went about in totally different ways.

Like how Jase was as much a planner as Alec, but where Alec tended to assume the wants and needs of others and then went ahead and made one perfect plan based on those assumptions, Jase assumed nothing and instead stacked contingency upon contingency to account for every possible outcome. I didn't even think he did it consciously sometimes; he was that proficient at it.

"It's not like that," I said, feeling a little weird reducing Jase to a sexy tree, even though I'd had more than one dream about climbing him. It wasn't my fault if my subconscious was a tree hugger who wanted to swing from his branches and slide down his trunk.

Food.

It was definitely time for more food.

Robin gave me a look. "So he sends out free appetizers to the entire restaurant, is that it?"

I waved her off. "He's just being nice because he feels bad

for me with the whole note thing. Just like you." I waggled an accusing finger at her. "Don't think I don't see through this weeknight drink invitation."

She brought her hand to her chest in mock offense. "I would never. I just needed an in to this swanky spot, and you were it."

"Ah, so you're using me," I said with an exaggerated nod.

"Yup. Purely selfish reasoning over here. And now that I've tried it, I'll have to start living off of canned beans and frozen peas so I can afford to come back every week."

"Wait till you try the food for the symposium," I said. "I'm still not recovered from the tastings, and those weren't even the finalized dishes."

Just thinking about how good they were was all the motivation I needed to push through these next two months and all this event would bring.

More press. Probably more hate mail.

More death threats…

I took a gulp of my drink.

Robin's eyes turned serious. "How are you doing with everything? I didn't get to see you yesterday after it happened."

"I'm…okay," I said, proud to realize it was true. Yes, I was still anxious, but—and maybe this was the booze—I was also content. Right at this moment, anyway. And a bunch of other times over the past six months, if I thought back on it.

It wasn't just the new job or this particular city or any one specific thing. It was that all of it together was starting to feel like it "fit." Like after years of trying to wedge myself into someone else's mold, I had maybe finally found the one that was right for me.

That was the feeling I wanted to hold on to—not the fear

squirming in my belly at what might happen, but the warmth spreading through my limbs as I sat next to my friend, and the giddiness bubbling in my chest as I savored this delicious drink.

I felt alive right now, more so than I had in a long time, and I didn't want to analyze it or worry about whether I'd feel this way again tomorrow. I just wanted to enjoy it.

Chapter Twelve
Jase

IT WAS A GOOD TUESDAY NIGHT. We'd had a decent number of reservations on the books, the walk-ins had been steady—a nice constant flow rather than two hours of dead space followed by an onslaught of diners—and not a single person had sent back a dish.

Plus, Dani had been smiling for hours.

I hadn't been sure if she'd stay like I suggested, and even when her friend showed and they'd settled into a two-top in the corner of the booth that ran along the far wall, I figured they might just get one drink and leave. But they were finishing their second round now, the appetizer I'd sent out devoured, and showed no signs of stopping.

I leaned outside the kitchen doorway, watching Dani's head fall back with laughter, her face glowing in the soft light of the dining room. The lightness in her expression eased the knot that had been pulling in my chest since she'd come in yesterday shaking. The fact that she'd found this level of peace in my restaurant gave me a smug satisfaction I probably didn't deserve but I'd take anyway.

This was the power of restaurants.

I'd learned it all the way back in my very first job as a dishwasher. It wasn't just the food or expensive wine, and it wasn't the fancy silverware or formal service. It was the atmosphere that was created when all of it came together perfectly.

It was the murmur of people and the backdrop of music against the sizzle of food as it came out of the kitchen and passed by your table on the way to another customer. It was the aroma of garlic in good olive oil and the clinking of wineglasses in celebration. It was the perfect symphony of the front and back of house working together, timing the courses just right so you were always ready for more but never left wanting.

It was art, and it was music, and it was imagination, and I wanted everyone to be able to experience it the way I did. Especially that woman across the room, who spent so much time in her own head that I wondered how often she got stuck there.

Neela approached the computer behind the bar, and I gave Dani's table a nod. "They order any food?"

"Putting it in now," she said, then gave a wry smile. "I don't think I've ever had a table be so excited about striped bass."

I bit back my grin. I'd never been so excited to make it.

"THEY NEED to make finding a therapist easier," Dani said. "It's as bad as dating."

Robin shook her head, the two of them sprawled on one of

the velvet couches in the middle of the dining room. "No way. Finding a therapist is notably *worse* than dating."

"Why's that?" Zach asked.

It was nearly eleven o'clock. We'd closed an hour ago, and some of the crew had decided to stick around for a shift drink. Neela had invited Dani and Robin to stay, which was going well for her if the gradually shrinking space on the couch between her and Robin was any indication.

Dani sat on Robin's other side, directly across from where I was on the opposite couch. Her body lounged easily against the cushioned armrest, her feet tucked under her, shoes forgotten on the floor. She'd taken her hair out of the low bun it'd been in earlier, her fingers mindlessly combing through the long strands.

"Because," Robin said with a sly grin, "at least with dating, there's the possibility of sex. All I get from my therapist is emotional exhaustion and, if I'm really lucky, a sinus infection."

The room chuckled, but I tilted my head in disagreement. "I don't know. I'd take my relationship with my therapist over anything I had with my exes."

Luis sucked air between his teeth as he untied the bandanna from his head and dropped it to the floor beside where he reclined against the couch. His thick dark hair fell across his forehead in waves. "That bad, Chef?"

I rocked my head from side to side. "Let's just say I'm no longer interested in anything that's not real."

My eyes flicked to Dani to find her watching me, gaze thoughtful. Her expression was less guarded than usual, her face as relaxed as the rest of her, though I couldn't tell if that was from the alcohol or just her getting tired. She'd stopped after her second drink with dinner and had been nursing the same cider for the past hour, so I doubted she was drunk. Maybe a little tipsy.

Robin raised her hands as if in surrender. "Fair enough. Doesn't change the fact that Dani here needs to get laid."

Dani's eyes went huge. "Oh my God, Robin, really?" She laughed as she covered her reddening face with her hand.

My lips tugged up.

"What? There's no shame in it," Robin said. "You're new here, and meeting people is hard. I'm just saying maybe you could redirect some of your therapist-search energy into the more beneficial of the two endeavors."

I picked at the label on my beer bottle with my thumb and tried to ignore the twisting in my stomach at the thought of Dani getting "benefits" with some random dude. It was bad enough I had the visual of her with my brother, which had apparently been "not a problem" for her. Thank God I knew I had a bigger dick than Alec. Dr. Ohara would scold me for caring, but if I didn't measure up to Alec there either, my inadequacy complex would be fucking crippling.

"I think our judgments on what qualifies as 'beneficial' somewhat differ," Dani mumbled.

"I see benefits to doing both," Aubrey chimed in diplomatically.

"Maybe at the same time?" Neela said, waggling her eyebrows.

Robin grinned, dangerous excitement filling her eyes. "Now we're talking. What we *really* need is a therapist dating app. To find shrinks in the streets and freaks in the sheets."

And that was my cue to exit. I pushed to my feet and collected empty bottles.

"There's no way that'd be ethical," Dani said as I headed for the bar.

I put the bottles in the mini recycling bin and set it by the kitchen door to take out back before I left so the bartender wouldn't have to deal with it tomorrow. My pocket buzzed, and I pulled out my phone to a text from my buddy Colin.

Colin: Definitely. Come by tomorrow.

"Sorry about keeping you here late." Behind me, Dani set empty glasses on the bar. "We've probably overstayed our welcome."

"No way," I said, turning to face her. I flicked my chin toward the couches. "I like letting the staff do this once in a while. It's good for team building, and it doesn't usually happen on the weekends since we're open later."

Her eyes sparkled under the twinkling of the chandelier as she tucked a strand of hair behind her ear. "They're a lot of fun. I get why this place means so much to you. I can tell it means a lot to them too."

For some reason, the words jarred me. I hadn't realized how much I needed to hear them until they came from her. I struggled to respond. "I try," was all I could come up with.

She shrugged a shoulder like it was no big deal. "You do a good job."

I dropped my gaze to my phone, suddenly overwhelmed, and remembered the message I'd gotten.

"Speaking of jobs," I said. "I have a lead on a silent auction donation for the gala."

Dani straightened. "Really?"

  Lacey Burke

"My friend just got back to me. We could check it out tomorrow night if you want?"

Something between amusement and surprise crossed her face. "Do you actually know a luxury car dealer?"

I chuckled. "No. But I think this could still work."

"Don't you *have* work tomorrow?" she asked, gesturing at the bar around her. "What about this place?"

"A and the guys can handle a Wednesday on their own." And I was due a night off.

Her smile filled her whole face, and for a second, I forgot to breathe. I'd only had one beer, but I was about to dig up the label to check how much alcohol was in it because my world felt off kilter, like it might tip over with a single glance.

Then she spoke, and everything snapped back into place.

"I'm in," she said.

Chapter Thirteen
Dani

THE SUN STREAMED through my studio's wall of windows as I made coffee, brightening my whole apartment to match the lightness buzzing inside me. I almost didn't need the coffee. Not when I still thrummed from the night before.

It had been the most fun I'd had in years.

Maybe that was sad that at thirty years old, I couldn't remember the last time I'd hung out like that with a group of people my own age. But it only made me more grateful for *this* group of people who had given it to me again.

For Zach, who had me keeled over laughing from his story about his first time on a food line and how he dumped scalding hot water over himself while trying to clean up a pot of burned caramel. And Aubrey, who'd brought out a leftover slice of chocolate mousse cake with raspberry sauce to share. It was only big enough for each of us to get one bite, but it may have been the best bite of my life.

That was true for everything I ate at that restaurant, but dammit, those people could cook.

They were kind and talented and *cool*, and I felt like the new kid in school, hoping they would let me keep sitting with them during lunch.

Which meant, naturally, I felt the need to work from home today—my actual home—so I wouldn't appear too eager to be a part of their clique and wear out my welcome.

Overthinking truly was my superpower.

It did have a plus side, which was that my brain's running loop of the things I did or said last night that could have been at all embarrassing kept me from fixating on the possibility of someone leaving death threats in my mailbox. Not that those particular nerves had vanished, but at this point, they'd more or less become my new baseline, an ever-present anxiety simmering on the back burner. The office was still getting hate mail, some of it addressed to me, but the fact that I hadn't gotten any at home made me think Geffery was right and whoever left the note on my car had no plans to take things further.

I might have felt relieved if it wasn't for the swarm of butterflies that had taken up residence in my stomach ever since Jase had invited me to his friend's art gallery.

They were different from my usual anxiety nerves. Less of an unrelenting squeeze of my ribs and more of a restlessness, like a hamster running wild on its wheel beneath my sternum.

Almost like excitement.

To go to an art gallery, which I hadn't done since leaving Chicago four years ago.

To potentially land a one-of-a-kind piece to include in the

gala's silent auction. Something that would make our event stand apart from the dozens of other fundraisers these donors likely attended, all offering some version of a spa package or a weekend getaway at a nice hotel.

To get a little dressed up and explore more of the city I'd lived in for six months and still barely knew.

To have fun like I did last night. To let my guard down a little and laugh, enjoy someone else's company.

Jase's company.

I liked Jase's company.

He was confident like Alec in a way that put others at ease, but Jase's was more of a quiet confidence. This bubble that slipped around you and lifted you up, bolstering you as it floated around the room. He never made me feel like I had to keep up, like I'd get left behind if I couldn't match the energy in the room or the pace of the conversation. There was no competitive edge, no display to present. He was just there as himself, making space for others to do the same.

I'd never expected it to be that way with him, especially after the disastrous start to our acquaintance. What I'd thought would be us gritting our teeth through the awkwardness long enough to get done what we needed to had become something almost like a friendship. One I found myself hoping I wouldn't have to give up once the symposium was over.

That was the thought I held on to as I got ready for the night.

I gave myself an hour, spending a little extra time curling my hair and applying a touch more makeup than usual. I tugged on a light pair of jeans and a strapless bodice, tying it together with a belt and sandals.

Nice, but still casual. This was technically a work meeting, after all, so I wanted to look presentable. But not like I was trying too hard.

Not like I thought this was a date.

I knew it wasn't. Sure, Jase and I could be friends, but more than that was…ridiculous wasn't a strong enough word. The only reason my heart was pounding was because I was eager to finalize the silent auction. And the only reason my palms were sweating was I'd started walking to the gallery Jase had texted me the address for, which turned out to only be a ten-minute walk from my apartment, and it was still hot out, the evening sun hanging low in the sky.

I was a block away when I spotted him. He leaned beneath the gallery sign, one heel propped on the wall behind him while he looked down at his phone. He wore dark jeans and a white button-down shirt, untucked, sleeves rolled up to his elbows.

My mouth went dry as I soaked him in. I always seemed to forget how attractive he was until he stood in front of me, making every cell of my body hum. It was like he was too much for my brain to process. Even the way he leaned was sexy—careless in his confidence as he waited like he had all the time in the world. And he'd waited for me to go in.

Alec wouldn't have done that.

The thought struck me with a jolt so hard I nearly stumbled. Alec would have gone inside and talked with his friend, assuming I'd meet him in there. It wasn't something about Alec that had bothered me when we dated, but in comparison, this was everything.

I didn't have to linger outside and wait for him to respond to my text. Or wander inside by myself without knowing if he was there yet. Or worry about making my own awkward introduction to his friend if he wasn't. There was nothing to over-think or second-guess. It loosened a layer of tension in my muscles as I approached.

"Hey," I said.

Jase lifted his head and froze. His eyes tracked their way from the top of my head down to my feet and back up again until they landed on my face, his gaze like a physical touch that scorched my skin and sent my pulse racing. When his stare connected with mine, it was nearly too much to hold, his eyes churning waves of blue intense enough to drown in.

I almost wanted to.

He pushed away from the wall and cleared his throat. "Hey." His deep tone sent a shiver across my collarbone and tugged at my core. "You look nice."

I adjusted the strap of my purse on my shoulder and tried to calm the pounding of my heart. "Thanks. You too."

He grabbed the handle to the gallery and pulled, holding the door open for me. "After you."

I stepped inside, catching the subtle spice of his scent as I passed. I fought the urge to close my eyes and breathe deep.

A blast of cool air hit me, raising bumps along my arms as I continued into the space, and the moment I did, color flooded my vision.

The gallery was one large room that extended to the back wall of the building with ceilings so high it felt like they weren't there. The floors were a polished wood, the walls simple white, but lining each of them were the most beautiful oil paintings, all in a similar style, probably done by a single artist. Additional paintings were displayed on dividers hung throughout the room.

I took it in with wide eyes until Jase placed his hand on my lower back, drawing all my attention to that point of contact and the warmth of his palm through my top. He guided me with gentle pressure toward a reception desk in the front corner.

"Jase, my man."

A British accent pulled my focus to a sharply dressed man about Jase's age who pulled Jase into a bear hug. Jase lifted his hand from my back to return the embrace, and I chose not to focus on the pang of disappointment in my chest as cool air replaced his touch.

"How are you, mate?" the guy said, giving Jase a final slap on the back before releasing him.

Jase's grin filled his whole face in a way I hadn't seen before —totally unrestrained. "I've been good. Been meaning to stop in for a while."

His friend waved him off and adjusted the cuffs of his royal blue shirt, the color playing off of the cool tones of his dark brown skin. Every detail of his look was polished, from his leather shoes to the short twists of his hair and his trimmed beard. "I know how it goes. I haven't made it to that fancy restaurant of yours yet, so we're even. Though I've heard some excellent things from a few clients of mine."

"Did you tell them they must be mistaken?" Jase asked.

His friend flashed his own wide grin. "Tried to warn them away multiple times. People don't listen to reason."

Eyes still alight, Jase gestured to me. "This is Dani. She's organizing the fundraiser I told you about. Dani, this is my good friend Colin Kentwood. Don't listen to a word he says that isn't about art."

"Excuse me," Colin said, "but whose mouth got us in trouble with the Italian police?"

"That is an extreme exaggeration of what happened," Jase said in defense.

Colin lifted my hand and dropped a kiss on the back of it. "It's not," he whispered.

I pressed my lips together to restrain my laughter.

Jase rolled his eyes with a smirk and reached for my hand. "She's too smart to be swayed by your flirting," he said as he slid my fingers from Colin's grasp. His touch lingered against my skin, thumb brushing my palm once before he pulled away. I clutched my bag to keep from reaching after him. "You going to show us some art, or what?"

"Apparently, that's all I'm good for," Colin said as he ushered us into the main part of the gallery.

Jase patted his cheek as he passed. "You're pretty too." He blew a kiss, and Colin swatted his hand away.

I was as enthralled by their back-and-forth as I was with the art. I'd seen Jase joke around with his staff before and laugh at their ridiculous stories, but he always remained one step removed, never forgetting he was their boss or crossing that line into something unprofessional.

With Colin, none of that power dynamic existed. They were straight-up playful with one another, even after not seeing each other for what sounded like a long time. It was kind of beautiful to watch.

"This showcase is for Mia Cordero, one of our local artists. She's built quite a following in recent years," Colin explained as he led us around the room. Benches were spaced throughout, some of which had people sitting on them, admiring the art.

"I can see why," I said. "There's such movement to them."

"Are you an art fan?" he asked.

"I'm not a collector or anything, but I do appreciate it. My dad's a photographer, so I used to go to a lot of art shows with him as a kid." I felt Jase watching me, taking in this new information.

"Oh, brilliant," Colin said. "The first gallery I ever worked at was a photo gallery in London. It's amazing how clearly some people see the world through a lens."

Bitterness mixed with longing in my chest as I studied the canvas in front of us. "And how much they can miss outside of it," I murmured.

When I turned, Colin had already moved on to the next piece, a smaller canvas displaying multiple women painted in a simplistic design, all in shades of reds, pinks, and purples. Their bodies were draped over one another, limbs intertwined in a human knot.

Jase stood behind me, gaze fixed on me. He studied me in that way of his that felt like he was staring into my soul.

For a moment, I let him. Then I followed Colin.

WE PERUSED the gallery for an hour or so, Colin giving us the vivid backstory on many of the paintings. He shared insights from the artist and revealed his favorite pieces.

Jase surprised me yet again by sharing his own thoughts on the art, and not just, "It looks cool." Don't get me wrong, that was a perfectly valid reason to like art—but he was talking color theory, composition, contrast, and texture. It reminded me all over again that Jase was an artist too, his food as layered and complex as any of the pieces in this gallery, and it suddenly made perfect sense why these two were friends.

"So," Colin said as we returned to the reception area at the front of the gallery. "What do you think? Would Mia's work be a good fit for your auction?"

Was he kidding? "It'd be perfect," I said.

"Great. We had four pieces in mind."

I waved him off. "Whichever one you decide on is fine by me. Seriously, they're all amazing."

Colin chuckled. "No, I meant we want to donate all four."

I looked at Jase, who was trying to hide his grin, then back at Colin. "Four? Of these paintings?" I pointed behind me.

Colin shrugged. "Mia feels strongly about your organization's mission, and it speaks closely to the themes of her work. She was excited to do it."

"That's…" My mouth hung open, waiting for words that never came.

These paintings sold for thousands of dollars each. Assuming they auctioned for over the market value—which they would, given the artist's popularity—this donation would bring in a huge chunk of money at the fundraiser. More than I'd thought possible. The flood of gratitude was too much for me to process.

"Thank you," I finally said.

I told him I'd be in touch tomorrow to arrange the details, and we said our goodbyes, he and Jase sharing another vicious hug before we stepped back out onto South Street and into the clear summer night.

A motorcycle roared by, the sounds of the city crashing upon us all at once, making the quiet serenity of jazz music and murmured conversation we'd left behind feel like another world. One I wasn't sure had even been real.

I stole a glance at Jase, who walked alongside me with his hands in his pockets. "I can't believe you got me four paintings for the auction."

He laughed quietly, triggering a flutter of something fuzzy in my chest. "All I did was send a text. Colin's the one who came through."

Maybe. But Jase had sent that text without prompting. He'd seen a way he could help, so he did. Just like he'd done for me again and again this past month and a half. It meant more to me than I knew how to say.

"How'd you two become friends, anyway?" I asked. We continued to stroll down the sidewalk with no particular destination in mind.

"I worked in London for a couple of years as a line cook, and he grew up there with one of the guys I worked with. We went out as a group a bunch of times, and the two of us just sort of clicked. He spent all his time in the photo gallery he mentioned, while I was working sixty-hour weeks at the restaurant trying to learn as much as I could and not get yelled at in the process. We both had these visions of what it would be like when we were the ones in charge."

"And now you are," I said.

He chuckled. "Yeah, by some miracle."

"That's right, you apparently came dangerously close to serving life in an Italian prison."

He huffed. "They *claimed* to be off-duty police, which I'm still not convinced of, and we were all plastered."

I laughed, my chest light. A soft breeze grazed my skin, carrying the lingering scent of summer with it. He moved closer to me so someone could pass by on the sidewalk, and I caught his intoxicating scent again too.

"You know how in high school, adults always said the friends you meet in college become the best of your life?" he asked.

I nodded.

"I always thought it was bullshit. Friends were just friends, you know? And then I met Colin, and I got it. It's been over ten years, and he'd still do anything for me, even when we haven't seen each other in months. I don't know why, but I'm fucking grateful."

I knew why. Because Jase was that way for everyone in his life. Staying under budget to protect Jillian's finances, letting me work at the restaurant when I would only get in his way, making sure his staff got fair wages and paid time off. He cared so much about others, and he didn't think anyone noticed.

"I have one friend like that," I admitted. "We didn't meet in college either."

I hadn't stayed close with my college friends. After graduation, we spread out to different parts of the country, and soon, our lives were all in different stages—some of us getting married, some having kids, others catapulting in their careers. And then there was me, just kind of…trotting along doing none of it.

"Where'd you meet?" Jase asked.

"Dance camp. Seventh grade." My lips tugged up at the memory. "We were roommates."

He pulled back in surprise. "I'm sorry, dance camp? Like ballet or hip-hop?"

"A mix. Ballet and contemporary mostly." It felt like a lifetime ago at this point.

"So why didn't you become a dancer?"

"No way," I said, shaking my head. "I wasn't good

enough." Which was true. Also true was the fact my mom would have developed a stomach ulcer if I'd tried for the arts. Following in my dad's footsteps instead of her own, shattering glass ceilings? Absolutely not. "I joined a dance club freshman year of college, but it didn't quite feel the same, and..." I shrugged. "I figured it was time to focus on something else. I just had a harder time than I thought I would finding what that something should be."

I'd switched my major twice before settling on marketing. It wasn't that I'd loved it so much as it seemed like a reliable way to make a living, and I hadn't been able to think of anything I might like better. My mom's easy acceptance of it hadn't hurt either.

"Rachel and I still talk, though. We send Christmas cards to each other and try to get together in person at least once a year."

And when I broke up with Alec, she'd been the only person who didn't second-guess the decision, including myself. She'd trusted my instincts more than I had, in a way not even my parents had before, and her trust in me was a huge part of why I didn't try to get back with him right away. Or rather my trust in her. Like if she believed in my judgment, maybe I should too.

I'd *thought* for a long time that I'd made the right call. Seeing how happy Alec was with Stephanie, like they were made for each other, made me think we were never really meant to be together. But it was only recently I'd started to *feel* that way too.

The sidewalk opened up to the main thoroughfare of Broad Street, and Jase and I both looked left and right, deliberating which way to go. My apartment was left. Ardena was right. I didn't know if that was where Jase would go or if he had other plans for his night off, but I figured this was where we would part ways. My stomach sank at the thought.

He gazed over at me, something almost shy in his expression. "You…wanna grab something to eat?"

That sinking feeling evaporated, my entire chest lifting as my lips tugged up. "I know a place."

Chapter Fourteen
Jase

We looped around a few blocks toward the Italian Market until we reached a quaint restaurant on the corner of two side streets. It had a white brick exterior and green awnings over the windows. Josie's was sprawled in black letters on the sign hanging over the entrance.

"Have you been here before?" Dani asked as she walked ahead of me up the three steps to the door. I tried not to stare at her ass as she reached for the handle and failed miserably.

Her outfit was driving me insane. I'd kept my hands in my pockets most of the night just to stop myself from touching her. Her belt emphasized the delicate curve of her waist that my palm would tuck perfectly into, and her top cupped her small breasts, which swelled against the fabric with every breath she took. I wanted to run my tongue along the edge like an ice cream cone. My cock throbbed in my jeans.

"No," I said, forcing the gravel from my voice as I followed her inside.

It looked like the quintessential Italian family restaurant. Tables draped with red-and-white checkered cloths were scattered throughout the narrow space, topped with shakers of grated cheese and chili flakes. The lighting was low, made homey by string lights hung across the ceiling, and framed photos and old movie posters covered the walls.

It was busy for a Wednesday night. The kind of busy that came from regular customers rather than college kids going out for the weekend or tourists visiting from out of town. The server, a teenager in a black T-shirt and apron, waved Dani over and pointed at an empty table in the corner. Dani waved back, then nodded for me to follow.

We weaved our way through the tables, so tightly spaced I could hardly move without bumping into someone's chair. It gave me the opportunity to check out the food on everyone's plates.

Hints of nutty parmesan and cracked pepper caught my nose from what appeared to be cacio e pepe. The salty scent of guanciale hit me from another table's pasta all'Amatriciana. The sautéed chicory greens I spotted really caught my attention. I hadn't had a plate of those since leaving Italy. A spark of nostalgia flared in my chest that had me moving quicker for the table.

Dani slid into the chair against the wall, giving me the seat with a little more legroom. The server came by to drop off menus and water glasses.

"You need some time?" she asked Dani, eyeing me. I was clearly the new one here.

"Yeah, but put in an order of the eggplant to start," Dani said. She lowered her voice. "Did he make it?"

The server flashed her brows. "Only three slices left."

"Can I call dibs on one?" Dani asked.

"You got it. I'll be back with your eggplant in a little bit."

The server left, and I raised a brow at Dani.

"The owner makes the best tiramisu in the state," she explained. "But he doesn't make it every day, so you have to jump on it when you can."

"How'd you find this place?" I asked. Philly's food scene was impossible to keep up with for even the most diehard, and this seemed like the kind of gem you had to stumble upon. The regulars probably hurled empty wine bottles at reviewers to prevent word from getting out.

"The owner's my landlord," she said as she played with a corner of the paper menu. "I live a block away, and this is pretty much the only place I've eaten at since moving here." She shot me a small grin. "He doesn't give me a discount or anything, so don't think that's it. It's just really good. Plus, his family runs it—his daughter's our server tonight—and they take good care of me. They're the only people besides Robin I really know here so far."

I knew what that was like, being alone in a new city. Sometimes one where English wasn't the native language and the only familiar thing to cling to was food. Even when the dishes were different from back home, at the core, food carried the same meaning no matter where you went. It was about community and connections, culture and customs. To feed others was to nurture them, and that was a very personal thing.

I lifted my menu. "Then as someone with the inside scoop, what do you recommend?"

She met my gaze over the papers. "What do you like?"

"Whatever's good."

Her eyes narrowed. "It's all good."

"So let's get it all."

"What?" She gave a surprised laugh.

I flipped over the menu. The back side was all drinks and desserts. There weren't that many entrées. "One of everything. We'll share, and anything we don't finish, you can take home."

"Their servings aren't small," she warned.

"Then I guess you'll have dinners for the week."

She looked unconvinced.

"Come on," I urged. "It's been way too long since I had good Italian food."

"Was that when you lived in Italy?"

"That's definitely where I had the best. There have been a few good places since. Nowhere that boasted the best tiramisu in the state, though."

She glanced to the side and bit her lip, a little color rising in her cheeks. My pulse kicked up.

The server returned and placed a plate of eggplant slices rolled with ricotta cheese in front of us, along with two smaller plates and rolls of silverware.

"You ready to order?"

I looked at Dani.

She held my gaze, sucking me in to where nothing else existed. Just the sea-green swirls of her eyes and the hint of a smirk pulling at her lips. Then she peered up at the server and said, "We'll have one of everything."

So what made you want to become a chef?" Dani asked. She scooped some pasta puttanesca onto her plate, one of the six dishes currently covering our table. We'd rotated through the appetizers already, the servings we'd decided to save compiled onto a single plate to make room for the entrées.

She'd set about the meal with the kind of organized approach I'd come to expect from her, taking a single spoonful of each dish to start so she could sample a little of everything before returning to the ones she enjoyed most.

I respected it. Even more, I appreciated the way she embraced the experience. Whether she'd initially done it to humor me or not, she'd fully committed, and every time she leaned forward to breathe in the aroma of a dish before tasting it, I was hit with the urge to reach across the table and kiss her.

Not that I would. This wasn't that kind of meal. The kind that two people who were into each other shared as a lead-in to something more.

I wasn't even sure it qualified as a meal between friends. More like a celebration between colleagues. Temporary colleagues at that. Who knew what would happen after the symposium was over? She might not step foot in Ardena again.

I pushed aside the sinking feeling in my stomach and scraped a pile of gnocchi onto my plate. My method was to go for whichever dish had my mouth watering the most.

"It mostly happened on accident," I said in answer to her question. "After high school, the only thing I knew for sure was that I didn't want to go to college, so I got a job at a pizza place in my hometown."

My parents had loved that. Their problem child throwing away his future to be a dishwasher. They took my not wanting to go to college as a personal affront to them, one I still didn't think they'd gotten over. In their world, a Michelin star would never be worth more than a college degree.

"I started off washing dishes and helping with food prep.

The owner was this older guy with the patience of a saint who showed me how to hold a knife and julienne a pepper. And doing it, something just clicked. I think I liked the structure of it, having a clear objective I could accomplish each day."

It didn't matter if the objective was only to chop a box of onions. Knowing I'd completed it to the standard set out and that I'd contributed in some way to the result going out to customers gave me a satisfaction I'd never found anywhere else.

"Eventually, I started cooking on the line," I continued. "I still remember the first time I saw someone enjoying a dish I made. It's all I've wanted to do since."

Maybe it was because I'd spent most of my childhood feeling like a fuckup. Like I'd gotten so used to expecting anything I did to be met with disappointment that realizing I could do something others might not only appreciate but actually admire was this seismic shift. One I was probably still coming to terms with. All I knew for sure was how grateful I was that Frank had hired and mentored me the way he did. I owed all of my accomplishments to him.

"And then you traveled the world, cooking as you went?" Dani asked.

I shrugged. "Basically. I was hungry to learn and willing to work for it. After I'd saved up a bit working for Frank, I moved to New York for a few years to get fine dining experience, and that took me to London and wherever else I heard about an opportunity after that."

"What made you come back?"

I took a bite of gnocchi and thought about how to answer. The creamy dumplings practically melted on my tongue.

"I reached the point where I wanted something more permanent," I ended up saying. "Something I could really build and shape. It was easier to get an executive chef job in the States, so it made sense to come back. I hadn't planned on Philly, but it's where an opportunity came up, and then Jillian offered me an even better one."

She'd attended business lunches at my old restaurant for years before I took over as head chef. Three months after I'd started, she'd gone back to the kitchen to pay her compliments to the new chef. She'd noticed the change in the food, enough that she popped in to say hello every time she dined there after that. A year and a half later, she came in with the offer to run her new restaurant. I'd known her well enough by then to trust her when she said my talent was wasted on a small man pretending to do big things, and that if I had the guts to take a chance on her, she'd repay the offer tenfold. So far, she'd been true to her word.

"I like what I have at Ardena with Jillian," I continued. "I like it here in general. It feels the most like home than anything else I've had."

"It's not an easy thing to find," she said.

"What, home?"

She nodded, and a hint of the somberness I'd caught in her eyes at the gallery returned.

"What about you?" I asked. "Why Philly?"

She twirled a long strand of spaghetti onto her fork. "Sort of the same as you. My last job was in Wilmington doing marketing and event planning for a company down there, and neither the job nor the city felt like a great fit." She let out a humorless laugh. "Neither had the four other jobs in the four other cities I'd lived before it. I didn't really know what I was looking for, but I knew I needed a change, and when I found the position at HBC, it seemed like maybe that could be it."

"Has it been?" I asked.

She glanced up.

"The change you needed?"

Her mouth curved, too softly to be a smile, but it lit up her face all the same. "Yeah. I think maybe it has." Her lips stretched wider, humor filling her eyes. "Although now I'm thinking I should have traveled the world first. I'll have to try that someday."

I swallowed the offer to take her myself. Colleagues didn't show each other their favorite parts of the world. The reminder formed an ache in my chest I was quick to rub away.

We finished a couple of the entrées before calling it, and Dani assured me I wasn't sticking her with her least favorite dishes for leftovers.

"I liked it all. Promise." The gleam in her eye had me shifting in my seat.

Once the server, Isabelle, boxed up our stuff and cleared the dishes, she brought out a slice of tiramisu as wide as my face. Dani straightened in her seat as Isabelle lowered the plate to the table, and as soon as Isabelle's back was turned, Dani snatched up one of the forks and slowly sank it into the corner of the slice. Her mouth closed over the bite, and her eyes fell shut as the faintest moan escaped her lips.

My hands squeezed into fists, stare glued to her face as she slid the fork from her mouth and flicked her tongue over her bottom lip. Her eyes opened slowly, as if coming out of a dream—a really fucking good one, apparently—and her gaze dropped to the dessert, then up to me and back again. She spun the fork restlessly between her fingertips.

Jeans now tight, I reached for the second fork.

"Be honest," I said, leaning my forearms on the table. I

pointed my fork at the tiramisu. "If I wasn't here, you'd be halfway done with this by now, wouldn't you?"

Her eyes narrowed. "I was giving you a chance to try it."

Fighting a smile, I grabbed a bite with my fork. She pinned her blue-green stare on me as flavor exploded on my tongue, the bitter notes of coffee and cocoa cutting through the richness of the cream and the sweetness of the sponge.

It was good.

Watching her eat it was better.

Almost as good as watching her eat my food. The way her head dropped forward on the first bite as she surrendered to the flavors. Seeing the pleasure sink into her whole body, her shoulders falling, breath sighing out, eyes fluttering closed. Knowing I was responsible.

It made me want to give her pleasure in other ways. See how her body would react to my fingers along her skin, my lips on her pulse, my tongue on her clit.

I'd never get to find out.

Not with her.

This at least I could have.

I took a few more bites of the dessert, leaving most of it for her, and by the time it was gone, so were the rest of the customers. Isabelle came over with the check, and I grabbed it off the table before Dani could reach it.

"Let me pay half," she insisted, palm open on the table for me to hand her the bill.

"No," I said simply.

"I owe you for the paintings."

I fished out my card and placed it in the folder. "It's not like I bought and donated them myself. Plus, it was my idea to order the whole menu." And as far as I was concerned, she'd never pay for another meal in my presence.

She studied me for a moment before leaning back in defeat. "Fine. I'll just find another way to repay you."

More than one idea flashed through my mind, and I reminded myself for the dozenth time since we sat down that no version of tonight ended with her bare skin against mine.

Isabelle came to grab my card. I left her a big tip, and we headed out, reemerging onto the sidewalk. The air had cooled a little, still warmer than the AC inside the restaurant, but no longer muggy.

"Let me walk you home," I said. I didn't like the idea of her being out here alone at night, no matter how safe the area was. Plus, I wasn't ready for the night to end just yet.

She nodded with a soft smile, and we started down the empty sidewalk. We took several steps in comfortable silence, just the dull clacking of her shoes on the concrete.

I glanced her way. "Can I ask you something?"

Her arms swung easily at her sides, her body seeming more relaxed than earlier in the night. I shoved my hands in my pockets to stop from clasping her hand in mine.

"Shoot," she said.

"It's about something you said at the gallery, about your dad missing things outside the lens." She'd said it quietly, almost like she hadn't realized she was saying it out loud. Like she normally wouldn't have, bottling it up instead behind the composed mask she showed the world. But the mask had slipped, and I'd seen it. "What did you mean by that?"

She took a deep breath. "That was…maybe not fair of me to say. His job wasn't the only reason he was distant." She looked up and explained, "My parents are divorced. I was thirteen, and it was *both* of them putting their jobs before their marriage that caused it to fail."

It sounded like maybe they had both put their jobs before their daughter too, but I stayed quiet.

"Because my dad travels so much for work, it made sense for me to live with my mom full time, and it got to the point where I only really saw him once or twice a year. Mostly at Christmas. If he had a show in the area."

She let out a chuckle, but disappointment weighed it down.

"The few times we'd talk on the phone, it was usually about his next project or the one he'd just finished, and it began to feel like the only way he'd ever see me was if I was in front of his camera." She shrugged a shoulder. "And I didn't tend to be his subject of choice."

Irritation flared in my chest, along with an ache of recognition I'd buried long ago.

I knew that feeling.

Of not being seen by your parents. Of feeling like the only way they'd ever relate to you was if you were something or someone different.

"What about your mom? Are you close with her?"

She let out a hard sigh. The same one I'd used a hundred times in the context of my own mother.

"She's not exactly a gentle personality. It's served her well in her career, running board rooms and landing executive positions. But the older I've gotten, the more I've come to accept that we just don't have much in common."

I tried to swallow against the knot of longing in my throat that still hoped the same wasn't true for my family, despite the part of me that had decided a long time ago it was. A more stubborn part of me was determined to keep trying. "Do you still see them for Christmas?"

She shook her head. "I stopped going home to Pittsburgh for the holidays during college. It was a long way to travel from Connecticut, and it was easier to just stay at school for breaks or go home with friends." She shot me a glance. "That was actually how we first met."

I gave a blank stare.

She grinned. "Don't worry, I don't think we were actually introduced. But it was the first time I saw you. I went home with Alec for winter break my junior year, and you were back home for a few weeks before going abroad again. To Italy, maybe?"

That was right. I'd only gone home because my parents had been on my case about it and offered to pay for the flight. The whole two weeks I'd spent texting Colin about our plans for Italy and counting down the days until I left.

"You weren't around the house much, but your parents had this holiday party, and I remember seeing you there."

I remembered that party. A bunch of my parents' friends and colleagues drank mulled wine and champagne, laughing over white elephant gifts and showing each other pictures of their kids and grandkids. I'd watched from the corner as my dad's work buddies patted Alec on the shoulder and asked him about his job plans once he graduated. I saw the way my dad's chest puffed up each time at Alec's response.

I'd felt like an outsider. The same way I'd felt most of my life. And the closer I tried to get to that inner circle, the more suffocated I felt.

What I didn't remember was her. How that was possible, I had no fucking clue, seeing as anytime I walked into the same room as her now, the whole thing seemed to reorient until she was at its center.

Honestly, it was probably a good thing I hadn't noticed her then. It would have been one more thing I ended up resenting Alec over. One more thing he didn't deserve to be resented for.

Not that it stopped me from resenting him for it now anyway.

"And?" I asked lightly, trying to ease the bitter taste in my mouth. Her steps slowed as we reached the stairs to a brick apartment building. "Has your impression of me gotten better or worse since then?"

She held my gaze as she grasped the railing and placed one foot behind her on the lowest step. She climbed slowly backward, studying me as she went.

I followed, one step behind, our eyes level the whole way until we reached the top. Her back hit the door as I rose above her, and I stepped in close, drawn to her by some gravitational force.

"Better," she said, head tipped back to hold my gaze, the curve of her cheek illuminated by the streetlights. The corners of her mouth lifted, and I shifted closer, less than a foot of space between us. "Definitely better."

Her impression of me before could have been trash enough that better didn't mean much. But from the way her gaze burned into mine, I didn't think that was the case. The way she'd said it made my chest expand with warmth I never wanted to fade.

She tilted her head at the building behind her and whispered, "This is me."

It was. Not the building but the breathtaking woman in

front of me. Her wide-open gaze was a beacon into her soul, inviting me to look at her. To see her.

All of her.

In a way I doubted even my brother had seen. Because if he had, he never would have let her walk away.

My gaze dropped to her mouth, and I swayed closer, her lips parting on an inhale, chest rising and falling with rapid breaths, nearly brushing mine.

Words fell from her lips, breathy and low. "You want to——"

My phone buzzed against my leg, jerking me back.

"Sorry," I said as I reached into my pocket.

Dani straightened away from the door, tucking her hair behind her ears, her cheeks turning pink.

I looked at my phone, and my stomach clenched. Of course, my mom was calling me right now. It went through to voicemail, but knowing my mom, she wouldn't just leave a message and wait for me to call back.

I shoved my hand through my hair and forced myself to meet Dani's gaze. "It's my mom. I'd ignore it, but she'll just keep calling."

Sure enough, the phone buzzed again in my hand as "Mom" lit up the screen.

"It's okay," Dani assured me with a soft smile. "It's getting late, anyway. I should probably call it a night." She turned for the door, then paused, casting her warm gaze back at me, rooting me in place. "Thank you," she said again. "For everything."

She rose onto her toes and pressed a soft kiss to my cheek. An electric charge ricocheted from her lips through my body, pulling my muscles taut and stealing my breath.

Before I could find it again, she was gone, the latch clicking shut behind her as she disappeared inside.

I listened to her footsteps climb the stairs on the other side of the door as I hung on to the moment a second longer. Then I blew out a breath and answered the phone.

"Hey, Mom." I descended the stairs to the sidewalk.

"There you are. I didn't think you were going to answer."

Then why did you call twice in a row?

I bit down my irritation. "What's up?"

"I need a final head count for the baby shower. Did you decide if you're bringing anyone?"

I peered up at Dani's building, the whisper of her lips lingering on my cheek.

There was no way. And not just because she was Alec's ex and that would be awkward as hell. But because as soon as she encountered the two of us side by side, she'd realize the same thing everyone else did: that I was nothing but a poor substitute for the person she really wanted.

The faulty brother, always on the outside. Someone who could be a colleague, maybe even friend, but one she'd always want to split the check with.

"Just me," I told my mom.

Why did it feel like that wouldn't be enough?

Chapter Fifteen
Dani

I was drunk.

Not my usual warm-tingly tipsiness, either. *Drunk.* I'd only had three tequila shots and a few sips of rum and Coke, but my dinner had pretty much consisted of chips and guacamole, and I hadn't been pacing my drinks like I usually did on the rare instances I had hard liquor.

I now understood why it was called that, by the way. Because that was how it hit—hard.

Robin and Kelly sat in the booth alongside me, more tequila shots lining the small round table of the karaoke bar. It was Saturday night, a week and a half since the art gallery "not date" with Jase, and if I'd had any doubts about just how much of a "not date" it was, those had been well and truly cleared up this past week.

Jase was avoiding me.

I hadn't been sure at first. I'd woken up Thursday morning feeling like a Disney princess, ready to fling open my windows and break into song while birds helped me get dressed for the day, still flying high on the incredible donation Jase had landed for me. I hadn't even been nervous to head into the office to share the news with Talia and finalize the details, worries about hate mail and death threats far from my mind. Geffery had escorted me to and from my car, but aside from his company, it had felt no different from the hundreds of other times I'd gone into work.

It had taken two days to get the silent auction finalized and squared away, and by Monday, I'd been eager to get back to Ardena. I could pretend it was just because I liked the atmosphere, which I did, but that wasn't what had put the flutters of excitement in my stomach. It had been the thought of seeing Jase.

For a "not date," that night had been more fun than any actual date I'd ever been on. And it wasn't just the paintings. It was how easy it was to talk to Jase. How effortlessly he made me laugh. How hours fell away with him without me noticing, and how never once throughout the night had I felt the need to hide.

Maybe I should have. Maybe I'd shown too much. Maybe I'd made him uncomfortable by kissing him on the cheek.

I didn't know.

What I did know was he hadn't been there when I'd shown up on Monday. And when he still hadn't come in by the afternoon, I'd asked Aubrey if he was sick. She hadn't heard anything from him.

I'd thought of texting him but then worried that'd be weird. After all, it *hadn't* been a date. He didn't owe me a phone call.

But when he'd come in Tuesday, perfectly healthy in all his tall, rugged glory, I'd gotten only a cursory "Hey" before he disappeared into the kitchen. Whereas before the gallery, he'd make hourly trips up to Jillian's office to get something, or sometimes just to check in, this past week, he'd only come up a grand total of two times, not even looking at me when he did.

That was what hurt the most, the not looking. Like he'd seen enough of me and wasn't interested in seeing more. Like he'd rather I was invisible.

Only, I didn't want to be invisible anymore.

Hence, karaoke.

I wore a pink slip dress that had hung untouched in my closet for years because I'd been too intimidated to wear it before tonight, and a pair of lace-up stiletto boots that spent more time on my shoe rack than on my feet for the very same reason. Robin and Kelly had convinced me I looked sexy, and you know what? I *felt* sexy. Free. For once in my overly analytical existence. And maybe it was the tequila, but I liked that feeling.

Someone on stage started a rendition of "Since U Been Gone" by Kelly Clarkson, and when the chorus hit, we all sang along at the top of our lungs before bursting into laughter.

"*Why* have we never *done* this before?" Kelly shouted, her blond hair crimped and pulled back in a messy half bun.

"Right?" Robin replied. Her red lipstick was the same bright color as her hair, both still managing to pop under the dim lights.

The three of us had already performed on stage once— "Say My Name" by Destiny's Child—something I never would have done a year ago for fear of sounding bad, of not being perfect. Which was exactly why *I'd* never done this before.

It was suddenly, blazingly clear. I'd spent my entire life

trying to be perfect, convinced I had to be in order to receive the affection I craved.

Want Dad to show up for my dance recital? Better nail that routine. Want my report card hung on the refrigerator? Only if I got all A's. Want Mom to show any interest in my career? Time to climb that corporate ladder.

It was a mask I'd constructed early on in an attempt to make order of the chaos my parents had dealt; one I'd only fastened on tighter with most of the guys I'd dated. No wonder I'd always been bored. They'd probably been doing the same thing as me, wearing masks of their own, presenting the versions of themselves they thought I wanted to see, leaving us with nothing but the performance of perfection between us.

Maybe that was why none of them had ever lived up to Alec.

Alec, who was so comfortable in his own skin. Who walked into any room and took ownership of it. Who knew exactly who he was and exactly what he wanted for himself. Alec, who, if I was honest with myself—and maybe the tequila was responsible for this, too, because I was all about the honesty tonight—had probably been a big part of the reason I'd felt the need for a mask at all. Or at least the need to keep wearing one. Because how could someone that perfect ever want to be with someone as ordinary as me?

Another singer got on stage, this one choosing a slower song I didn't know, and Kelly drew our attention back to her.

"All right, ladies," she said as if calling an official meeting to order. "Who are we serenading tonight? I call dibs on Mr. Man Bun in the back corner."

She pointed across the room at a guy with muscles usually only seen on NFL linebackers, his dark blond hair pulled back into a messy bun that matched his gruff beard. He was all hers. I preferred lean muscle. Like the kind an infuriating chef I knew had.

Robin held her palms out in front of her. "No serenading for me. I want to see how things play out with Neela."

My lips rose. "You two going on another date?" They'd been on one so far since the night we'd stayed late for drinks at Ardena, and from the bubbly smile on Robin's face, it had gone well.

"Brunch tomorrow. Which means I need to cool it on the tequila shots. I'd like my hangover to be curable with waffles and hash browns and not the kind that requires half the day with my head in the toilet."

"We'll allow it," Kelly decreed before turning to me. "That leaves you, Dani. Who's it gonna be? Or are you holding out for a certain ex-boyfriend's super-hot brother?" She crawled her fingers across the table. "Robin told me you two were making eyes at each other the other week."

Robin and I shared a look. I'd filled her in on the whole Jase-avoiding-me situation, but I didn't feel like rehashing it now. Tonight wasn't about him. He'd made it clear where we stood, which was apparently as far from each other as physically possible, and that was fine by me. I didn't need him to see me. I'd make sure someone else did instead.

"No brothers," I said. I tossed back another tequila shot, letting the burn dissolve Jase from my thoughts. "Let's go serenade it up." I headed for the stage.

"Here, let me."

Robin took the keys from my hand and opened the door to my building. I wasn't fall-over wasted, but I'd hit that sleepy stage of drunkenness where even the wooden doorframe outside my apartment looked like a nice comfy place to lean my head and rest my eyes for a minute. She held the door open and ushered me up the stairs to my apartment, opening that door too and dropping the keys on the end table before flicking on the light.

I stepped into my small space and sighed, the familiar coziness like a warm embrace.

"You good?" Robin asked as I tossed my clutch onto the couch. "Want help getting your shoes off or anything?"

I smiled a lazy smile and shook my head, ambling back over to wrap her in a tight hug. With my heels on, I towered over her by a good three inches. Her hair smelled *amazing*. Like cotton candy and bubble gum.

"Thanks for getting me home," I mumbled with a sigh. "You can black out on my couch any time."

She chuckled before pulling away. "Noted. Drink a glass of water before you fall asleep, yeah?"

"Yes, ma'am." I still had to take off my makeup and brush my teeth anyway. I didn't care how drunk I was—even drunk me knew waking up with clumpy mascara and sour alcohol breath only made the morning after worse.

"And no drunk dialing Hot Chef McFart Face," she added, leveling her finger at me.

I huffed. Like I would ever call him for anything again. I was done with him. Not that there was anything to be done with in the first place.

The door clicked shut behind Robin, and I flipped the lock before shuffling into the kitchen. Grabbing a cup, I turned on the tap and watched the water line rise in the glass.

What would I even say to Jase anyway?

Nothing. Except that he was being a total dickwad who deserved for his showers to run cold every morning.

I chugged down the water in one go and plunked the glass into the sink, then headed for the bathroom.

Or maybe I'd demand to know why he was avoiding me in the first place. I deserved to know that much, didn't I? Grown adults didn't get to just stop talking to people they had a problem with. We weren't in second grade. He couldn't pretend I didn't exist.

The thought stewed as I quickly washed my face and brushed my teeth. It solidified in my mind as I sank onto my bed to take off my boots. The softness of my comforter was almost enough to make me screw getting up for pajamas and just strip out of my dress and crawl under the covers naked, but my studio was practically all windows. Flashing my neighbors wasn't really the approach I was going for when it came to meeting new people.

I managed to change into a baggy T-shirt and slid under my cool sheets, a gentle breeze grazing my cheek through the open window above my bed.

Why shouldn't I say all that to Jase? Why should I have to sit with this jumbled mess of rocks in my stomach when this was all his fault in the first place? He'd invited *me* to the gallery. He'd walked *me* home. He had no right to treat me this way, and he should have to hear it…or at least read it.

Robin had said no to drunk dialing, which, of course. But a text was fine, right? I mean, a text was different. He wouldn't be able to tell I was drunk from a text. Not if I read it over extra carefully before I sent it. He'd get the truth, I'd get the last say, and my dignity would remain intact. It was the perfect plan.

My phone was in my hand with the screen unlocked before I had time to second-guess that logic. I winced at the brightness as I pulled up my messages and opened my conversation with him.

The last text exchange between us had been when he sent me the address of the art gallery. I'd responded with a smiley-face emoji. Somehow, that made everything worse.

My fingers itched to start typing, to send him the message that would take whatever this *thing* was battering around inside me and shove it into him instead. Make him deal with it.

Embarrassment.

Shame.

Rejection.

Disappointment.

But when I tried to think of the words, my brain could only come up with three.

Me: I miss you.

I stared at them typed out, knowing I couldn't send them but not wanting to send anything else. Not really. All that anger and hurt were only covering up this one truth, and I couldn't bear to admit it, no matter how drunk I was.

I'd deleted half the message when a loud bang erupted outside over the low city rumbles. My body froze, my thumb hovering over my phone screen as my tequila-muddled brain stumbled to identify the sound. It boomed again, louder this time, rising up from below my window, and it was only when the shouts started alongside it that I realized what it was.

"Let me in!" yelled a deep voice I didn't recognize followed by three more bangs. Someone was slamming against the door to my building.

My pulse hammered at the base of my throat as I stared into the darkness of my apartment.

The glare from the streetlamps provided just enough light to make out the edges of my furniture, only instead of comforting shapes, they were looming shadows that might lunge at any moment.

Another bang, and this time, I flinched.

Could it be the person who'd left the death threat on my car? *Had* they followed me home? It wouldn't have been hard. Maybe they'd just been watching me, waiting for the right moment or building up the courage to…what?

What happened if they got inside?

I closed my eyes against the thought and tried to stay calm, but hard angry slashes of black ink flashed across my lids, recounting every word of the note in vivid detail. All the ways they hoped I would die. All the things they'd do to me first.

Murdering whore.

Fucking cunt.

Get ready to get r—

"Come on!" The slamming was a constant now, what must have been their fist connecting with the wooden door and rattling the latch.

No air reached my lungs.

How strong was that door? How long until they got fed up and kicked it down?

With silent gasps, I tried to unlock the darkened screen of

my phone. I shook so badly it took three attempts for it to accept my fingerprint.

Jase's text conversation glowed back at me, and I didn't pause to think before tapping the phone icon in the top corner.

"Open the fucking door!"

I squeezed my eyes shut and brought the phone to my ear. A tear escaped, trailing over my cheek and onto my pillowcase. "Please," I whispered at the first ring. "Please."

The slamming switched to jangling, like whoever was down there had grabbed the door handle and was trying to rip it off.

I dragged air through my nose as the line rang twice, trying to control my breathing and gather my thoughts.

What if they got in? Did I have anything in my apartment I could use as a weapon? The standing lamp by the couch, maybe? I had knives in the kitchen.

Oh God.

Would I have to stab someone? *Could* I stab someone?

Bile burned the back of my throat.

The line rang again, my whole body shaking as my breaths grew shallow. Each pound against the door rattled through my bones, echoing the pounding of my heart against my ribs. I clutched the phone to my ear, clinging to the silence between rings, and willed the line to connect.

Chapter Sixteen
Jase

I THREW the metal pan into the sink, where it clattered against other pots, ringing angrily through the kitchen. Aubrey snapped her head up from where she was breaking down the cold station for the night, brows drawn together in surprise.

Tightening my hands around the edges of the dish pit, I lowered my head and forced in a deep breath. I never wanted to be one of those chefs who threw hissy fits, breaking shit and screaming at their staff. Especially when my frustration wasn't their fault.

The problem was me.

I'd been fucking up all week, breaking sauces, burning pans, overcooking scallops. It was like I was a line cook all over again, and not a fucking good one. My balance was off. What used to come to me as easily as walking now felt like stumbling through muddy, tangled weeds, just trying to stay on my feet.

"You could call her, you know," Aubrey said.

I clenched my teeth against the pinch in my stomach. "No, I can't."

I blew out a breath and headed over to break down the sauté station. The kitchen had technically been closed for an hour, but it had been a busy night, and we'd had tickets open until a few minutes ago. I'd let Zach and Luis go home first to make up for all the slack they'd had to pick up from me this past week. Just thinking about it made me want to throw something else. I was supposed to be teaching them, helping them grow as chefs, not making their jobs harder.

"Why not?" Aubrey challenged. Her own frustration and no lack of judgment filled her voice. She'd made it perfectly clear how she felt about me dodging Dani the way I was, and I didn't blame her. It was a dick move. No—a cowardly one.

Turned out I was a fucking coward.

"Because…" How did I explain what even just a friendship with Dani would be like? How every single day would feel like that night at Colin's gallery all over again—one minute, the most right something had ever felt outside the kitchen, only for the next to be a jarring reminder of all the ways it was wrong.

Wrong.

Dr. Ohara would probably challenge me on that word. Ask me who I was hurting by having a friendship with Dani.

I didn't have an answer. All I knew was how my parents would react if they ever found out.

Dani had *met* them, for fuck's sake. She hadn't been just some casual fling of Alec's. They'd been serious enough for him to take her home for all of winter break. And even if he wasn't bothered by the situation, which I honestly couldn't guess whether he would be or not, my mom would never accept it. Not when it might make her precious baby boy uncomfortable.

And I'd be the insensitive older brother who couldn't help stirring up drama.

That was what I was in my parents' eyes. The instigator. The fuckup. To them, every decision I made was a way to stick it to the family, never mind whether it actually had anything to do with them or not.

The irony was most of my decisions lately had been about trying to connect with my family. I'd left that part out when I told Dani why I moved back. Yes, I'd wanted the chance to build something of my own as an executive chef, but there'd been more to it than that. A nagging desire to see if maybe I could still have the kind of relationship with my parents and brother I'd wanted growing up. One where I could stand apart from them and still be on equal footing. Where I could be different from them but no less loved.

I was still trying to find out. The struggle was finding a way to do it that was healthy for all of us. But I didn't see how Dani might fit into that equation. And honestly, I wasn't sure I had it in me to find out.

"Well, in that case," Aubrey said when I didn't answer.

I shook my head. "It's complicated."

"Not as complicated as you're making it."

She was probably right. But I didn't know any other way to handle it.

We shut down the rest of the kitchen in silence, labeling food items, putting them neatly away in the walk-in, and sanitizing every surface. I was mopping the floor when my phone buzzed in my pocket.

I heaved out a breath, not up for a chat with my mom right now. But she didn't usually call this late.

I leaned the mop against the prep table and dug out my

phone, heart jumping at Dani's name on the screen. Why was *she* calling this late?

I caught the call on the last ring. "Dani?"

There came no answer, only her shaky breaths.

My pulse spiked. "Dani, what's wrong?"

Aubrey looked up from wiping down the inside of the prep fridge, concern in her eyes.

"Someone…" Dani started, but her voice faltered, so quiet I almost couldn't hear. "Someone's trying to get into my apartment."

My apron was over my head before she finished the sentence. "Where are you?"

"In my bed. I'm afraid if I move, they'll see me."

"Stay there. I'm on my way."

I shot a glance at Aubrey, who motioned for me to go, then I was running out of the kitchen, through the mostly empty dining room, and up the stairs.

"Talk to me. What's going on?" I said as I reached my locker. I didn't bother changing; just grabbed my wallet and keys and was back down the stairs. I put Dani on speaker just long enough to pull up a ride service app. Her apartment was close enough to walk, but a car would get me there faster.

"They've been banging on the door and sh-shouting," she said, then inhaled sharply. "I don't know w-what…" She choked on her exhales, sounding seconds away from a full-blown panic attack.

"Hey, just breathe for me, okay?" I forced my voice steady, even as I shook with adrenaline. The car was a minute away. "I'll be there soon."

I rushed out onto the sidewalk as the car pulled up and was

inside before it fully stopped. I could hear Dani pulling in breaths, still fast and shallow but better than a second ago.

"That's it, breathe," I said. My eyes were glued to the GPS, counting the blocks. "I'm almost there." I hadn't thought through what I'd do when I got there. For all I knew, the guy was armed. Maybe not with a gun, or he would have used it to get inside by now. But he could have a knife.

At this point, I didn't care. I just had to get there.

"The pounding stopped," she said a minute later. "I think…I think they might have left."

The car turned onto her street. "I'm pulling up now." There was no sign of anyone outside her building when I exited the car. I took the steps to the front door two at a time. "Can you buzz me up?"

The lock clicked, and I sprinted up the stairs, pocketing my phone as the door at the top of the landing opened, Dani's small frame shaking on the other side.

I crossed into her apartment and pulled her into my arms. She collapsed against my chest, torso heaving with quiet sobs.

"It's okay. I'm here," I said to calm myself as much as her. I could feel her heart racing against where my own was trying to punch its way through my chest.

I shuffled us a few more steps into her apartment and closed the door behind me, making sure to lock it. Then both my arms were around her again, one tight across her shoulders, the other rubbing small circles against her spine as I swayed slightly side to side.

Her hands clung to the back of my chef jacket, but her breathing had slowed, her shoulders no longer shaking.

"He wasn't here for me," she said against my chest, voice

muffled and still thick with tears. "It was a drunk guy at the wrong building. A woman next door came out and got him."

I blew out a breath, relief finally easing into my muscles.

We stayed like that for another minute before she sniffed and pulled away. I wasn't ready to let her go, but I loosened my arms as she stepped back, her head angled toward the floor. I could see the moment she drew her walls back in place.

"Sorry for calling," she said, her red-rimmed eyes flicking to mine before she headed for the corner of the studio that made up her kitchen. "I didn't mean to pull you away from the restaurant."

"It's fine—"

"No, I—" She coughed out a laugh. "I don't know why I didn't just call the police. It would have made more sense than bothering you. Blame the tequila shots." She grabbed a tissue from the box on top of her fridge and turned away to blow her nose.

"You didn't bother me," I said firmly, taking another step into the apartment. "I'm glad you called me." Though now I was curious who she'd been doing tequila shots with. I hated that I wanted to know.

Her arms wrapped around the front of her stomach, hands clinging to her sides. "Still, you don't have to stay. I'll be fine." Except she was trembling.

"Let me stay with you tonight. I don't want you to be alone."

She shook her head, still facing away from me.

It killed me not seeing what was going on in those eyes, to not know whether she was really okay. "I'll sleep on the couch. You won't even know I'm here."

"You won't fit on my couch."

I glanced behind me at the small two-seater that occupied the living space. It was only a little larger than a loveseat and left just enough room to comfortably maneuver between it and the queen-size bed that filled the other half of the space. I could probably fit on it if I wanted, but only if I didn't mind having a fucked-up back for the next week.

"Then come stay at my place," I offered.

I didn't care that it had been a false alarm. She hadn't known that while it happened, and with the hate mail she'd been getting, it made sense that she'd be scared. All I wanted was for her to feel safe. And to know she was safe for myself.

She sniffed again, tightening her arms around her torso. I wanted to go to her, to tuck her against me and offer her more comfort. I didn't think she wanted that right now, and after the way I'd acted this week, I didn't blame her.

But I *had* been the one she'd called, and I wasn't leaving her alone while she was still this shaken.

"Dani," I pleaded.

She gathered a shuddering breath and let her head fall back on her shoulders as she released it. Like she was giving in, or maybe asking for strength.

She gave a single word in response. "Okay."

Chapter Seventeen
Dani

The cab ride to Jase's apartment was short, his building only a few blocks from Ardena. We rode the elevator to the fourth floor in silence, him in his chef clothes, me in my sleep shirt, pajama shorts, and flip-flops. Whereas I was still shivering—and not from his building's AC—he appeared totally relaxed, leaning against the railing along the elevator wall, eyes casually tracking the numbers as they lit up above the doors.

When we reached the fourth floor, he led me down the hallway to his unit and unlocked the door, holding it open for me as he flicked on a switch. The track lights above his kitchen island brightened, illuminating the rest of his living space with a warm glow.

It was simple and masculine with mostly gray and black furniture, but little touches brought the space to life—potted plants on the windowsill, framed posters on the walls, a throw blanket folded over the back of the couch.

It felt comfortable.

Lived in.

My shoulders lowered another inch as I took in a full breath. I was safe here.

This was why I'd called Jase, I realized. Maybe I should have called the police instead, but I couldn't bring myself to regret it. Not when Jase was the one who managed to slip protective blinders around me again and again, blocking out everything that made me want to run. Even when he wanted nothing to do with me.

There was every chance he would go back to avoiding me tomorrow, but tonight, I was just grateful he'd answered my call.

"You can go ahead and sit on the couch," he said, walking into the kitchen. "I'll make you some tea."

I started toward the living room when a flash of gray caught my eye.

"Who's this?" I asked, kneeling to extend my hand. A large, fluffy cat with storm-gray fur rounded the corner of the island, rubbing against the wooden leg before stretching its nose to sniff my fingers.

"That'd be Baxter," Jase said, leaning across the counter to glimpse at us as he filled the electric kettle. "He's a shameless flirt, so if you have a problem with cats, let me know, and I'll shut him in the bedroom."

Baxter brushed his head against my hand, then slid his soft body down my arm and between my legs before going back the other way, a purr rumbling through his chest.

I smiled. "No, I love cats. I've wanted one for a while, but I've moved so frequently over the years that it never seemed like a good idea."

"The same was true for me before this year. When my ex

and I split, I thought of getting a dog, but it would have been a nightmare with my hours. Then I saw this guy at the shelter, and that was it."

My curiosity piqued at the mention of his ex. He hadn't talked much about his past relationships before.

Not that he had reason to. Just like I had no reason for asking.

It didn't stop me from wanting to know.

Baxter followed me to the couch, which was easily twice as large as mine, and quickly curled against my side as I settled onto the cushions. A minute later, Jase approached with two mugs, handing me one and setting the other on the coffee table before disappearing down the short hallway. He reemerged wearing a black T-shirt and gray drawstring pants, a soft-looking navy blanket bundled in his arms.

"Here." He set the blanket on the couch beside me. "So you can get cozy."

Emotion tightened my throat. I couldn't remember the last time I'd been this cared for by another person. Or even the last time I'd put myself in a situation to allow it.

I tucked the silky fleece around my shoulders, carefully maneuvering it over Baxter, who eyed me as if to warn me I wasn't allowed to move from my spot. It gave me the time I needed to compose myself enough to speak.

"Thank you," I said as Jase lowered onto the opposite side of the couch.

He did a quick scan of my bundled-up form before meeting my gaze. "You feeling better?"

I nodded. An electric charge still coursed through my body, keeping my nerves on edge, but it was easing with each moment that passed in his presence. Baxter's weight and continued purrs helped too.

"So…" His brows rose. "Tequila shots?"

A laugh burst from my chest, shaking loose more of my body's tension, and I lowered my eyes to the warm mug in my hands. "Karaoke night," I explained. "I may have gotten a little carried away."

He shot me a grin. "Been there. Just be glad you don't have to be on your feet all day tomorrow picking and chiffonading twelve quarts of cilantro with an asshole of a boss screaming in your face every ten minutes."

I laughed. "That a regular experience of yours?"

"It used to be. More than I care to admit."

"I wouldn't have guessed that. It seems like you hardly ever drink." I'd only seen it twice—the afternoon after the *Citizen Daily* interview and the night the staff had drinks. Both times, he'd stopped after one beer.

He took a sip of his tea. "I don't much anymore. Not since last year. I wasn't really in the healthiest place."

"How so?" I asked before taking a sip of my own tea. Chamomile with honey and lemon. It soothed its way down my throat.

He hesitated, scratching the back of his neck.

"Sorry, you don't have to—"

"No, it's fine," he said, shaking his head. "It was just a lonely time. Which isn't how you expect to feel when you're living with your girlfriend of two years." He traced his thumb along the rim of his mug. "You know that shift drink we had after close the other week?"

I nodded.

"It's a regular thing in the industry. Staff going out and having a few drinks after shift, maybe more. I did it all the time when I was a line cook, but when I was at my last restaurant, I started going hard. Didn't really think anything of it. I was just having fun, you know? I thought I was happy. It's not like I had any reason not to be. Good job, beautiful girlfriend, all the boxes checked off like they were supposed to be. But then every night, I would go out and drink until I couldn't see straight 'cause *that's* a happy thing to do."

He tried to say it lightly, but there was a strain to his voice.

"One night, I had borrowed my ex's car to get to work, and I tried to drive home drunk. Aubrey was the one to take the keys from my hand. She dragged my sorry ass to her place so I could crash on her couch."

The corners of his mouth lifted, and mine followed suit. Something in me warmed at the knowledge he and Aubrey were "get sloppy drunk and blackout on your couch" friends.

"The next morning, she reamed me out. Told me I needed to change something or I would end up losing everything I'd worked for. Or worse. When I got home, my girlfriend was looking at wedding dresses. She didn't ask where I'd been, just turned to me and said she thought we should get married. When I asked her why, she said, 'Well, why wouldn't we?' I puked in the toilet, then broke up with her. And then I moved out, changed jobs, got a cat, and found a therapist. I swapped out drinking for going to the gym too. Seemed like a better use of my time."

"Wow," I said. That was a change all right. One most people wouldn't have been brave enough to make.

His gaze dropped to his lap. "I probably could have handled it better. It's not like my ex was a bad person; she didn't deserve to be blindsided like that. But I realized our entire relationship had been surface level. Just us going through the motions that had been scripted out by someone else, and I couldn't do it anymore. I don't ever want to be back in that place, living under a layer of smiles, pretending."

His words from the night of the shift drink floated back to me. Something about him not being interested in anything that wasn't real. It made more sense now. Spoke to the part of me that hadn't been willing to settle for the few guys I'd dated since Alec, none of whom had sparked anything within me despite all the figurative boxes they'd ticked. Maybe even spoke to the part of me that had broken up with Alec in the first place.

Jase shifted in his seat. "Sorry. You didn't need to hear my life's story."

"Don't be." I lifted a shoulder. "I asked."

He peered at me, our stares connecting for the first time since he'd begun his story. We studied each other quietly for a moment before he turned away. "I'll let you get some sleep." He leaned forward to get up.

"Wait," I said quickly.

Forearms on his knees, he glanced back.

"Stay a little longer?"

My muscles no longer trembled, and my pulse had returned to normal, but the thought of being alone just yet had my stomach clenching in knots that made me want to cling to him like I'd seen baby pandas do to their zookeeper's legs.

His eyes filled with understanding, and he sank back into the cushions. The knot around my stomach loosened.

"What's your favorite dish on the menu to cook?" I asked.

He raised an amused brow. "Why do you want to know?"

I gave another shrug. "I like hearing you talk about food." Almost as much as I liked watching him cook it. Where I saw a zucchini, he saw unlimited possibilities. It was fascinating getting a peek into his mind in that way.

He fought a smile but humored me, telling me all about the pear and chestnut agnolotti and how it reminded him of cooking in Italy. Then he moved on to which dish he liked least and what he might replace it with. I shifted to face him, my shoulder pressed against the couch, and tilted my head to rest against the back cushion.

I didn't notice my eyes close as the low, steady cadence of his voice enveloped me like a blanket. At some point, I registered the mug lifting from my hands and strong arms wrapping around me. Then weightlessness, nothing but the solid warmth beneath my cheek tethering me in place. A moment later, I sank into a cloud of softness, my mind following close behind.

Swaddled in the comfort of safety, I slept.

Chapter Eighteen
Jase

I TOSSED around on the couch, bunching the pillow under my head for the fourth time in as many minutes, trying to get a little more sleep. It was still early. Especially considering how late Dani had finally passed out.

She would have fit easier on the couch than me, but I wanted her to have the bed. Mostly so she'd sleep better, but also so on the unlikely chance last night hadn't been a false alarm and she *did* have a stalker, they would have to go through me before getting to her.

The desire to protect her still burned in my chest. She never told me what was written in the note that had been left on her car, but scrolling through some of the comments on her social media had been enough to give me an idea. I wanted to shield her from it. Pull her back into my arms and keep her there so I could block out anything that might harm her.

There was a good chance I was on that list.

I owed her another apology for last week. Probably an explanation too.

Honestly, it was hard to remember my reason for avoiding her when my mind kept wandering back to the thought of her sleeping in my bed. I could practically smell her on my sheets already. Lightly floral with an underlying sweetness I wanted to lick.

My groin ached, and I ran a hand over my face, officially giving up on more sleep. I sat up and scanned the room for Baxter, expecting him to jump on my lap and demand to be fed like he did most mornings at my first signs of stirring.

The morning sun filtered in through the large windows of my living room, brightening the apartment with natural light. No sign of my troublemaking cat, though.

I got to my feet and shuffled down the short hallway toward the bathroom, pausing when I spotted the bedroom door. I must not have closed it all the way last night, because it'd been pushed open, just wide enough for a small feline to squeeze through.

Through the crack, I spotted Dani sound asleep, dark hair peeking up over my gray comforter, one hand resting beside her face on the pillow. Nestled in the crook of her arm was Baxter. He had his head resting below her chin, body splayed along hers, blissed out like it was the only place he wanted to be.

Careful not to make a sound, I took my phone from the pocket of my sweats and snapped a picture.

I wasn't sure what made me do it. Just that I wanted to be able to look back on this moment and remember this feeling. Like a molten lava cake had split open in my chest, its warmth oozing everywhere. To wake up to this every morning and have the same peace settle over me at the sight.

Only there wouldn't be an every morning.

Not with her. Not like this.

Just whatever could be captured in a single photo on my phone and the knowledge that it would have to be enough.

BY THE TIME Dani emerged from the bedroom, I had banana pancakes keeping warm in the oven, fresh fruit sliced and set out on the island, and eggs cooking in the pan. Mornings were the only time I consistently cooked at home, so while my fridge wasn't stocked with much else, I had plenty of breakfast foods on hand.

"Smells so good," she mumbled, rubbing her eyes.

I fought back a smile. "Coffee?"

"God, yes." She slid onto a stool as I set up the French press.

"You sleep okay?"

Her eyes were puffy, but she gave a nod. "Mmm, yeah. Baxter's better than a weighted blanket."

As if summoned, his furry highness strolled out of the bedroom. He stopped in front of his food bowl and gave a stretch before leveling me with a stare and letting out a demanding meow.

I leaned against the counter and crossed my arms over my chest. "Don't look at me. You chose her," I said, nodding at Dani. "As far as I'm concerned, she can feed you."

He let out another yowl, apparently not happy with that suggestion.

"Oh yeah? Well, how do you think I feel?"

His next meow was short and definitive.

"Do I at least get morning cuddles?" I scooped him up and butted his forehead with mine. He rubbed his whiskers against my face, a purr rippling through him, and I pressed a kiss to his soft cheek.

Dani's eyes were bright with amusement as she watched us.

"I can't let him win too easily," I said in defense, lowering Baxter to the ground and giving him a scoop of food. "He's spoiled enough as it is, aren't you?" He was too busy eating to reply.

She focused on him a moment longer, then glanced at me, our gazes locking. Her hair was in a loose ponytail, pieces falling out around her face. She had no makeup on. Her sleep shirt was big and baggy.

She'd never looked more beautiful.

A faint blush rose to her cheeks, and I shifted my gaze, turning to get her coffee and a plate of pancakes.

"Thanks," she said as I placed both in front of her. She picked up her fork, but instead of eating, she spun the fork between her fingers. "Look—"

"If the next words out of your mouth are going to be 'I'm sorry,' I don't want to hear it," I said.

Her mouth snapped shut, surprise and a little hurt flashing across her face.

I swallowed. "I'm the one who owes you an apology. I shouldn't have avoided you the way I did last week."

She studied her fork. "Why did you?"

I exhaled through my nose, dropping to my forearms on the island. "It was nothing you did. That night at the gallery and then dinner afterward—it was amazing. The best night I've had in a long time. But all the stuff with you and Alec…" An invisible hand wrapped around my throat and squeezed.

She watched me, waiting.

"It felt like a lot," I finally managed. "And I tend to push people away when that happens. I know I shouldn't, but I do. I *did*. And I'm sorry."

She nodded, staring at her plate again.

I wanted to tilt up her chin and peer into her eyes, see what she was feeling. Not being able to felt like being locked in the walk-in, muscles going cold and numb while all I could do was wait.

"I get it," she said after a minute, one corner of her mouth lifting in a way that was almost sad. "I know all about feeling overwhelmed and pushing people away."

Right.

Like when she'd broken up with Alec. Her mistake. The thing I'd told her *wasn't* a mistake since it had been what she'd needed at the time.

That was what I was doing now, wasn't it? What I needed?

"And you're right," she went on, still talking at her pancakes. "It is a lot. So maybe we take a step back. You've done so much to help me with the symposium, and I feel like we make a good team when it comes to the event stuff, so maybe we just stick to that from now on. Not overcomplicate it."

"Sure," I agreed, mouth suddenly dry. "Keep it simple."

It was what I'd wanted. The whole point behind avoiding her in the first place. To pull things back. And now we were on the same page.

I should be relieved.

So why, as I watched her pick at her pancakes, her gaze still avoiding mine, did I feel as though a gaping hole had been carved from my chest instead?

Chapter Nineteen
Dani

"Hey, Dani."

Neela rounded the bar and filled the three-compartment sink used for glass washing, her long dark hair slicked back in a neat braid that made her thick brows stand out against her golden-brown skin.

"Hey. Sorry, I'll get out of your way in a minute," I said, gesturing to my laptop and event binder sprawled out across the bar in front of me. The servers would be here in twenty minutes to open the rest of the dining room, and I liked to be upstairs by then, but I'd hit a stride on the guest welcome packet design and wanted to see if I could get it done.

Neela waved me off. "Don't worry about it. You're fine."

It was only this week I'd worked at the bar again instead of up in Jillian's office. Something about the atmosphere drew me down here, particularly for my more creative tasks. Maybe it was the colorful paintings on the walls or being able to hear the bustle of prep work in the kitchen—another kind of creativity all its own—but being down here made it easier for me to plug into my artistic juices.

It was *possible* a small part of me also liked being nearer to Jase. For no other reason, of course, than I'd come to appreciate his professional opinion, and I'd missed it last week when he avoided me. I'd meant what I said when I told him we made a good team. I would hate to lose that over something that should never have been a possibility in the first place.

Just then, he strolled out of the kitchen on the way to the office, tossing me a nod as he passed. I nodded back.

It was our new dynamic. Or maybe our old one. He'd ask me to taste a new dish he was workshopping, and I'd ask for his opinion when I needed a second set of eyes on the symposium's menu design. He gave me a heads-up when the cleaning crew would be in so they wouldn't disturb me, and I let him know when I was leaving for the night so he could use Jillian's office to run reports.

No hugs.

No talk of exes.

Simple.

Just like we'd agreed.

"Look who it is," said Neela, shifting my attention to the front door and the guy who'd just walked in. "Where have you been, hot stuff?"

He was about my age and handsome in a movie star kind of way—lean but fit, short dirty-blond hair styled to look effortless, his strong jaw clean-shaven with the hint of a cleft in his chin. He'd be right at home on the cover of *GQ*.

He flashed Neela a dazzling smile, raising his hands as if in surrender, a bundle of dark fabric gripped in one hand. "I know, I know. It's been a while. I've been meaning to stop in, but things at work have been all over the place."

"I won't hold it against you as long as you draw my niece another sketch the next time you eat here. She framed the last one you did on the back of your receipt."

The guy's face lit up with genuine delight. "Yeah? Done."

Neela flicked her chin at whatever was in his hands. "Those for Aubrey?"

"Yeah. She in the back?"

Neela nodded. "I can take 'em to her if you want."

He passed the bundle across the bar, and Neela disappeared with it into the kitchen. His gaze fell on me, blue eyes glancing at my laptop screen.

"That looks good," he said, nodding at the welcome packet design. "It for the event this place is catering next month?"

I blinked in surprise. "Yeah, actually. How'd you know about that?"

"Aubrey told me." He stepped closer, leaning his forearms against the back of the stool two seats down from mine. "You design this yourself?" he asked, studying the screen.

I nodded, scanning the design. It was basically finished, but something about it still felt off.

"You open to suggestions? Feel free to tell me to fuck off," he added lightly. "You just look like you're stuck, and I happen to be a graphic designer."

My lips twitched. "Go for it."

"It's the title. It's getting washed out by the border, which is throwing the rest of it off balance. Try making it a darker color."

I did as he suggested, selecting the title and darkening it by a few shades. It did the trick. The whole design clicked into place.

"Huh." I looked up at him. "Thanks."

"No problem." He shot me that dazzling smile of his, dimples on full display. If he wasn't careful, he could hurt someone with it. "I'm Evan, by the way." He extended his hand.

I shook it. "Dani."

He nodded at my laptop. "If you've got any more designs you're working on, I'm happy to help. Aubrey made it seem like this event is sort of a big deal, and I have fun doing this kind of stuff. Only if you want, though."

"That'd...be great, actually." I'd done enough design work for events over the years that I could hold my own, but I was all for having a professional's input. Especially for this event that *was* a big deal, for me as much as HBC. Its success would be confirmation I belonged here—at this job, in this city, serving an actual purpose. Failure would prove I was never meant for any of it. I'd accept any help at my disposal to keep that from being true. "How long have you and Aubrey been together?" I asked.

Given the familiar way he'd talked about her, it hadn't seemed like a ridiculous assumption. Not until his face contorted like I'd told him to pop into the bathroom and lick the urinal.

"God, no, we're not together. We're practically related at this point." He cocked his head. "Well, we did get married in second grade, but my older brother divorced us a week later, so I'm not really sure that counts."

"Let me guess, your brother's a lawyer now?" I asked.

Evan scoffed, his mouth twisting. "Not even close."

"If only," Aubrey said, emerging from the kitchen and saving me from whatever I'd unknowingly stepped in. The front of her pants was soaked with some sort of orange liquid. "Then maybe I wouldn't have gotten completely ripped off by that deal. I didn't get any of your Halloween candy despite neither of us signing a prenup."

"That was your own fault for trusting my brother to actually consider how his actions might affect others," Evan replied.

"Yet *he* shared his Halloween candy with me."

"Yeah, because he knew you were in love with him and felt bad about it."

She shrugged a careless shoulder and headed for the stairs. "I still got candy out of it."

"Hey, I brought you pants," Evan called after her. "You want candy too?"

"If it's chocolate, then yes." She held up the bundle of fabric I now understood to be chef pants. "Thank you!" she hollered over her shoulder before disappearing up the stairs.

Evan shook his head and returned his focus to me. "If you want to see a sample of my work, I designed most of her tattoos."

I'd seen them. The ones on her arms, anyway. She had others she'd told me about, but her chef clothes hid them. The ones on her arms, at least, were breathtaking.

"You're hired." I tilted my head. "I mean, I can't pay you. But I'd welcome your input."

"I have some time right now. We could get started?"

"Sure." I dipped my chin to the stool beside me and slipped my laptop his way as he sat.

"Evan, hey."

Jase stood at the end of the bar nearest us, probably on his way back to the kitchen.

"Hey, man," Evan said. "How's it been?"

Jase glanced from Evan to my laptop to me. "What are you…?"

"Evan volunteered to help me with some design stuff for the symposium," I explained.

Jase's brows drew together. "I thought you did most of that already?"

"There are a few things I haven't gotten to yet. Plus, only the invites have been printed, so there's still time to incorporate his suggestions for everything else."

A muscle flexed in Jase's jaw. He opened his mouth to say something, but Luis stuck his head out of the kitchen.

"Hey, Chef, your timer's going off."

Jase's gaze locked with mine, holding it for a long moment before he broke contact and retreated to the back.

For a second, I thought I saw something like regret in his eyes, and my pulse kicked up at the possibility. I quickly shook it away. It had probably been nothing. And even if it had been something, regret wasn't it. That would be the opposite of simple, and simple was what we were keeping things.

Chapter Twenty
Jase

I washed my hands in the small sink inside the door to the kitchen, stare fixed on Dani and Evan where they sat at the end of the bar. He pointed at the laptop screen between them and said something that made her burst into laughter, her face lighting up the same way it had the other dozen times he'd made her laugh in the past hour.

My stomach churned with acid as if I'd chugged a bottle of vinegar. I wanted to punch something. Or tear it apart.

"You're not allowed to dismember my best friend," Aubrey said as she came up beside me.

I raised my brows.

"You're glaring," she explained. "Also, you've been washing your hands for a full five minutes. I think they're clean."

I smacked the faucet off and snatched a paper towel from the dispenser. "I'm not glaring." I might have been glaring. "I just don't want him messing with her."

"He's not going to mess with her."

I shot her a look. "I've seen him pick up a different girl six nights in a row."

"And? They're consenting adults. They have a nice night; sometimes he sees them again, and sometimes they agree to part ways. Just because you don't have a sex life doesn't mean he's not allowed to."

I rolled my eyes. "You know what I mean."

"I know that you're jealous."

"I'm not," I said, dismissing the punch the word landed to my gut. "She deserves more than to be some fling."

Aubrey let out a derisive snort. "She can decide for herself what she deserves. You're the one who seems to be having trouble making decisions."

"What are you talking about?"

"Jase." She said it like *are you serious?* "You either can't take your eyes off her or you're completely avoiding her. One minute, you're saying you can't be friends, and the next, you're running to her apartment to fight off a potential stalker."

What was I supposed to have done, let her fend for herself? *You could have called the cops*. But it wasn't like I'd stopped to think about it. I'd acted on instinct. And besides—

"That was before," I said. "We talked since then. Agreed to take a step back."

"Is that what this overprotective thing you're doing now is?" Aubrey asked, gesturing at my wide stance and crossed arms. "Stepping back? Because from where I'm standing, the only person messing with her is you."

I watched as Dani's smile filled the whole dining room, her silky brown hair falling down her back in waves, blue-green eyes bright with interest. My shoulders sank.

Aubrey's voice softened. "It's only as complicated as you make it, Chef."

She went back to work, and after one last glance at Dani, I did the same. Neither of us brought it up during service. I avoided looking into the dining room altogether.

It was a steady Thursday night—not hectic but busy enough to keep my mind occupied. Until every so often when Dani's laughter would reach my ears, floating on the murmur of conversation from the dining room, and it was like someone grabbed my rib cage and squeezed. It made me want to stick my head in a pot of boiling water. Or better yet, Evan's head.

He'd probably emerge looking every bit as much like Prince Charming, an easy smile on his face like nothing could touch him.

He reminded me of Alec in that way. In a lot of ways, actually. Both had that easygoing charm that could let them step into a brawl and have the guy about to pound their face in one minute laughing with them like they were best buds the next.

They had the same laid-back charisma that drew attention to themselves without even trying. They were both good at whatever they set their minds to, not because they were determined not to fail so much as it never occurred to them that failure was even an option.

They were both good guys.

Aubrey was right. Evan wasn't some player who would lie to Dani or try to manipulate her into bed. He was the kind of guy who would find twenty dollars on the sidewalk and ask everyone around if they'd dropped it rather than keep it for himself.

She was right about me too. I needed to let Dani go. Fully. Let her take a chance with a guy like Evan who *did* deserve her.

He was exactly the kind of guy who could live up to the shadow of my brother still lingering in her mind, the kind of guy who could make her happy.

She deserved to be happy.

I didn't know what I deserved. I was still trying to figure that out. But I couldn't expect her to hang around in limbo while that happened.

So I left them alone.

I pushed through service, ignoring the clench of my stomach when their food orders came in and Dani's favorite dish was printed right there on the same ticket as his. I cooked it, pretending it didn't feel like holding my hand over a lit burner, searing my skin raw with every one of her laughs.

And then the laughing stopped.

Each minute, I braced myself to hear it again, and each minute that I didn't added more pressure to the weight slowly sinking to the pit of my stomach, until a full hour had passed and I finally accepted that was it. She'd left with him.

I stabbed the last open ticket for the food that had just gone out and untied my apron, turning to Aubrey as I pulled it over my head. "I'm going up, if you need me."

She nodded, and I headed for the office, planning to bury myself in sales reports until my brain went numb and could no longer form images of Dani and Evan together. Her fair skin under his touch. Her full mouth against his lips. Her long legs tangled in his sheets. I ground my teeth against the fire in my chest and lengthened my stride.

Only to freeze outside the door to the dining room.

There, sitting before me—laptop open, glass of sparkling water in hand—was Dani.

She sat alone, Evan nowhere in sight, and whatever delusions I'd built up over the past few hours crumbled as my chest expanded with what felt like my first full breath all night. Hell, all week.

We'd agreed to keep things simple. And while the logical side of my brain knew this was anything but, the rest of me couldn't imagine anything simpler than how completely I wanted her. The fact that she was still here made me think maybe there was a chance she wanted me too.

Complicated or not, that was all I cared about right now.

And I wasn't willing to deny it any longer.

Chapter Twenty-One
Dani

I wasn't sure why I was still here.

Evan had left an hour ago after we'd successfully reviewed the rest of the symposium designs. He'd had a good number of suggestions, mostly small changes that had made a huge impact, and my ribs still hurt from laughing.

It wasn't that Evan was funny so much as he had an ease to him that brought levity to even the smallest things. Alec was a bit like that too. But despite some definite flirting on Evan's part, I hadn't found myself drawn to him in that way.

Yes, the guy was gorgeous, with his subtle dimples and bright blue eyes. But looking into his eyes didn't stir anything inside me. There was no sensation of being swept up in a storm I never wanted to escape, both exhilarated and emboldened by its winds. It was more like looking out onto a calm lake. Certainly enjoyable, but not what I wanted to feel about a romantic partner.

A friend, sure. Evan seemed okay with that. He hadn't

pushed when I'd dodged his more flirtatious comments or appeared offended when I insisted on paying for my meal. And when he'd gotten up to leave, pausing with his brows raised in a final invitation, he hadn't rolled his eyes or stomped away when I'd shaken my head. He'd just smiled in understanding and said good night.

Six months ago, I probably would have talked myself into going with him. Rationalized my way into his bed and hoped whatever "more" I craved materialized later.

But I was tired of rationalizing myself into things. Especially when my gut was finally starting to speak up. Or maybe I'd just finally given it enough space to be heard. Whichever it was, I wasn't ready to silence it again.

All of which left me sitting alone as the restaurant wound down around me, changing the heading colors of my production spreadsheet instead of going home to sleep.

I *should* go home. It wasn't even that I was afraid to; I just… wasn't ready to leave yet. Almost like I was waiting for something. Only I had no idea what.

"You ready to close out?" Neela asked.

I startled out of my haze. "Sure, here." I scrounged around in my bag for my wallet and slid her my credit card.

When I sat back up, Jase stood in the doorway to the kitchen, apron in hand. His eyes locked with mine, icy blue and burning, and all at once, I was caught in the storm again.

He swallowed as he approached the bar. "I didn't think you'd still be here." His voice was low, almost soft, grounding me after the high energy of my night.

"I know, it's late. I was just…" I shrugged, trying to find the right word. "Unwinding."

He nodded, eyes never leaving mine, his gaze waking up the

nerves in my body one by one like light switches being flipped on until every part of me was lit up with awareness.

This was what I'd been waiting for. This connection flowing between us. I craved it the way I did doughnuts after someone brought them into the office too many days in a row. I'd gotten used to having it and hadn't realized how much until it wasn't there anymore.

"Here you go." Neela laid the credit card folder beside me.

"I have some stuff to do in the office," Jase said as I filled out the tip. I left Neela a big one to make up for occupying a seat at her bar all night. "But I won't be long. You could stay if you wanted. Unwind a bit longer."

My gaze returned to his, unable to resist the churning waves. "Yeah," I said, a little breathless. "That sounds good."

I didn't know if the pounding of my pulse was simple, or the warmth rising to the surface of my skin as his eyes flicked to my mouth for the briefest of seconds before he walked away. All I knew was the same pull in my stomach that had told me *not* to go with Evan was telling me to *stay* now, and nothing within me wanted to resist.

The rest of the customers left, and I made my way over to one of the couches in the dining room, kicking my shoes off and sinking into the cushions. Somehow I'd come to feel as much at home here as I did in my own apartment. A few minutes later, the kitchen staff said their good nights, and Neela headed out, locking the front door on her way.

I rested my head against the padded arm of the couch and gazed up at the nearest chandelier, my stare dancing between the hundreds of tiny crystals reflecting the light like stars clustered throughout a galaxy. I felt as though I could reach up and touch them, float into the endless sky, and drift among their light. It was a little like being drunk, my body and mind completely relaxed, but without the haze of alcohol. Something else was in its place, a current of energy thrumming beneath my skin, locking me in the present moment.

I sensed, more than saw, when Jase joined me, his presence filling the room, wrapping around me like a heated blanket. My gaze dropped to where he lowered himself onto the opposite couch, sinking down enough to rest his head against the back cushion while still looking at me, his long legs relaxed out to the sides. He'd changed out of his chef clothes into a pair of dark jeans and a navy T-shirt, everything about him unassuming yet impossible to look away from.

Music played over the dining room speakers, mellow and flowing, drowning out the city streets and anything else beyond these walls. It felt like time had stopped and the only things that currently existed were in this room.

I tracked my eyes back over the lights and gave a lazy smile. "I love it here at night."

His deep voice washed over me, bathing me in warmth. "You don't have to work twelve hours straight to experience it, you know. You could just come in an hour before we close."

I smiled wider and caught his amused gaze. "I like it here during the day too. It's a good thing you don't serve tiramisu, or Sal might get jealous."

His lips rose. "Maybe I'll start."

"You'd have your work cut out for you. I don't know if you've heard, but his is the best in the state."

His smirk grew. "I like a challenge."

A small thrill shot through me at the way he said it, all confidence and resolve, and we stayed like that, studying each other for a moment before he spoke.

"It seemed like you and Evan got along." His voice stayed even, but the lightness in it had turned forced.

I shifted onto my side to face him. "We did. I'm going to talk to Talia about offering him some freelance work."

His brows rose. "Wow. So you're keeping him around, then."

"Should I not?" A teensy part of me hoped he'd say no. The same part that hoped it had been regret in his gaze earlier. That he'd been jealous. Probably because that was how I felt whenever I imagined him dating another woman, caring for her, making her laugh. Cooking for her.

Something like liquid-hot metal scorched my chest and pooled in the pit of my stomach.

Jase stared at his hands in his lap, one thumb rubbing into the opposite palm. I fixated on the movement, mesmerized by each tiny flex of his fingers. "He's a good guy," he finally said, nodding. "A good friend to Aubrey."

I swallowed a hint of disappointment. "I could use a good friend."

His eyes shot up to mine. "You have one."

"That's true." I tucked my hands between my face and where it lay against the armrest. "I'm lucky to have Robin."

"I wasn't talking about Robin."

I knew. But to acknowledge what he did mean felt wrong somehow, like it was only half the truth, and I didn't want to look at all of it only to have to turn away again.

My voice grew light. "I mean, I like Zach a lot, but I don't think of us as being 'good friends' yet. We haven't even had any sleepovers."

Jase's mouth twitched. "You're missing out. He's a hair-braiding pro."

I smiled. "Yeah?"

"Oh, yeah. Killer dancer, too. If the gala falls flat, we can send him out there to fire things up on the dance floor."

"You mean that's not your job?"

He made a face. "You wouldn't want that. I'm a terrible dancer."

I huffed out a breath. "I don't believe that for a second." I'd spent too many hours watching him move in the kitchen, flowing with a confident grace that was hypnotic to watch.

"Okay, then." He got to his feet, shaking out his arms and rolling his neck. "I'll prove it." His eyes gleamed as he extended a hand. "Dance with me."

"What?" I laughed.

He waved me up. "Come on. Give me your professional opinion."

"I was never a professional," I said, but I set my hand in his anyway.

He tugged me to my feet, catching my waist with his other hand. "Still better than me," he murmured.

My response evaporated from my lips as he stepped closer, his hand on my waist wrapping around to rest on my lower back, pulling me into him so our chests brushed. I slid my free hand over his shoulder and let myself lean into his warmth.

The room fell away as our bodies rocked gently side to side, his nearness like a drug. One whose high I'd been chasing since the first time he'd wrapped his arms around me after the note on my car and made me feel safe.

I breathed in his scent, catching the slightest hints of garlic and rosemary over his usual spice, and felt high all over again. His cheek grazed mine, the scruff of his jaw lightly scraping my skin, and my nipples pulled tight.

"You're such a liar," I breathed as a shiver ran through me. He was a fantastic dancer.

He released my hand and trailed his fingers up my arm, raising goose bumps in their wake. His thumb stroked my jaw, and he tilted my head up, drawing my heavy-lidded gaze to his. I was putty in his hands, practically melting as his eyes dropped to my mouth.

The first press of his lips against mine was so soft it was almost a question. I had no answers. My brain had whited out, no longer capable of thought, and I didn't care if I ever got it back as long as I could keep kissing him.

I chased his mouth and pulled him to me, his tongue grazing my lips, and I moaned, opening to him, needing him closer, to taste more of him. I arched forward, running my hands into his hair, clinging to him as his tongue brushed mine.

It felt so good. *He* felt so good, his arms tightening around me, one hand cradling my face as the other molded my body to his, steadying me and making me dizzy all at once.

I never knew kisses could be like this.

The ones I'd had before had mostly been fine. Nice. Something I'd enjoyed well enough but that had always managed to feel mechanical, like assembling a couch. Slot mouth A against mouth B. For the passionate variation, use tongue.

But this.

This felt not only good but necessary. Like instead of air, the thing I needed to breathe was him.

He broke away from my lips to trail kisses down my neck as his hand sank into my hair and gently tugged. I panted for breath, tilting my head to the side so his mouth could close over my racing pulse. He sucked lightly, and my knees practically gave out, my hips shooting forward as my hands twisted in the fabric of his shirt.

I tugged his mouth back to mine, moaning again at the glide of his tongue as if maybe I'd imagined how good it was, only to be proven wrong.

His answering groan was like a stroke against my clit, and all I wanted was to hear it again. To stay locked in the back and forth of this kiss that was both gentle yet demanding, seeking yet allowing, urgent yet unrushed, forever.

It was only after he pulled away, who knew how long later, that I registered the latch of the back door clicking shut and the footsteps in the kitchen growing nearer. He rested his forehead against mine, our heavy breaths mingling, before giving my hip a final squeeze. Just as he stepped back, Aubrey strolled into the dining room.

"I'm surprised you're still here," she said, head lowered toward her phone. "I forgot my pants that I need to wash—oh." She stopped in her tracks as she looked up, eyes widening at the sight of the two of us standing so close. She fought to keep her lips from rising. "I'm just gonna…" She pointed toward the stairs and scrambled across the dining room, leaving us alone again.

I bit back my grin and peeked at Jase. I wasn't sure what expression his eyes would hold, and a part of me braced for embarrassment or regret. But all I found was the same steadiness that occupied my own body.

My gaze dropped to his mouth, and that steadiness melted into a simmering heat that pooled in my core and had me biting my lip.

He let out a soft groan. "You really need to stop looking at me like that."

"Why?" My voice was all breath.

"Because," he said with a dangerous smile as his thumb brushed over my bottom lip. "If I start kissing you again, I'm not gonna stop, and you've had a long day. You should get some sleep."

He was right. The buzz still radiating through my body from our kiss was already struggling to fight off exhaustion, and even the temptation to kiss him again wasn't enough to stop a yawn from escaping. Plus, Aubrey would be down here again soon, and I didn't want her to feel awkward.

"See you tomorrow?" I asked.

I didn't want to believe he'd avoid me again, but it'd be a lie to say a sliver of worry didn't still taunt me with the possibility.

He must have seen it because he held my gaze, his eyes open and honest as he said, "I'll be here."

Chapter Twenty-Two
Jase

I didn't remember getting home. Hardly remembered locking up the restaurant after walking Dani to her car and saying good night. Aubrey had been gone by the time I got back. The rest of the night was a blur, faded to the backdrop of that kiss.

It was all I could think about as I lay in bed the following morning, early light drifting through my windows, a part of me wondering if it had all been a dream.

It hadn't been. I knew because I could recall exactly how smooth Dani's cheek had been against mine. Could still feel the give of her breasts against my chest, how her arms had tightened around my neck. Could still taste the moan on her lips.

Her fucking lips.

Just the memory was enough to make me hard, my cock throbbing as I recalled those lips on mine. I wrapped my hand around the base of my shaft and squeezed, a groan catching in my throat. I heard the tiny inhale she'd taken the second before my lips had touched hers, and the memory of her taste flooded my mind.

I gave myself a slow stroke. *Fuck.*

It was like that kiss had unlocked something inside me, shifted something fundamental, only I had no idea what.

Whatever it was burned through me, coaxing my hand to move faster, my hips thrusting up to meet my strokes.

Fantasies of Dani I'd been suppressing for months bombarded me, heightened by the truth I now possessed of the way her tongue moved against mine, the silkiness of her hair between my fingers, the openness in her gaze when I'd pulled away. I imagined that gaze on me now, staring up at me as her hand squeezed my cock, jerking me off at a frantic pace.

I came. So hard I couldn't breathe.

An hour later, I was at the restaurant, changing out of my street clothes. It was earlier than I usually got in, but I'd wanted to make sure I got here before her. To eliminate any shred of doubt in her mind that I might have regretted one moment of last night.

I'd just closed my locker when I heard her on the stairs. A moment later, she was there, standing in the open doorway in a caramel-colored dress that accentuated her soft curves and ended just above her fingertips. Her luscious hair framed her face in chestnut waves, and a rosy color was high on her cheeks.

Our eyes locked, and everything in me stilled. The rest of the world was silenced by the blue-green of her stare.

Then we were kissing.

We moved as one, her arms around my neck, mine low across her back, our lips connecting like they'd never been apart. It wasn't hurried or frantic, just inevitable. Necessary. Like two magnets finally coming together, a missing piece snapping into place. As satisfying and dizzying as it had been last night and better than every one of my fantasies to date.

I pressed her against the lockers, pinning her body with mine to deepen the kiss. She curved against me, tightening her arms around my neck, lifting on her toes to get closer.

My cock stiffened, the urge to wrap her legs around my waist and grind into her enough to make me lose my mind. I wanted to trail my hand up her thigh and push my fingers inside her. Lay her across the bench behind me, bury my head between her legs, and worship her with my mouth.

Not yet, though. First, I wanted to talk.

I dragged my mouth from hers, skating kisses along her jaw as she caught her breath, drinking in her sweet floral scent. My lips brushed her ear. "Let me cook for you," I said in a low voice.

Her chest heaved against mine. "Now?"

The corners of my mouth lifted. I'd do that too if she wanted. "This weekend. My place." I could take her out to eat, but I selfishly wanted to be the one to feed her, to be the only one to draw moans from her lips.

Her eyes met mine, and my chest swelled at the excitement shimmering in her gaze. "Like a date?" she asked. Her kiss-swollen lips tipped up.

I claimed them again, dipping my tongue inside her mouth for another taste.

"Yeah," I said when I pulled away. "Like a date."

Her body swayed into me, head tipping back against the locker. "What should I bring?"

My first thought was nothing. I wanted to spoil her completely. But I liked that she wanted to contribute, for this to be something we did together.

"How about a board game?" I murmured, trailing kisses along the side of her neck.

She tilted her head to the side and sighed, the sound a caress to my cock.

"Is that a yes?" I asked against her collarbone, my hands roaming the swell of her ass before brushing along the edge of her skirt.

Her grip tightened on the collar of my chef jacket. "Yes," she breathed. "*God*, yes."

The low, throaty words sent my heart racing as I slid one hand under her dress, the desire to touch her a physical strain that pulled my muscles taut. I skimmed my fingers up the inside of her thigh and watched her eyelids flutter shut as I reached the edge of her panties. She licked her lips, and my knuckles brushed her core, the fabric already damp.

"This okay?" I whispered.

Her eyes blinked open, heavy with arousal. "Don't stop."

Holding her gaze, I slipped two fingers under the elastic and trailed them through her slick heat to circle her clit. Her eyes fell closed, breaths coming harder as her hips started to move.

My attention slid to the open door. No one else was scheduled to be here for another hour, but I kept an ear out for a creak on the stairs. We'd already been interrupted once.

Shifting my thumb to her clit, I eased one finger inside her. She clenched around me and whimpered, one hand burying into my hair, grasping at the short strands. "Jase."

My name on her lips was my new favorite thing. Right along with the little moans she was making and the flush rising in her cheeks, the way her whole body responded to my touch, setting my blood on fire.

With my free hand, I hooked her knee around my waist, then added a second finger, curling them both against her inner wall. She squeezed her leg around me, rocking her hips to meet my hand's seeking motion, my thumb still working her clit.

"*Jase*," she said again.

I brought my lips to her ear. "You want more?" My other hand moved from her leg up to her breast, finding her nipple through her dress and teasing it with soft tugs.

A moan rolled up her throat as she arched her back, pressing her breast into my hand. Her hips were eager, driving my fingers deeper, her breaths heaving, eyes squeezed shut like the pleasure was too much. "Please——"

I pulled the top of her dress aside and closed my mouth over her nipple, circling the tight peak with my tongue before giving it a suck. Her muscles clamped around my fingers as I sucked harder, keeping steady pressure on her clit. Her mouth fell open on a silent cry, back arching, muscles locking as the rhythmic pulses continued, helpless moans falling from her lips.

My cock was steel in my pants, every nerve searing as I watched her come apart so openly, her pleasure mine alone to witness. I wanted to stand in that moment forever, make her come again and again, and see the same bliss painted on her face.

I eased the movement of my fingers as she clenched around them a few more times, pressing kisses along her jaw, her cheeks, her forehead, and finally to her lips. Her eyes fluttered open, blue-green jewels beneath dark lashes that trapped my breath in my lungs.

"You're so fucking beautiful," I whispered.

A smile broke over her face like sunlight bursting over the horizon. Our hands roamed each other, savoring the intimate touch for one more moment. She dipped her fingers beneath my shirt to graze the skin above my waistband, and my abs flexed almost painfully, goose bumps breaking out along my body. My cock throbbed, the loose fabric of my pants doing nothing to hide my erection as her hands teased lower.

She leaned in and pressed her lips to mine, slow and deep, driving my body higher with a need we didn't have the time or space to satisfy right now.

I pulled away with a groan, dropping my forehead to hers. "We should get to work."

She chuckled, making my own smile rise. "You're probably right."

I took one more inhale of her sweet scent, then pressed a final kiss to her lips. "See you later."

I forced my hands to drop, forced my feet to step back, forced my body into the hallway and down the stairs to the kitchen.

Forced myself not to focus on anything but the warmth in my chest and the rightness of the moment we'd just shared.

I didn't know what would come of this, but I did know—more than ever—I wanted to find out.

Chapter Twenty-Three
Dani

For the rest of the day on Friday, Jase and I worked in our respective spaces—me in Jillian's office and him in the kitchen. Neither of us ventured to see the other, knowing we wouldn't be able to keep our hands off each other if we did.

The restaurant's phone was flooded with calls from people trying to reserve a table for the already booked night, and not wanting to be a distraction during an especially busy shift, I decided to leave before service began. At four o'clock, I headed out, swinging by the bar to wave goodbye to Jase. He dragged me by the hand up to Jillian's office, pressed me against the closed door, and kissed me until I couldn't breathe.

Saturday, he texted me to ask what I wanted for dinner on our date. I told him to go with whatever he was in the mood for. I'd eat absolutely anything that man cooked, and then I'd ask for more.

Now it was Sunday evening, and I was on my way to his apartment, board game in hand, a change of clothes, makeup wipes, and a toothbrush rolled up in my purse. I'd decided to walk so I didn't have to worry about overnight parking, the complete opposite of how I usually felt before a first date. Normally, I'd want the excuse for not being able to stay the night, a buffer to keep things slow without having to come right out and say as much.

Tonight, I didn't want slow. I was past the point of dipping my toe in the water. I wanted to dive right in and be fully submerged in Jase. In the calmness of his presence and the steadiness of his confidence. In the fresh spice of his soap that made me want to rub my face against his neck like a cat in heat and then drop to my knees to find out how he tasted. To make him smile and then make him groan, make him lose himself as completely as I had against that locker.

It was a foreign sensation. Instead of the sharp buzz of my usual anxiety putting me on edge, something else rolled through me. A steady hum that vibrated low in my belly, craving everything he and I had already shared and more. Like something had awakened within me, some sensual being who had long been asleep and now needed to feed. It had my pulse thrumming as I made my way up the elevator of his building.

Outside his door, I adjusted the thin strap of my blue sundress, one that made me feel sexy but was still casual enough for a night in. It was another dress I'd bought a while ago but hadn't worn, never quite believing I could pull it off.

Tonight, it fit like a glove.

The door swung open, and my heart kicked at the sight of him. He wore dark jeans and a light blue button-down that made his eyes stand out, the sleeves rolled up to his elbows, leaving the defined lines of his forearms on display. It was a devastating combination.

He was frozen too, his gaze slowly moving from my hair down my body and back up again, his eyes burning with so much intensity that it raised the hair on my arms.

He wanted me.

The knowledge simmered my blood with arousal until it was thickly flowing magma in my veins.

It was only when Baxter slid out the door to rub against my leg that the moment broke. Jase took a step back and cleared his throat. "Hey, come in."

All sorts of delicious aromas greeted me as I trailed him into the kitchen, making my mouth water—onion and garlic and fresh herbs, and other combinations of ingredients I couldn't place. I set the board game on the island, careful of the candles and wineglasses laid out alongside a plate of some sort of appetizer.

I sent him a sidelong glance. "I'm impressed."

He gave a shy laugh as he reached for a glass of white wine. "I try." He handed me the glass, then picked up an appetizer off the plate. "Come here," he said softly.

I settled against the warmth of his body and let him place the bite in my mouth. As soon as it hit my tongue, my eyes fell closed on a moan, an explosion of umami richness bursting to life in my mouth.

"Oh my God, what is this?" Seriously, he could feed me anything, *anything*, and I would eat it.

"Fried parsnip crisp with sunchoke crumble and porcini puree," he answered as I licked my lips, catching the few crumbs stuck there.

I opened my eyes and found him watching me as if he'd never seen anything more beautiful. He leaned in and caught my mouth in a blistering kiss.

"You like feeding me or something?" I asked as he pulled away.

He rested his forehead against mine. "You have no idea." He nodded to the stools on the other side of the island. "Go ahead, take a seat. The next course is almost ready."

"Course?" I perked up as he moved to stir something on the stove. "As in more than one?"

He rested the wooden spoon on the ceramic saucer and crossed his arms over his chest, the corner of his mouth rising. "There are five."

"You know," I said, closing the distance between us and wrapping my arms around his waist. "You're playing a dangerous game. I might start expecting this level of culinary performance on every date."

He smirked, bringing his mouth to my ear. "I'm counting on it."

A delicious shiver ran up my spine.

I took a seat so he could serve me the next course of spicy tomato and pepper jam with charred flatbread that was—shocker—delicious. It continued that way for the rest of the meal, us eating together, talking about everything and nothing, him getting up to serve the next dish—first a watermelon and berry salad with chili lime dressing and herbs, and then summer corn tortellini with homemade pasta, all of it so good I could cry. He moved around his kitchen with the same controlled grace as at the restaurant, but even more hypno-tizing because I could watch him openly here.

Somehow it felt like we had done this a dozen times already, eaten dinner together at his place, his thumb brushing back and forth across my thigh, me refilling his wineglass without having to ask.

I offered to help wash dishes, but he refused, insisting there weren't that many. It was true only because he was as immaculate with caring for his kitchen as he was his food. He cleaned as he went, his sink never filling more than halfway before he put items in the dishwasher or rinsed them out by hand.

"I'm not this on top of the rest of my apartment," he admitted. "But one of the chefs I used to work for said it was like artists cleaning their brushes. It's about respect for your craft." He shrugged. "It stuck with me."

By the time we finished dessert—a dark chocolate brownie still warm from the oven that had me literally licking the plate, much to Jase's satisfaction—I couldn't eat another bite yet mourned there wasn't more. Not just because the food tasted so incredible, but because of all of it. Of how much I enjoyed talking to Jase. How easy it was to open up to him. How being around him somehow made me feel more myself. A self I hadn't known before yet recognized right away as the one I wanted to be.

It turned out it wasn't just Jase's food I couldn't get enough of; it was all of him.

Eventually, we made our way to the living room to set up the board game. He insisted on reading the rules to make sure I didn't give myself an unfair advantage, not that I would have. I planned to kick his ass fair and square.

By the end of the first hand, it was clear he was as competitive as I was.

An hour later, I jumped up from where I sat on the floor, arms raised above my head. "Hell yeah, baby, eat it!"

He threw his cards on the table. "I call foul play. You expect me to believe you just *happened* to draw the exact two cards you needed *exactly* when you needed them?"

I put my hands on my hips. "It's called luck."

"It's called cheating." He pointed an accusatory finger at me. "You stacked the decks, didn't you? When I got up to get us waters? It's okay, you can admit it. I won't tell anyone."

I skirted around the coffee table to where he sat on the couch and lowered myself in his lap. The glint in his eyes turned heated as I straddled him, his hands falling to my bare legs where my dress bunched at my hips.

"Don't feel bad," I said, nose brushing his, our mouths a breath apart. "Not everyone can be good at board games."

He squeezed my thighs, his thumbs skimming closer to where I was already growing wet, his touch igniting my skin. "I'm amazing at board games," he said, voice low.

My own voice was practically a whisper. "Then it must just be lousy luck." I rocked against him once with the slightest tilt of my hips. He was already growing hard, the pressure a delicious jolt to my core. I swallowed a moan. "But don't worry. That's about to change for you."

His gaze dropped to my lips. "Yeah?"

I nodded as I slid off his lap and settled on my knees between his legs. My hands flicked open the button of his jeans, the heel of my palm rubbing against him before I lowered his zipper.

A groan escaped his lips, low and deep, sending a pulse of heat between my legs.

I'd never been turned on by giving a blow job before. They were always more something I'd felt I *should* do rather than something I *wanted* to do. An item to check off the list so I wouldn't have to do it again for a while.

But this—the hunger in Jase's eyes, his whole body tense

with anticipation, chest rising and falling with heavy breaths—had me more than willing. Eager, even.

I eased down the waistband of his boxer briefs to reveal his hard length, precum shining on his tip, and wrapped my palm around the base, studying his face as I gave a light squeeze. His hands curled into fists at his sides, knuckles going white as his jaw flexed.

He was big. Alec was too, but it turned out Jase was the bigger brother in more ways than one. I forced down my smirk, aware of how inappropriate it was on so many levels, not least of which was that Alec was my ex, and I was about to feast on his brother's dick like it was my last meal.

I didn't care.

I'd never felt as good as I did at this moment, as powerful or as desired, and for once I was letting that instinct call the shots. The one that yearned to give this generous, protective man even an ounce of the pleasure he'd already given me.

I held his gaze as I leaned in and flicked my tongue over his tip.

"*Fuck.*" His head dropped back against the couch, chest falling as his stare remained glued to my mouth.

I licked up his length and swirled my tongue over the head, then closed my lips around him and lowered. His hands flew to my hair, fingers gentle as they brushed it from my face, clutching the strands as I eased out and back down. I took him deeper, sliding my tongue up and down his cock, wetting the base for my hand.

A groan caught in his chest, setting my skin on fire.

"Jesus." His hips began to move, small thrusts matching my steady rhythm, filling my mouth with his salty taste. I pumped faster, squeezed my hand harder, watched his brow furrow in what would almost look like pain if not for the scorching pleasure burning in his eyes.

My own hips squirmed in time with his thrusts, my thighs wet with arousal. The empty space between my legs ached for his hardness, clenching on nothing as a moan caught deep in my throat.

His grip on my hair tightened. "Stop," he gritted out, pulling me back. "Stop. Come up here."

I hopped to my feet and straddled him, our mouths connecting in a frenzied kiss as I rolled my hips against him, the friction driving me wild. He pressed forward, his rock-hard length rubbing against my clit with nothing but my plain white thong separating us. It was the sexiest underwear I owned, and right now, I'd never hated a piece of fabric more.

His hands found my ass, squeezing and kneading, yanking at my thong, grinding me against him in a way that had me gasping for breath. One strap of my dress fell off my shoulder, and I yanked the other off with it, peeling the top of my dress down so it bunched at my waist.

Cool air grazed my fevered skin, stiffening my nipples. He lowered his mouth around one, kissing and sucking it before taking it in his teeth and gently pulling.

"Oh God," I breathed. My hands tightened around his shoulders, thighs clenching with need. "Condom."

He moved to my other breast, laving it with the same attention until I was shaking in his arms.

"Jase, please," I moaned, tugging at his shirt, desperate to get it off him.

With a low chuckle, he unbuttoned it. The moment he had it open, my hands flew to his chest, fingers exploring his smooth, tanned skin, trailing across his dusting of hair and over his tightened abs.

He was too much—too attractive, too masculine. My body didn't know how to handle it, my hips frantic as he dragged his shirt the rest of the way off and dug into his pants pocket.

He barely got the condom on before I pulled my panties aside and sank onto him in one smooth motion. I whimpered at the fullness, the stretch almost too much. It only made me want more.

"That's it," he murmured, running his hands up to grasp my breasts as I sank lower. His thumbs flicked over my nipples. "Take what you need."

I did.

Oh God, I did, filling myself all the way, rubbing my clit against his groin as pressure built inside me unlike anything I'd felt before. A churning ocean of pleasure ready to drag me under and drown me in its depths.

I ground against him, hands clutching his shoulders, gripping his hair, desperate to hold the shards of myself together that threatened to fracture with each roll of my hips.

He grazed his hands down my spine and gripped my ass, tilting my pelvis forward enough so his lips could reach my neck, my collarbone, my breasts.

"Yes," I breathed, picking up speed. "*Yes.*" The new angle of my hips had him hitting a spot inside me that made me cry out. I gasped his name. "Jase—"

He closed his mouth over a nipple and sucked.

It was like crashing to shore and catapulting through the sky all at once, wave after wave of pleasure rushing through me in terrible relief. My muscles seized, toes curling, and I ground down faster, tightening around his cock again and again, his hardness both the cause and the cure of this agony I never wanted to end.

When I finally came down, he was brushing my hair from my face, trailing his touch over my skin, kissing the underside of my jaw, my temple, my neck. Worshipping me.

His lips brushed over mine, and I sank into the kiss, wanting closer, even as I caught my breath. I pulsed with aftershocks around his still hard erection, and whatever being had awakened within me stirred, hungry for more. My hips churned in response.

It seemed as though, with all things Jase, I couldn't get enough.

Chapter Twenty-Four
Jase

DANI ROCKED AGAINST ME, almost imperceptible moans catching in her throat with each back and forth as she came down from her orgasm. Watching it had nearly sent me over the edge with her, but I'd managed to hold off, my muscles straining with the effort. No way was I ready for this to end.

Easing forward on the couch, I hooked her legs around my waist and carefully rose to my feet. Still buried inside her, I carried her to the bedroom, her tight heat clenching around me with every step.

She draped her arms over my shoulders, bare breasts pressed to my chest, face burrowed against my neck. Her mouth closed over my pulse, sucking gently before she licked up to my earlobe and tugged it with her teeth.

My cock throbbed, the feel of her unreal. Not just the way she clasped around me but the way she moved and chased her pleasure. How she'd completely let go on the couch and taken what she needed, leaving me to sit back and let her. To watch her and coax her on until she slipped over into ecstasy.

Every experience from my past had been the opposite. Me feeling like I had to be the one to take charge and dominate. To fulfill a specific role during sex—this composed, assertive, hypermasculine guy I'd worn like a filter throughout all my relationships because it was what I'd thought I had to do to keep my partner happy.

I hadn't realized how much pressure it had been until Dani lifted it.

I lowered her onto the bed, Baxter thankfully nowhere in sight, and rocked into her once, pinning her to the mattress as I kissed her slow and deep. Her mouth chased mine, seeking more, but I didn't give it to her.

Instead, I pulled away, her pout making my lips twitch as I stood. She'd had her time to play; now it was mine.

I worked her dress and panties over her hips, leaving her gloriously naked, the small mounds of her breasts rising and falling with her rapid breaths. My eyes drank in her slight curves and toned legs, following the soft line of her abdomen. She rubbed her thighs together as I kicked off my jeans, her eyes consuming me with equal hunger.

Once naked, I braced myself above her, not letting our bodies touch as I took in how beautiful she was—her skin flushed, lips swollen red, dark hair billowing around her face, framing those blue-green eyes.

She whispered her fingers along my chest and down my abs, making them clench as her touch drew close to where my cock strained for her.

Goose bumps lifted along my skin. Her eyes rose to mine,

glinting in the light filtering in from the living room, and the openness of her gaze tightened my throat.

A slow smile spread over her lips. "Hi."

I lowered to my forearms on either side of her head, pressing our bodies together, no barriers between us. "Hi."

This, right here. This was what I wanted. No roles. No masks. No performances.

Just us.

I sank back into her one inch at a time, watching her eyes widen and mouth fall open as I rocked out slightly, then pushed in almost painfully slowly, wanting to draw this out as long as both of us could bear.

On my third thrust, I dropped my forehead to her shoulder, shaking with restraint. "Goddamn." Her knees squeezed my hips, legs hooking around mine like she was trying to fuse herself to me.

"Please," she moaned, hand clutching my hair as her head fell back.

I picked up my pace, no longer able to resist, the need to pump harder and faster growing with her every moan.

Sweat coated our skin. Our bodies slapped together, her wetness easing my way, driving me higher, my thrusts faster, until I could feel my climax closing in. It hovered just over my shoulder, ready to devour me. I refused to let go until she did.

I rose to one hand, tweaking her nipple with the other before dragging it down to circle her clit. Her head rolled to the side, eyes squeezing shut as her voice rose. "Jase. *Jase.* Oh God —" A tremble rolled through her, and then her muscles locked, back arching, mouth open, the pulsing of her perfect heat severing the last of my restraint.

"*Fuck.*" I braced myself on both hands, snapping my hips, white flashing before my eyes as I buried myself in her and spilled into the condom. My arms gave out, and I collapsed on top of her, managing to hold myself up enough to not completely crush her.

When I'd caught my breath enough to form words, I asked, "Are you okay?"

She blew out a breath that turned into a chuckle, light and free, her belly moving against mine. It ended with a sigh. "I'm amazing."

I smiled against her neck. "Yeah?" I lifted my head so I could meet her eyes.

Relaxed features gazed back at me, almost drowsy, a grin lighting up her face. She bit her lip as if to contain it and nodded.

"Amazing enough that you'd want to stay the night?" I asked.

"That depends." She traced a finger over my shoulder. "Will there be breakfast in the morning?"

My lips rose higher. "Any requests?"

She gazed up at me through long, dark lashes. "Surprise me."

I pressed my lips to hers once, then again, kissing her softly before finally pulling out. "Be right back."

On my way to the bathroom, I spotted Baxter at his water bowl. I shot him a wink of gratitude for the privacy. The guy had a fresh tuna treat headed his way.

When I returned to the bedroom, Dani stretched from the bed and crossed to the door, rising on her toes to press a kiss to my cheek. "My turn."

"I have an extra toothbrush you can use."

She shot a smirk over her shoulder. "No need. I came prepared."

I fought a grin. Of course, she had.

She returned a few minutes later without any makeup and crawled into bed beside me. I almost got hard all over again. I'd seen her without makeup before, but this felt different. How even now that we'd slept together, she didn't feel the need to hide, no matter how thin the mask.

A perfect calm washed through me as we sank into the pillows, her head on my chest. I tried to think of the right thing to say to encapsulate this feeling seeping into every part of me, but no words did it justice.

Before I could get anything out, her limbs grew heavy and her breath slowed into the steady rhythm of sleep. It looked like I'd just have to show her instead.

Chapter Twenty-Five
Dani

Morning greeted me with a hard chest at my back and a warm bundle pressed to the curve of my stomach. Eyes still closed, I reached out and encountered soft fur. A purr rumbled to life, rolling its way up my torso.

"Morning, Baxter," I mumbled.

The body behind me shifted, and soft lips pressed to the back of my neck. "Do I get a 'good morning,' too?"

I smiled, the low gravel of Jase's sleep-heavy voice washing over me like warm honey. His erection pressed against my ass, and I nudged my hips backward just a little, his groan lifting the corners of my mouth higher.

"Certainly feels good," I said.

He let out a low hum and brushed his hand down my side, his palm gliding over my thigh and back up to rest in the dip of my waist. "How'd you sleep?"

I let out a deep sigh. "So good."

As soon as my head had hit the pillow—the pillow being

Jase's deliciously firm chest—I'd been *out*. Even now, my body was fully relaxed, my muscles loose and languid. More notably, my mind was quiet. The incessant chatter usually rattling off my to-do list the second I woke was blissfully silent, and the quickly mounting stress that accompanied it was absent as well.

Did everyone know the cure to anxiety was really good sex? If not, studies needed to be conducted and official research published because it felt goddamn groundbreaking to me.

He placed another kiss below my ear, then whispered, "Too bad Baxter's here, or I'd show you exactly how glad I am to hear it."

The memory of him above me, thrusting with a frantic pace as his pleasure hit its peak, had my body eager for more. "Why not show me anyway?"

He chuckled against my neck, the low sound raising tingles along my skin. "He's far too innocent to witness that."

Right on cue, Baxter curled tighter into a ball and covered his face with his paw. It didn't deter the warmth blooming in my stomach as my feverish need from last night built again.

I arched, pushing my ass harder against Jase's cock. "What about if we stay under the covers?"

Grabbing his hand, I slipped it beneath the sheet, guiding it between my thighs where I was already growing wet. He felt as much and growled, rocking his stiff length against me.

Before his fingers could explore deeper, his phone buzzed on the bedside table. He dropped his forehead to mine with a sigh. "Hold that thought."

I followed him as he rolled away, propping myself on my elbow as he reached for his phone.

My gaze raked over his body, admiring the definition in his arms and chest as he lounged against the headboard. His stomach flexed, and I wanted to run my tongue along each and every groove, down to that V peeking out above the sheet, then lower to where his erection tented the covers. I'd banish Baxter to the living room myself if that was what it took to get my mouth around him again.

The image vanished as soon as I caught sight of his phone.

Mom.

I tensed, heart lurching in my throat. My mind flashed back to the steps of my building the night of Colin's gallery. Her name on Jase's screen. The way he'd avoided me after.

Baxter stood, arching in a stretch before hopping off the bed and strolling out of the room.

Maybe I should follow. Just walk into the living room and keep walking out the door, back to my own apartment, and pretend this never happened.

I didn't know what Jase's relationship with his parents was like, but I got the sense there was tension there. Maybe even tension with Alec. Tension that this—*me*—would likely only make worse.

Not for the first time, I wished Jase could be not Alec's brother. Not *anyone's* brother. That he could just be some guy I'd met who had no connections to my past and wouldn't cause complications for either of us.

Maybe he wished that too. And if he decided the complications were too much, I'd get it.

It would hurt. But I would understand.

He silenced the phone and ran his hand through his sleep-mussed hair. The gesture tugged at something tender behind my ribs.

"She was probably calling about my travel plans for when I

go home in a few weeks. For the, uh…" His eyes flicked to mine, then back to his phone. "The baby shower."

Right.

Stephanie's baby shower. That Alec would be at because Stephanie was his pregnant wife.

And Jase was his brother.

I should leave.

I should find my dress and go home, where I'd work from now on so Jase didn't have to worry about avoiding me, and we'd only have to interact again at the symposium—

"Hey."

My attention snapped back to Jase as he tossed his phone aside.

He slid down beside me on the bed, his body warm against mine, and tucked a lock of hair behind my ear. "I don't want to think about that right now," he said, voice quiet but firm. "Not after last night."

His eyes held mine, open and sincere, searching. Always searching. *Seeing.*

Screw it.

I kissed him. My mouth sought his like it belonged to me, and he let me have it, opening to me immediately as he pulled me against his chest. In one smooth motion, he rolled me onto my back, rising above me and blocking out the rest of the world.

Maybe it could be like Robin suggested, where we just enjoyed each other and moved on. No need for his family to ever find out.

Simple. Like we'd agreed.

His lips left mine, letting me catch my breath as he kissed his way down my throat, pausing to suck each breast before continuing lower. The sight of him between my legs was almost enough to make me come before his tongue even touched me. When it finally did, he had to hold my hips in place to keep them from bucking off the bed.

His mouth moved against me, tongue seeking, and my body twisted away to escape the mounting pleasure even as I ground against him for more.

It was too much. Too much and not enough. Too much and everything I needed all at once.

"Jase!" I cried out, covering my eyes with my hand.

He closed his lips over my clit and sucked as he slid two fingers inside me, drawing me to the edge of an excruciating fall.

That was the thing about keeping it simple—it only worked if no feelings were involved.

The problem was I had already started falling, and there was no stopping it now.

We fell into a routine.

I continued working from the restaurant, wanting more than ever to be close to Jase, to witness him in his element and be part of his world. The hate mail had died down enough that Geffery thought it was safe for me to return to the office, but Talia was happy with the progress I'd made and had no problem with me working remotely until the symposium. I planned to take advantage of every moment it allowed me to spend with Jase.

I craved him, not just with my body but also with my mind.

With something else, too, that scared me too much to think about.

Because for every part of me that recognized how *right* this felt, being with him in this way, another part couldn't help but feel like our time was running out. That feeling of being in a dream you never wanted to wake from but knowing in the back of your mind that your alarm would go off at any second.

I didn't want to wake from this.

He cooked for me most days, breakfasts after nights spent together—usually at his place since he had Baxter to take care of and the better kitchen—and lunch, which he'd bring to me in Jillian's office.

More nights than not, I ate dinner at the bar in what had become my regular seat nearest the kitchen. Despite Jase's protests, I insisted on paying, though I did let him give me an employee discount. It was still more than I would have spent on meals out before, but with the amount I saved on groceries from his cooking for me, I figured it balanced out.

Robin joined me for either dinner or drinks at least once a week, usually on a night Neela worked, and it was on those nights especially that it struck me how different my life was from two months ago.

Two years ago.

Ten years ago.

That I had found a space for myself where I felt full with people who filled me up. That I was, for once, content to sit here in this moment instead of pushing and planning and rushing to the next. Even when an email came in the following Monday afternoon that should have had me scrambling.

"Did he say why?" I asked Talia over the phone. I was

cross-legged on Jase's couch, wearing one of his T-shirts with my laptop on his coffee table, said email filling the screen.

"Some sort of family emergency. He didn't give details, but he was firm in his withdrawal."

I blew out a breath. "Okay." There really wasn't much else to say. The main speaker for one of our symposium panels had just pulled out, and unless we replaced him, we'd have a huge hole in our schedule.

It was doable but not ideal. Especially since everyone on our list of backups was located on the other side of the country, and coordinating the logistics this close to the event had the potential to be a nightmare.

A month seemed like a lot of time, but it almost always took a week just to hear back on an initial inquiry, and most people needed time to work out their schedule before they could commit, which meant it would likely be a little over a week out from the symposium before we had a confirmed speaker to book travel for. Not to mention how the programs would need to be updated and printed at the last minute, along with a million other details that would need to be adjusted.

"I'll make some calls," Talia said. "See if anyone gets back to me quickly."

"All right. I'll hold off on emails until I hear from you. Let me know if anyone bites."

"I'll check in again later today. It'll work out," she assured me.

"Yeah." I didn't sound convinced. I guess I wasn't. Not that we wouldn't find someone, but whether we should.

Talia hung up, and I clicked over to a new tab in my browser and opened my social media accounts. Like the hate mail, the nasty comments and DMs had slowed way down, but

I could still see the ones from before. I hadn't bothered to delete them, instead choosing to ignore them altogether, rarely looking at my accounts.

I looked now, though, not entirely sure what I was looking for until I saw it. Not in every comment, but in enough.

"Everything okay?"

Over at the island, Jase was making us his version of grilled cheese—the kind that used sourdough bread and three different cheeses, and that he stuffed with various fruits or veggies and then drizzled with a balsamic glaze. His hair was still damp from his post-gym shower, and he hadn't put on a shirt, leaving his lean muscles on display, a few of them flexing as he cut up a nectarine. I let my eyes take in the view.

"Not exactly," I replied. "One of our panelists canceled."

He brushed his hands off and rounded the island, a clean pair of gym shorts riding low on his hips. I didn't even pretend not to stare.

He came to stop in front of the couch and held out his hand. "Come here."

"What?" I asked, placing my hand in his.

He pulled me to my feet. "You look like you could use a dance."

Just like that, I softened, the tension surrounding my thoughts loosening under the warmth of his gaze, that contentment I found so often lately seeping its way in. I looped my arms around his neck, and his hands rubbed slow circles against my spine as we swayed.

"You also don't look as worried about this whole panelist situation as I would have guessed you'd be," he said.

It was true. A lot of planning went into organizing all five panels—determining the right topics to have the greatest impact on moving the conversation forward, finding the right combination of experts for each one that would provide valuable perspectives and complement each other's strengths. This sort of hiccup this late in was exactly the sort of thing that would normally spin me out.

Instead, I found myself wondering if this wasn't an opportunity for something else. Maybe even something better.

"I…have this idea," I admitted, still working through it in my head, the pieces coming together more solidly with each second.

His brows rose. "But…?"

I sighed, sinking a little more into his arms. "But it'd be a big change from our original plan. One that could create noise, and not all good. I'm not sure it's worth mentioning to Talia."

Except the more I thought about it, the more I wanted to. And our plans had already changed. Why not do something big with it?

"It's worth it," Jase said easily.

My eyes narrowed. "What makes you so sure?"

"Because you have the same look on your face that you did during your interview with Bill Sewick." His mouth tilted up. "The one that says to get the fuck out of your way because you're on a mission, and no one's stopping you."

I closed my eyes and shook my head like he was ridiculous, but also so I could catch up with the sudden rush of emotion surging through my chest. Because he was right. What coursed through me now was exactly what I had felt during that interview. The same boldness to speak up and be heard, to be unapologetic in my actions.

It had scared me then, how reckless it had felt. It was still unfamiliar to me now, and yet…I kind of liked it.

I peered up at him. "That's really what you saw?"

He nodded. "Still do."

The way he looked at me as he said it, the steadiness of his gaze, the tone of his voice—he said it like he meant it. Admired it, even.

Admired *me*.

I pulled his mouth to mine, kissing him deeply before sinking to my knees. Then I spent the rest of my lunch break showing him how much I admired him back.

"A VIRTUAL PANEL," I said to Talia the following morning. We were in her office with my proposal laid out on her desk. "One that's open to the public. We stream it live and accept questions from viewers in the chat for our experts to answer."

Right now, the symposium was invite-only, intended as an opportunity to further the conversation around maternal health issues within the industry by those in positions to enact change. But too much of that change was being challenged from the outside by people who didn't understand the full picture.

"It would certainly get a lot of attention," Talia agreed, reviewing my notes.

My proposed topic was "Abortion as Healthcare: What It Is and Why It's Crucial to Comprehensive Medical Care." It was intended to grab attention, and no, not all of it would be good. But that was the point.

"This is a chance for us to address all the misinformation out there about abortion," I said. "Challenge the stigma it's been brandished with and get the truth out there about what it actually is and the specific circumstances it's carried out under.

This is so much broader and more complex an issue for health-care as a whole than I think most people realize, and they should get to hear the perspective of the medical providers dealing with these situations every day."

"Is your hope that this will minimize the amount of hate mail we get toward the clinic? Because I don't see that happening. Most of the people who wrote those letters aren't interested in being educated. They have their own version of the truth and won't be swayed by another."

I shook my head. "This isn't about them. It's about the people who *are* willing to listen. Who are seeking to understand better, or maybe don't even realize what they've been told isn't all there is to this." I knew those people existed because I'd seen them in my social media comments, trying to ask questions but getting drowned out by all the enraged voices.

"I mean, half the stuff I know now I didn't learn until I started working here," I added. "This issue is so inflammatory that it's hard to ask questions and get actual, reliable answers without one side of the internet or the other coming down on you. *That's* what this panel is for. A safe place to have this discussion without judgment or preaching. We can monitor the chat and only pull legitimate questions for the panelists, keep the trolls and hate out of it. Focus only on answering questions from the medical perspective about this procedure and why it's necessary for effective healthcare for people who can get pregnant."

Talia's arms were crossed, but she nodded along, looking more thoughtful than opposed. "We'd have to get the board's approval. It's an approach we've never taken before."

No, we'd been tiptoeing around the issue because of how polarizing it was, hoping to avoid things like hate mail and death threats for as long as possible. That's what I'd done during the interview. Tried to talk around the truth instead of coming right out and saying it. It hadn't made a difference.

"It isn't enough for us to brush this aside," I said. "Not anymore. We need to stop acting like we're doing something wrong that needs to be kept hidden. The best way we can do that is to not only join the conversation but lead it. No more hiding."

She studied me for a long moment, one that previously would have had my insides folding in on themselves as I second-guessed my every word. On the other side of this silence was her approval or rejection. And up until now, I'd held that above all else. I'd never fully believed my ideas were good unless Talia agreed with them, needing that approval to validate my own judgment.

Not this time. Whether Talia and the board approved the virtual panel or not, I trusted the urging in my gut that said it was the right call.

Talia smirked. "You really believe in this, don't you?"

"Yes," I said without hesitation.

She released the cross of her arms. "I do too. I'll see how quickly I can get the board together. Keep prepping for this. Let's be ready to pull the trigger as soon as we get their okay."

I nodded and turned for the door.

"And, Dani?"

I glanced back to find her smiling.

"Good work."

My chest swelled, pride surging through me at those two words in a way it never had before. Probably because this time, I believed them.

Chapter Twenty-Six
Jase

Me: Got plans for the day?

I SENT the text and looked out at the bouquet of yellow balloons swaying in the breeze at the end of my parents' driveway. I'd been parked along the street of their house for five minutes already, working up to going inside. More cars lined the edge of their lawn, the baby shower in full swing. Ideally, I'd slip in unnoticed, give my brother and his wife my best, then spend the rest of the party sitting along the wall sipping a beer until it was late enough that I could justify needing to head out.

Dani: Not really. Just taking advantage of some me time.

Me: Me time? Is that code for masturbating?

Dani: Don't know yet. Depends where the day takes me.

She ended the text with a winky face, and my lips rose. I'd give up six months of my salary to be back at her place, in her bed, watching her pleasure herself until neither of us could take it and I sank slowly inside her. I could practically feel the way her hips would rock helplessly against mine, urging me to take her harder, faster, to fill her completely, the way I had last night and the night before. Nearly every night for the past three weeks. My cock twitched at the thought, and I had to tear my mind away from the image and remember why that wasn't how I'd be spending my day.

Me: Have a good time.

Dani: You too.

I didn't have high hopes. I think she knew it, too. I hadn't exactly hidden that I wasn't thrilled to be going home to Connecticut, and I was sure she'd noticed how many of my mom's calls I'd ignored in favor of returning them later. Or the fact that I wasn't staying the night at my parents' house even though I wasn't working this weekend.

Maybe she found it strange my mom hadn't asked me to help with food for the shower, despite my offering. I'd rather spend my time here in the kitchen, but when I'd put it out there, my mom had said she'd think about it and then never mentioned it again.

A part of me wanted to tell Dani how much that stung, to let her see the tender skin my family always managed to poke. It was a vulnerability I'd only ever shown Dr. Ohara. One I still had a hard time facing myself.

How much of it would she really want to know? How awkward would any mention of my family be for her?

Maybe it wouldn't be awkward at all. Maybe the certainty that it would be was all in my head. Maybe I should try letting her in and see how it felt for both of us.

I had to make it through this shower first.

I took a deep breath and pushed my way out of the rental car, grabbing the gift bag off the front seat. Hot August air pressed in around me, plastering my button-down shirt to my back, the stiff material offering no breathability. The only reason I'd worn it was because my mom had given it to me, which meant it might be one less thing she'd find to criticize me for. I wasn't up for that today. All I wanted was to celebrate Alec's growing family and leave without any added drama.

Michael Bublé's singing greeted me over the speakers as I pushed open the front door. The same muted-toned furniture and ornately framed artwork I'd grown up with filled the space as if no time had passed, every throw pillow and decorative trinket precisely arranged into the picture of domestic bliss.

My chest constricted as memories barraged me. I was sixteen again, seventeen, eighteen, slipping silently past this same room as I snuck out the front door, slowly pulling the latch closed behind me, relief flooding my lungs the second I was on the other side. As if I could breathe again.

It was a calling I desperately wanted to answer as the ivory walls with their crown molding squeezed in around me.

I made a straight line through to the kitchen instead, out the sliding door and onto the deck, where my breaths came a little easier in the fresh air.

What had to be at least fifty people mingled throughout the

backyard. Buffet tables were set up on one side of the deck, covered in metal trays of catered food, while high tops and round tables draped in white tablecloths were scattered across the grass. At the center of each was an arrangement of white and yellow flowers, matching the yellow balloons tied all along the yard's white fence. It looked like something straight out of Martha Stewart. I had to hand it to my mom—it was impressive.

And the complete opposite of anything I would plan or want for myself. Not really surprising at this point, but it still made my shirt feel that much tighter.

With a quick sweep, I was able to spot my parents. Dad stood just off the deck with a few of my uncles and a man I recognized as Stephanie's father. Mom was across the yard with most of the ladies, orchestrating what looked like a game involving diapers. At the center of the chaos sat Stephanie under the shade of the large oak tree.

I crossed the deck to deposit my gift on the table with the others, then headed to the cooler beside the food and grabbed a beer. I'd just twisted off the top when my brother stepped through the sliding door, grinning when he saw me.

"You made it, man." He pulled me into a hug, slapping a hand against my back before pulling away.

"Yeah, I—" I started to say *I wouldn't miss it*, but I probably would have if Mom hadn't been so insistent. "Yeah."

Guilt gnawed at me. My little brother was having his first kid. I should want to celebrate with him. Should feel proud of him instead of wishing he'd do one thing that didn't meet my parents' expectations. Should be able to look at him without bitterness twisting my stomach.

I wanted him to be happy. He'd never been a bad brother to me, had never antagonized me or judged me for my decisions, at least not to my face. It wasn't his fault he had the kind of relationship with our parents that I'd never managed to build.

We stood next to the food table in silence, peering out at the yard.

"Congratulations, by the way," I spat out. "I don't know if I've said that to you yet." I hadn't. Add it to the list of ways I was a terrible big brother. Right below me fucking his ex-girlfriend.

What would he say if I told him? Just laid it all out right now:

So hey, remember Dani, your college girlfriend who I'm pretty sure at one point you planned to marry? I woke her up this morning with my tongue between her legs, then drove my cock into her until neither of us could speak. Oh, and also I can't stop thinking about her.

Would he care? Be angry? Feel betrayed?

Or maybe he'd just think I was pathetic, like I was chasing who he'd been, trying to be the same.

Not that I was about to find out. This would be about the worst possible time for that particular conversation, not to mention I wanted to discuss it with Dani first. Another conversation I wasn't sure how it'd go.

"I'm really happy for you and Stephanie," I said instead.

Alec beamed. "Thanks." His gaze landed on his wife, his whole face softening as if the rest of the party faded away. "We're really excited." He clapped me on the shoulder. "And, hey, maybe you're not so far behind, now that you're back with Gabby."

My brows pulled together. "What are you talking about?"

"Gabby," he said again, sounding confused. "Mom said you were back together. That's why we invited her."

My hand holding the beer bottle froze in midair. "You what?" Every inch of my skin grew tight as my pulse shifted into high gear. "Tell me she's not here, Alec." My eyes flew to the group of women across the yard.

"She…I'm sorry," he said, voice panicked. "I swear to God, I thought you were back together."

Just then, I caught a glimpse of raven-black hair and tanned skin in the middle of the pack of women, head thrown back, laughing at something my mom had said.

I should have turned around, marched through the house, and left that very second. Nothing good would come of this. But before I could retreat, my ex-girlfriend looked over her shoulder and spotted me.

She smiled like she was expecting me. Like this had been the plan all along. Like it hadn't been a year since we'd last spoken. She stood and tapped my mom's arm before pointing in my direction, and my mom's eyes lit up as they both started across the yard.

"This is not fucking happening," I said, ready to scream except for the fact that I could no longer breathe.

This is not fucking happening.

If I thought it enough times, maybe it would come true. And then pigs would fly.

"What can I do?" Alec asked, eyes wide, face pale with guilt. I had nothing to do with this, yet I still managed to ruin his party. All by not being with the person my mom thought I should.

"Don't worry about it. I just need to duck inside for a bit. I can't—" I glanced at Mom and Gabby, now halfway to the deck. "I just need a few minutes. Please, just enjoy your party, okay? Please."

"Are you sure? Because I could—"

But I was already stepping inside, setting my beer on the island as I headed for the staircase to my old room. If I walked out the front door, I'd get straight in my rental car and wouldn't stop until I was back in Philly. The desire was so strong I had to grip the railing to stop myself. I refused to do that to Alec.

"I'll go get him," Gabby said from the kitchen, her voice and the swift clicking of heels on the wooden floor following me up the stairs.

I reached my room, now void of the Green Day and Blink-182 posters that had hung on the walls in high school, and clasped my hands behind my head. I was able to drag in two full breaths before the door clicked shut behind me.

"Hey, handsome."

My arms dropped. "What are you doing here, Gabby?"

Her smile was predatory as she stepped toward me, hips swaying in her tight dress. "What, I don't even get a hello?"

Sure, if we'd stumbled across each other in the grocery store. But she was here, in my parents' home, at my brother's baby shower. My muscles were granite, my lungs hardly able to expand. "Whose idea was this? Did my mom call you?"

"You know the two of us were always close." She lifted a shoulder. "We've stayed in touch a little. She thought I might like to come, and it seemed like a good idea."

"Why?" I practically begged. "And why didn't you call me first?"

"Would you have answered if I did?"

Probably not, no. Not right away. I would have needed some time to brace myself before a conversation with her. But I would have at least texted her back.

"That doesn't explain why you're here," I said as she got closer. "We broke up over a year ago."

"So? That doesn't have to mean anything." She laid her hands on my chest, and I flinched. "Not if we don't want it to."

"It means we're not together anymore," I said, pulling her wrists away and stepping back.

Growing up, this room had never felt small to me. If anything, it had felt the opposite, been the one place where I could cast off everyone else's expectations and have the space to be myself. Right now, that space was getting sucked out, the walls shrinking around me, leaving me trapped with more than one of my pasts.

She took another step, cornering me against the twin bed. "We could be—" she started, but frowned as she saw my face.

I was already shaking my head.

She dropped the flirtatious act. "Jase, come on. We were together for years, and then we hardly even talked about it before you left. One day, everything was great, and the next, you were ending it. Do you seriously not regret it?"

"No," I said, stepping to the side to put another foot of space between us. I grimaced at the harshness of my tone. I *did* regret some of how I left. But not *that* I left. And I didn't trust her to care about the difference.

She saw my grimace and jumped on it. "We can talk about it now," she said, hope rising in her voice. "I get we had a few issues, but we were good together. We deserve another shot."

"No."

She reached for me again. "Look—"

"I'm seeing someone." The words left my mouth like a gavel, striking hard and fast.

Gabby's face fell. Her hands dropped to her sides. "Your

mom said…" She folded her arms over her stomach, shoulders drawing forward. "Why didn't you bring her?"

I shoved my hands in my pockets, a bit of steadiness returning with the thought of Dani. "It's new," I explained. "And despite what my mom thinks, she doesn't get a say in my relationships."

Gabby lowered her chin, eyes drifting to the small desk along the wall to her right. "But it's serious?"

Yes. My instinct was to say it. To fucking scream it. Burn Dani's name into my skin and bare it for the whole world to see.

But the truth was I didn't know. The way I felt about Dani was new to me, and it was entirely possible she didn't feel the same way.

Even if she did, she might not see a future for us. Not with her history with my brother and the unknown of my family. "Serious" implied marriage and houses and babies and all the things Gabby wanted from me that I didn't have in me to give. Not when that was all she wanted me for. When she could take or leave the rest of me without it mattering to her bigger picture.

I'd never felt that from Dani. Like an object to be obtained.

"It's real," I replied.

"And I wasn't, is that it?" Her eyes went glassy, and my shoulders sagged.

"*We* weren't, Gabs," I said as gently as I could manage. "We were convenient. I wasn't there for you the way you deserve, and you…"

Her red eyes held mine, waiting.

"We *both* deserve to be with people who make us feel good.

More than just 'not alone.' Can you honestly say that's what we were for each other?"

Her gaze swept the room before dropping to her feet. She dug one heel into the plush carpet. "I'll go," she finally said.

I nodded, not knowing what else to say.

She walked to the door, pausing as her hand touched the knob. "I hope it works out for you, Jase. But maybe ask yourself, how real can it be if you won't even bring her home for your brother's baby shower?"

She didn't wait for an answer. Just opened the door and was gone, leaving me to wade through the doubt she'd left in her wake like a lingering perfume.

I'd barely made it downstairs before my mom was in my face, demanding an explanation.

"What on earth did you say to Gabby to make her leave?"

I strode past her toward the kitchen. "Leave it alone, Mom. Please. You never should have invited her in the first place. In fact, I asked you not to."

She scoffed. "So I'm the bad guy for not wanting you to be alone forever? To have a future? She was good for you, Jase. She has a stable career, is nice and attractive. What reason is there to not be with her?"

"A stable career?" I rounded the island, keeping it between us like it might protect me in some way. "And I don't? You think I need someone to support me after I fail miserably as a chef like I do at everything else, is that it?"

Her mouth hung open for a beat as she crossed her arms.

So that's a yes.

"How would you even know how my job is going?" I challenged. "When was the last time you asked me about the restaurant? It's good, by the way. So you can stop trying to find someone to pay my rent."

"I just want you to be happy." She gestured out the window to the backyard. "Look at Alec. Look how happy he is with Stephanie."

I clenched my jaw, refusing to blow up within earshot of the party. "He is happy. And this party is for him, so how about we get back to it and forget this?"

"But if you go after Gabby right now, you might—"

"*Mom*, drop it, okay? I don't love Gabby. I don't want to be with her. I was miserable with her. You don't get to decide I wasn't just because it's what you'd prefer."

"Jase." My father stepped inside from the deck, sliding the glass door closed behind him. Guess I was really in trouble now. Just like old times. "That's not how you speak to your mother. She was just looking out for you."

My hands rolled into fists on the cold granite as I strained to keep my voice even. "She completely disregarded everything I said about Gabby. Either she wasn't listening to me or she didn't care. Neither of you do." I drew my arms wide. "What am I supposed to do with that?"

My mom showed me her palm and turned away. "I can't talk to you when you're like this."

"Your mom's right," my dad said, placing a hand on her shoulder. "It's disrespectful to your brother to discuss this now, anyway. He's the one we should be focusing on today."

I blew out something too bitter to be a laugh, focusing anywhere but at them. If I looked at them right now, I didn't think I'd be able to hold in my scream.

"Come on, dear." He led my mom toward the sliding door.

"Stephanie was going to start opening presents. I know you had a plan for that."

Because opening presents needed a plan. Apparently, *opening them* was too simple.

I watched out the kitchen window as my mom plastered on a smile and took up her place as ringleader, coordinating the move of presents over to the oak tree where Stephanie still sat. She waved Alec over, and he took a stance behind his wife, bending to drop a kiss on her cheek as his hands rubbed her round belly. The ladies circling them all awed, and the men all cheered him on, the perfect son living his perfect life while I was on the outside once again.

I stayed for another half hour, watching them open presents from the rear of the deck before I slipped into the house and left. Chances were I'd be back in Philly long before anyone noticed.

Chapter Twenty-Seven
Dani

I PULLED the last box off the top shelf of my closet and wiped it with the dust rag. Early 2000s pop music filled my apartment from the portable speaker on my coffee table, and I bounced my hips to Britney's voice as I flipped the lid off the box to see what was inside. I'd spent most of the day cleaning my apartment, getting rid of things I no longer wanted or needed while reconnecting with some hidden gems I'd forgotten I had.

In a normal way this time, not a nervous fit.

It wasn't that there was nothing to be nervous about. HBC's board had approved my virtual panel idea, so we were officially in hype-building mode. The first thing I'd done was post a single sentence on my social media: "Abortion is healthcare."

As expected, the trolls who'd started following me after the interview took it and ran, which re-sparked the whole online debate so that by the time we made the official announcement, people were eager to take part. Hundreds had already registered to attend the panel, many sending in genuine questions for our speakers to answer. It was shaping up to be the highlight of the symposium.

Maybe that was why I was in such a good mood. Or it could be that I'd been at my apartment so scarcely lately that giving it some attention was grounding. And okay—it had the added bonus of keeping my mind off Jase and the baby shower.

It wasn't that I was *nervous* about the shower. I didn't really know how I felt. Weird, I guess. Mostly because I couldn't be there with Jase.

I knew he felt weird about it too, but neither of us seemed to know what to do with that weird, so it just sort of existed between us, like when Baxter wedged his way between our legs to cuddle with us both on the couch—not *bad*, but something we had to maneuver around. Especially if we wanted to get closer.

I'd thought of texting him a few different times today, but I didn't know if that would be helpful for him or add more stress—a reminder of the thing he was still keeping from his family. A thing we hadn't yet defined or looked too closely at. We'd seemed to come to an unspoken agreement that if this bubble had to eventually pop, we wanted to enjoy it while we could.

So instead, I cleaned. I'd turned it into a ritual, with comfort music and a glass of wine, savoring the enjoyment of being in my space.

After I finished with the closet, I planned to shower and head over to Jase's apartment. He wasn't getting home until late and would probably be too tired to cook, so I thought I'd get something ready for him that he could quickly reheat before going to bed. He'd given me a key to take care of Baxter in case of an emergency, and I figured he wouldn't mind me using it for this.

I removed the lid from the box and, one at a time, took the items out to sort through. It was mostly college stuff—an old paper I had been particularly proud of, some photos of me with my roommates from junior and senior year, the tassel from my graduation cap. I'd saved it to turn into a Christmas ornament, but I guess never having my own Christmas tree had limited my motivation on that one.

My hand smacked against something hard, and I pulled out a long, flat jewelry box. A memory came with it: my birthday during spring semester of my junior year, Alec and me studying on his dorm bed, him placing this box in front of me. I opened it now just as I had then.

The necklace looked exactly as I remembered. A thin sterling-silver chain with a single heart pendant, one side of the heart embedded with tiny diamond studs.

"It's a promise charm," he'd told me. "I know we're not ready to get married yet, but hopefully soon we will be. And until then, this can let everyone know how much I love you."

It was beautiful. The necklace and the gesture. Yet I'd lain there with no clue what to say, my brain spinning like the cursor on a computer when it freezes, a pinch of nerves or doubt or *something* pulling in my belly.

It was the first time I'd felt it about our relationship. The first time the smile for him on my lips had been forced. I'd just kept staring at the necklace, exactly as I was now, unable to shake the fact that it wasn't a style I'd ever have picked for myself. It felt significant somehow, like if he didn't know my taste in jewelry, how well did he really know *me*?

More interesting was how I always forgot that detail whenever I fantasized about my relationship with Alec and what might have been if I hadn't ended things. It hadn't crossed my mind in over a month, but all the times before, I'd only ever seemed to focus on the ways he had been perfect for me. His good looks, and his warm smile, and how easy it had been to be with him.

I'd never stopped to consider how it had probably been so easy because I'd let him make my decisions for me. How we'd never fought because I'd brushed off the things that bugged me, discounting them as trivial. How the necklace wasn't the only gift he'd gotten me that I'd had to pretend to like more than I actually did. Like the milk chocolates he'd gotten me for Valentine's Day when I preferred dark. And the geometric patterned scarf he'd given me for Christmas in colors I never wore.

In my head, the important thing had been that he'd gone through the effort of getting me gifts at all. The fact that they weren't perfect shouldn't matter. But looking back now, it had never really been about the gifts; it had been about me not feeling seen. And as comfortable as I'd thought I felt with him, I hadn't been comfortable enough to mention it, to tell him I liked nutty chocolates better than cream fillings, or that I wanted to be in a job for two years before I started thinking about marriage.

I'd felt like the bad guy for so long, the heartless monster who'd broken up with the perfect guy for no good reason, who couldn't even put the why into words. How good a reason could it have been if it was that obscure?

Maybe that was why I'd kept the necklace for so long. Not because I was hanging on to Alec but because getting rid of it would feel like equating our relationship to trash or signifying that what we'd shared had meant nothing to me. Like it might hurt him in some way, and I didn't want to do that again after he'd done nothing wrong to deserve being dumped in the first place.

But none of that was true. I could get rid of an item from my past without minimizing the importance of that time for me. I could say goodbye to Alec and still be grateful for everything we'd shared.

Above all, getting rid of this necklace didn't hurt Alec. Whether I held on to it or not had no effect on him. My guilt didn't impact his happiness. He'd moved on. And here I was, hanging on to things that kept me from doing the same because, why? I was afraid letting them go would somehow add to his pain or hurt him again? I didn't have that kind of power over him. Not anymore.

The only person I hurt by not letting go of the past was me. Maybe that had even been the point, some demented part of my subconscious punishing me for hurting a good guy, for letting him go for reasons I didn't believe were "good enough." Like maybe I didn't deserve love again after throwing it away so carelessly before.

No more.

It was time I stopped punishing myself.

Better yet, it was time I forgave myself altogether.

Maybe it had been a mistake to end things with Alec, although more and more, I was starting to think Jase was right about that not being true. I'd made the best decision I could for myself at the time, and as much as those dreams about Alec had haunted me, I didn't regret where my life had ended up. It wasn't always simple or picture-perfect, but it was one I had built for myself, one I no longer felt the need to constantly measure against someone else's standards.

That was worth just as much as any relationship. Maybe more.

I traced over the necklace with one final touch, appreciating it for the gift it was before closing the box. Then I put it in the pile with the rest of my giveaways and headed for the shower.

I'D JUST REMOVED the lasagna from Jase's oven when the door to his apartment swung open. I jumped so hard the casserole dish nearly slipped through my oven mitts. Jase froze in the entryway, his keys dangling from his hand.

"Oh, hey." I slid the hot dish onto the stovetop. "I didn't think you'd be back this early."

His eyes tracked my movements as I took off the oven mitts and dropped them onto the counter, his gaze flicking briefly to the dirty pots on the stove and the dishes in the sink before returning to me. "What are you doing?"

I couldn't tell if he was angry. He seemed oddly blank, almost shell-shocked, like he wasn't all here, and it occurred to me that his being home so early might have something to do with why.

"I figured you'd be tired when you got home, and I wanted you to have something to eat." I glanced at the lasagna still bubbling in the dish, a few dark patches scattered around the edges that would crisp up as it cooled.

He followed my gaze. "You cooked for me?"

I trailed my fingers through my ponytail, suddenly self-conscious. "It's not five courses or anything, but I got the recipe from Sal, so it should be okay."

Assuming I'd followed the recipe correctly. Jase seemed to like the lasagna well enough when we'd eaten at Josie's, and I figured comfort food was a good call after a family event.

"And sorry about the kitchen being a mess," I continued when he didn't say anything. "I'd planned to have it cleaned up and to be gone before you got home, but if you give me like ten minutes, I can get it done and be out of your hair—"

He gripped the back of my neck and devoured my mouth with his kiss. I hadn't even noticed him move. One second, he was across the room, frozen in what I'd been sure was horror at my clinginess, and the next, he was surrounding me, filling my lungs with the scent of him that my body seemed to need more than air.

His lips met mine with urgent presses, and I melted into it, letting him consume me as eagerly as I consumed, hungry for him in a way I'd never been for anyone.

He backed me into the island and pressed more fully against me, his hard bulge grinding into my belly. Goose bumps broke out along my body as his hands slipped beneath my tank top and unclasped my bra.

"I need you," he breathed, skimming his mouth down to the sensitive skin below my ear and sucking. My legs threatened to give out.

I nodded enthusiastically, throat tight with arousal, and he wasted no time pulling my shirt over my head and tossing my bra aside like it should never have been there in the first place.

That was how I felt about his shirt, currently in the way of my hands that craved his skin. The material was stiff and somehow wrong across his shoulders, too constrictive and unyielding. I tore at the buttons, wanting it off, wanting him free of whatever else clung to him that didn't belong.

There was more. I could see it in the pain of his gaze, taste it in the desperateness of his kiss.

Whatever it was, I'd take it from him. Let him pour it into me and find comfort in my body, take from me what he needed in kind.

His shirt gone, he worked down the zipper of my jean shorts and tugged them off as he sank to his knees, pressing kisses along my stomach. I braced myself on the island behind me, head falling back as his tongue teased my core over my panties. His hands slid under the elastic to squeeze my ass, pulling me to his mouth.

"Please," I whimpered, breaths ragged. It was almost too much to watch him on his knees, cool blue eyes gazing up at me with something close to reverence as he eased my underwear down my thighs one agonizing inch at a time.

The next pass of his tongue was a shock of pleasure. I dropped to my elbows on the island, legs already shaking as he lifted one knee over his shoulder, then the other so my lower half was suspended off the ground and splayed open to him while he feasted.

There was no other word for it. His mouth was relentless, moving over me like he couldn't get enough but planned to die trying. His tongue filled me, teasing a spot that had me grinding against him, soaking his lips with my arousal. I moaned in protest as he retreated, but only until his mouth closed over my clit, sending me into a new kind of madness.

I came once, a slow-building wave that had me crumbling beneath its swell, continuing to break me apart until I was a trembling mess.

Jase rose to his feet and gently set me on the island, pulling my legs wide for him to step between. He reached for his wallet as I dropped kisses to his chest, scraping my teeth along his nipples and roaming my hands over his shoulders, my every touch an attempt to express how completely I wanted him.

Admired him.

Was grateful for him.

He rolled the condom on, then lifted my chin and kissed me again, just as deeply and fully as before, communicating the same to me. At least it felt that way, even if he didn't mean to say it.

Then he tilted my hips forward and sank into me, and there was nothing left to say. No words to describe how good he felt, no phrases that could capture his fullness inside me, no way to encompass this absolute truth of us together.

He moved, slow and deep, grinding our pelvises together with each thrust. The friction sent me to another plane, then somehow higher as he leaned me backward in his arms to take my breast in his mouth. He drew the nipple to a peak, swirling and sucking before moving to the other.

"Jase." It was barely a whisper. My next orgasm was already building, gripping me too tightly to speak. Sweat coated our skin, sticking my hair to my neck, making me slide against the counter as I helplessly rocked my hips.

He steadied me with his palms on my ass, his muscles flexing beneath my touch as he moved inside me and pressed his forehead to mine. "I've got you."

My fingers threaded through his hair, eyes squeezing shut against the approaching onslaught.

"Look at me," he breathed against my lips. "Please. I want to see you."

I forced my eyes open as the pleasure swelled, gaze locking with his, and that was it. Everything ceased to exist except for ecstasy and him. There was no escaping it, no navigating it, no way out.

There was only the tightening of his arms around me as he snapped his hips faster, pumping into me with abandon, and the agony breaking over his face as he found his own pleasure. Groans fell from his lips, filling my head like a prayer.

"Dani, fuck. *Dani.*"

When I found my way back to the present, my back was flat against the island, his forehead resting on my sternum, both of us heaving in air like we'd just burrowed our way out from below ground and drawn our first breaths. I held him to me, one hand buried in his hair, the other gripping his shoulder, not wanting to let go.

But more than that, something told me this was what he needed. For me to run my fingers through his hair, rub my palm over his back, and make him feel cared for. Loved.

I didn't analyze how easy it was for me to do. I just did it.

"Well? How is it?"

We were sitting on his couch, me in my tank top and panties and him in his gray drawstring pants, each with a plate of lasagna on our laps. I hadn't touched mine yet, too concerned with watching him finish his first bite, trying to tell if he liked it.

I'd rate my cooking skills somewhere around average; I could usually follow a recipe to a decent result, but it was nothing to write home about. Sal had assured me this recipe was foolproof, but I suddenly doubted every step I'd taken. Had I overcooked the noodles? Was there enough sauce?

If the way Jase's eyes fell closed was any indication, I'd done okay. Then he confirmed it by leaning over to kiss me, a short and sweet press to my lips. "It's delicious. Thank you."

I tried to suppress my smile as I cut into my own piece. "And the shower?" I asked, hesitating a little. "How was that?"

My plan had been not to ask. The last thing I wanted was for him to think I was fishing for gossip about Alec and Stephanie. Especially after today, when I felt like I'd finally made true progress toward closure. But there was no ignoring that something had happened to upset him, and I wanted him to know he could share it with me.

He let out a deep sigh. "Not good. My mom…" He shook his head.

"What?"

"She invited my ex."

My spine snapped straight as something ugly swept through me. Something eager to pull hair and scratch faces. I tried to hide it by cutting another bite out of my lasagna. "Why would she do that?"

"Basically, she thinks I'm a loser who will never be able to trick someone else into being with me, and since my career is doomed to fail, I need someone who can carry me through life so my parents don't have to continue to be embarrassed by me. I'm paraphrasing, but that was pretty much the gist of our conversation." His tone aimed for flippant but came up short. There was pain there—old and deep-seated.

I lowered my fork to my plate, bite of lasagna still on it, and put the plate on the coffee table. "How could she possibly think that?"

He shrugged one shoulder, poking at his own lasagna without moving to eat more. I'd be worried he lied about liking it, except I didn't think he was actually seeing it right now. He was back at his parents' house, reliving whatever that conversation had been with his mom.

"I never…fit into their world. No matter how much I tried as a kid, I just always liked different things and thought in a different way. By high school, I'd stopped trying."

"And Alec?" I didn't have any siblings, so I couldn't know firsthand, but I imagined that Alec's relationship with their parents had to have an impact on Jase.

"He fit."

It was the way he said it, like he was somehow a failure for not being his brother, that cleaved my heart in two.

I took his plate from his hands and set it on the coffee table next to mine, then climbed onto his lap and straddled his legs. His eyes fell to my collarbone, and I took his face in both hands and forced him to meet my gaze.

"You're the best man I've ever known." I held his stare so he could see I meant every word. "One of the best *people* I've ever known."

He swallowed, his Adam's apple bobbing.

"And if your parents can't see that, it's their loss." I bit back the other words I had for them. *They're fools. They should be ashamed. They can go fuck themselves.* Something told me Jase wasn't ready to hear those. He still wanted a relationship with his parents, still sought their approval despite all he'd already accomplished not being enough to get it. And it wasn't for me to tell him not to want that, as much as I wished I could.

A tear rolled down his cheek, and his eyes fell closed as I

brushed it away with my thumb. I kissed his cheek where it had been, wanting to replace his hurt with something gentle.

He pulled me to his chest, locking his arms around me as my head came to rest on his shoulder. We stayed like that for a while, the steady beat of his heart against mine, our chests rising and falling in tandem as we breathed.

I would have given almost anything to stay like that forever, at peace in his arms. Would have given just as much for him to feel that same peace with his family. For him to no longer believe his place was along the edge of the room, looking in at the party from the outside.

I didn't know if that was possible. Parents didn't always change. Mine hadn't.

What I did know was he'd never find that peace with his family with me at his side. And for every moment like this we shared together, it was going to be that much harder when I had to let him go.

Chapter Twenty-Eight
Jase

"The blackened green beans are running low on the banquet table, Chef," Dani said, poking her head into the hotel kitchen off the event space where the first night of the symposium was currently underway.

She'd taken to calling me Chef tonight, I'm sure to maintain professionalism in front of her bosses and event donors, and it went straight to my dick every time. I wanted to hear her say it in that breathy cry she gave right before she came on my cock.

"Already?" I asked, soaking her in with my gaze. She was glowing, a blush to her cheeks, eyes radiant against the deep green of her sleek jumpsuit. I'd watched her all night as she coordinated every last detail of the cocktail hour, reaping the payoff of all the hard work she'd put in these last months, making it look as easy as pouring a bowl of cereal.

"They can't get enough," she said with a gleam in her eye, her smile just for me. It took all my self-control not to pull her into the kitchen, press her against the door, and kiss the hell out of her.

It had been like that for weeks, ever since the baby shower, my need for her a constant, tangible force trying to burst through my skin.

I'd been prepared for the opposite. For the shower to be the crack that grew into a wedge between us. But then I'd gotten home to her cooking for me, and…it still overwhelmed me to think about.

No one had ever cooked like that for me before. Sure, Aubrey and the line cooks prepared staff meals that I ate, and my mom had cooked dinners for our family growing up. But no one had ever cooked something just for *me*. As something nice to do, as a way to take care of me. And especially after the mess of the shower, to feel seen like that? It was more than I knew how to say.

So I'd shown her instead. I hoped I had, at least. Hoped I'd said it with every kiss and every embrace, every morsel I fed her since. And I'd continue to try, starting with doing everything in my power to make sure this symposium went off without a hitch.

"I'll start sending out smaller batches so we don't run out as fast," I told her.

"Thank you."

"Whatever you need."

Her lips inched higher as she turned away, allowing me the briefest glimpse of her ass before the door swung closed.

"Half tray?" Aubrey asked from down the line, already pulling out more green beans.

"Yes, Chef."

"Heard."

A server came in with an empty tray for me to refill, and we fell back into it. Zach and Luis kept up with food prep while I worked on plating, and our well-oiled kitchen machine operated as smoothly as ever.

By ten o'clock, all the food had been sent out, including the desserts, and I was pleased with how little had gone uneaten. For one, it told me people liked it, but it also meant minimal waste of both food and money, which was how I aimed to run things.

"I liked this," Aubrey said as we cleaned up. She stacked the empty sheet trays we'd brought from Ardena to take back with us.

This was the first weekend since we'd opened that Ardena was closed for dinner service, but I didn't fixate on that. Jillian was right about this event being a growth opportunity for the restaurant. I chose to focus on that instead.

"What, catering?" I asked, wiping down the counters.

She lifted a shoulder. "Yeah. It still has a flow to it like at the restaurant, but I could sink into this more. Maybe because we knew what we'd be putting out instead of waiting for individual orders."

"Probably." Personally, I preferred the individual orders. A spike of anticipation went through me each time the ticket machine started printing, that second before the first dish came into view, when I wondered what it would be. Some nights, we sold an even spread of menu items. Others, it seemed like I cooked the same two dishes all night. Never knowing what any particular service would bring was part of the fun.

When the kitchen was in good shape, I made my way out to the event room to see how things were winding down. Dani planned to spend the night at her place since tomorrow would be an early morning and it would be easier for her to get ready there. I wanted to make sure I saw her before I left.

A couple of the high-tops scattered throughout the room still had people conversing around them, empty drink glasses in hand, but the waitstaff had cleared the rest, including the banquet tables lining the far wall. Dani slid up beside where I stood and joined me in my perusal. I crossed my arms to keep from reaching out to touch her. She clasped her notebook with both hands.

"A success?" I asked.

"Without a doubt. The food was a huge hit. Maybe you should be a chef or something."

I stole a glance at her, catching the smirk on her lips, unable to resist staring at her for several breaths before tearing my eyes away. "You look beautiful, by the way." I hadn't had the chance to tell her yet tonight.

"Thank you," she said softly.

My eyes strained to look at her again, see if a blush tinted her cheeks, but I'd have to touch her if I did that. Not want to but *have* to, and she was still working.

"I kind of wish you could get dressed up too," she admitted quietly.

I quirked a brow. "Yeah?"

"I'd drag you onto the dance floor for a proper dance."

I grinned. "You like dancing with me or something?"

She paused long enough that I finally gave in and glanced her way, expecting to find a teasing glint in her eyes. Instead, they shone with the same sincerity in their depths that filled her next words.

"Yeah. I do."

My breath left me as the simple statement almost knocked me over, those three words electricity in my veins.

Moments like this, I wondered how much a relationship with my parents was worth.

My mom had been calling me almost daily since the shower. Alec had tried a few times as well, but I'd ignored them both, not ready to hash it out. I knew whenever we finally did, I'd walk away feeling like shit.

Dani made me feel the opposite. Like the man I wanted to become, the man I'd tried my whole adult life to be. A man I felt good about being—*liked* being. A man who might actually deserve someone like her.

It was sad how difficult that was for me to accept. I wasn't all the way there yet, but I wanted to be. And it gave me an idea.

After saying good night to Dani, I headed back into the kitchen, where Aubrey was putting away the mop.

"Hey," I said. "New plan for tomorrow."

Chapter Twenty-Nine
Dani

I needed pens.

The volunteers for tonight's gala had arrived a half hour ago to finish setting everything up, and the box of silent auction materials was mysteriously missing pens. It was mysterious because I specifically remembered setting a bundle of HBC pens wrapped in a purple rubber band next to the stack of clipboards in the conference room for the volunteers to pack while I'd been running the panels yesterday, yet they still hadn't made the trip.

But honestly? Considering all the things that could have gone wrong over the past three days of the symposium, missing pens was a problem I'd happily take.

I crossed the ballroom toward the hotel's reception, the skirt of my gown grazing the carpet behind me. Tonight was the grand conclusion to this event and probably the most important part. The first two days had gone exceptionally well, starting with a lively cocktail hour followed by yesterday's speakers, both punctuated by Jase's spectacular food. The virtual panel had especially been a success.

Of the hundreds who had registered, I'd expected maybe half to actually attend live, but it had been more. The panelists had led with the pre-submitted questions, and I'd pulled follow-up questions and comments from the chat to turn it into a true discussion. The chat itself had been a bit of a mess with plenty of arguments between attendees, but our speakers were never subjected to it, which kept things moving smoothly.

Talia, Director Gardner, and the panelists had all been thrilled. My favorite *Citizen Daily* journalist Bill Sewick had been in virtual attendance and had lots to say in a new article he'd published this morning—pretty much more of the same. But other outlets had covered the panel too, most sharing at least some of the information our experts had spoken about, which had been the point of the panel in the first place: to get the truth out there.

Now, it was time to raise some cash so this clinic could become a reality.

Just as I reached the ballroom doors, Jase emerged from the kitchen and stopped short. His stare latched onto me, and my heart stumbled in my chest.

I missed him.

Which was completely absurd. It wasn't like I'd gone weeks without talking to him; I'd seen him every day of the symposium.

But I hadn't been sleeping in his bed these past few nights, hadn't been eating breakfast with him these past mornings, hadn't been telling him about my day when I got home. We'd hardly had the time to text with both of us going nonstop to pull this event off.

Tonight, though. Tonight, I could go home with him, collapse in his arms, and let him peel my dress off me the way he looked like he was imagining doing right now.

When I'd checked in on the kitchen a few hours ago, I'd still been in the jeans and tank top I wore to set up. I'd since transformed, changing into my deep purple gown with a slit up one leg, my hair twisted into a low bun that Robin pinned for me, my makeup a little heavier, a little more glamorous than usual.

"Hi," I said, stopping a few feet away from him.

I itched to get closer, to stand within his grasp and breathe in his warm scent, but I liked the way he was looking at me more.

He made a slow prowl of his eyes down my body and back up again like he'd never seen anything so beautiful. It made me *feel* beautiful. Not self-conscious like I sometimes felt when I dressed up, as if I'd put on another mask even less recognizable from the one I wore every other day.

Instead, his gaze made me feel *real*. Grounded in myself more than ever. Proud of who I was and what I'd accomplished this weekend. Beautiful for more than just the dress I wore or the color on my lips.

His hand tightened around the strap of the duffel bag hanging from his shoulder, and when his eyes finally reached mine, they burned bright enough to light me on fire.

He cleared his throat. "Hi."

Tonight.

Tonight, I could gaze into his eyes for as long as I wanted and fall asleep under their tender watch. Then tomorrow, he and I could figure out what came next.

But first, I needed pens.

I flashed him a smile. "I'm on an errand. The kitchen's all set?"

"Good to go. The first course will be ready at six on the dot."

"Been looking forward to it all day." I dreamed about this menu sometimes. Not even kidding.

He smirked. "Let's hope it lives up to expectations."

"You always do."

His nostrils flared, and he nodded down the hall. "Go. Before I start kissing you, because God knows I won't stop."

My lungs expanded with warmth, and I forced my feet to take steps backward before turning from him altogether. I shot him a last glance over my shoulder, bubbles of giddiness fluttering in my chest at how tensely he held himself as he watched me walk away. Like it took physical effort for him not to follow.

As I neared reception, commotion from outside reached my ears, growing louder with each step. A single glance out the lobby doors told me pens weren't my biggest problem anymore.

Protestors lined the sidewalk in front of the hotel. A lot of them.

There had been a handful outside during yesterday's panels, holding signs with graphic images depicting the very misinformation about abortion the virtual panel had aimed to correct. We'd expected those same people would come out again tonight, but I wasn't looking at a handful of people. There was a whole crowd, wearing blue T-shirts with "Abortion is Murder" across the front in white block letters, some holding the same graphic signs as yesterday.

I stepped outside and their chants hit me like a wave, growing louder as the ones in front spotted me. I wouldn't be surprised if a few of them had contributed to the more colorful comments left on my social media.

Right now, I didn't care. I just needed to find Geffery.

He was a few feet down the sidewalk, talking to a police officer and one of the hotel's staff. As soon as he saw me, he waved me over.

"What's the plan?" I asked him over the noise. "We're minutes out from guests arriving."

The ones who had traveled from out of town were staying at the hotel and wouldn't have to pass through the protestors, but plenty of the guests were local. They wouldn't even be able to pull up to the valet right now.

"This is Officer Liang." Geffery pointed at the police officer, whose hand I shook. "He's got men setting up barriers to keep the protestors back. Trevor here," he said, gesturing to the young hotel employee, "will be at one end of the block, directing guests to the rear of the building where the new valet station is being set up. We'll have someone else at the other end of the block doing the same. The goal is to have guests avoid the protest altogether. I'll be here in case any show up at this door and need an escort."

I nodded, fully in agreement. "Thank you. Let me know if you need anything from me."

"I've got this. Go do your thing inside."

Normally, that'd be a tall order with a potential crisis looming, but there was nothing for me to do out here, no way for me to fix this on my own. I trusted my team to take care of it, and maybe more surprising was how good that felt compared to doing it all myself.

Geffery had my back, and so did Talia, so did Robin, so did Jase. Success or failure wasn't mine to carry alone, and it didn't stand on a single incident or stumble. I still had one hell of a fundraiser to pull off, and I had every intention of doing just that.

I'd taken two steps toward the hotel entrance when a flash of red caught the edge of my vision.

"Dani!" Geffery shouted.

I had no time to react before something exploded against my side.

Chapter Thirty
Jase

My hands were shaking.

That was how nervous I was. Like I was about to ask a girl to prom. I guess, in a way, I was.

I messed with my collar a few more times, not making it better or worse, just needing the excuse to stand here another minute so my heart could stop pummeling my rib cage. I wasn't *proposing*, for fuck's sake.

Though, the fact that the thought didn't have me lurching to empty my stomach in the stall behind me was interesting.

One last look in the mirror, one more deep breath through my nose, and I picked up the duffel now holding my chef clothes and pushed my way out the bathroom door.

"Are you sure there's nothing I can get you?" an alarmed-sounding voice said from around the corner. "Security is going through our camera footage to find the person responsible. If you want to press charges—"

"No, really, that's not necessary," Dani replied. Her voice

had my strides lengthening as worry shot through my chest. "I'll manage. Just please take the pens to the ballroom. I appreciate it."

We practically bowled into one another as she rounded the corner to the bathrooms. I caught her by the elbows, giving me a clear view of the red liquid splashed across the front of her dress.

"What happened? Are you okay?" Concern fell from my words even though whatever covered her was too bright to be blood. If it had been, she'd be bleeding out on the floor, not standing in front of me, calmly dictating tasks to hotel staff.

"I'm fine. It's just paint." She studied the stain. "My dress is ruined, which sucks, but I have an extra with me, and who knows. Maybe a dry cleaner will have some luck with this." She pulled the skirt of her dress to the side, inspecting it closer.

I ran my hands gently along her arms, trying to comfort myself as much as her. "Where'd the paint come from?"

"A bunch of protestors outside have water balloons filled with it. I think it's supposed to look like blood. Probably because I'm a murdering whore and all." I saw red for an entirely different reason at the thought of anyone calling her that, but I pushed my anger aside as she let out a flat chuckle. "I guess the virtual panel didn't change their opinions on the situation, huh? Not that we really expected it to."

She glanced up, her eyes amazingly calm given the situation, not a trace of fear there even after referencing what I assumed was the note on her car. Then her gaze shifted below my jaw, running down my chest all the way to my toes. Her brows pulled together.

"What are you…?"

Oh, yeah. That.

"I, uh—" I cleared my throat, once again painfully aware that I was in a suit for the first time since my brother's wedding five years ago.

Her gaze met mine, this time with a mix of curiosity and affection. It was the latter that calmed my nerves enough for me to speak.

"I wanted to dance with you too," I said softly.

It was the simplest truth I knew. I wanted to dance with her here, tonight, where she looked like a goddess, even with paint dripping down her dress. I wanted to dance with her tomorrow morning in my kitchen as I made her crepes with caramelized plums and vanilla cream, listening to her moan in my arms with each bite. I wanted to dance with her on lazy Sunday afternoons with Baxter cradled in our arms, and at the restaurant after close, and on holidays, and birthdays, and to cheer her up when she was sad, and to celebrate with her when she was happy.

I wanted to dance with her always, in all ways, to every single song.

Her brows lifted, tears gleaming in her eyes as her lips rose and her fingers threaded with mine. She squeezed them tight. "I hate that I have paint on me right now," she said through a laugh. "I want to kiss you so badly."

I couldn't care less about paint. I cupped her face in my hands and dropped my mouth to hers, easing her body against me as if we were dancing right now. My lips brushed softly over hers, sinking everything I felt into the kiss. She gripped my waist, her smile continuing to grow until she couldn't kiss me back anymore, setting my chest on fire. I opened my eyes but kept her close, sweeping my gaze over her face.

She peered up at me, eyes bright. "Hi."

My lips tugged up.

"Jase?"

Cold shocked my system like I'd been blanched in an ice bath. My brain froze too as the last voice I expected to hear echoed through my ears and landed like a meat hammer against my stomach.

He shouldn't be here.

Not at this hotel, not in this city, and definitely not at this event.

Not at this moment of all moments that was supposed to be about Dani and me and the months we'd put in to get to this place—at the finish line of a successful event and the start of something so much more.

Something I'd had to push him aside in my mind to convince myself I could have in the first place.

Yet as I dragged my gaze over Dani's shoulder, there he stood, wearing his own perfectly tailored suit, his pregnant wife's hand clasped in his.

The ultimate Beauford in the flesh.

My brother.

Chapter Thirty-One
Dani

ALEC WAS HERE.

In person. At the symposium.

Alec was *here*, with Stephanie, his extraordinarily pregnant wife who, wearing flats and a simple black gown, managed to look more elegant than any person of royalty I think I'd ever seen.

The two of them stood at the entrance to the bathroom hallway with identical looks of open-mouthed surprise on their faces, which, if my inability to move my jaw was any indication, perfectly matched the expression both Jase and I wore.

Jase, whose arms I was still in after he'd told me he wanted to dance with me, only I'd heard something entirely different in those words, felt it in his kiss, just before Alec—his brother and my ex—interrupted.

Alec was *here*.

How was Alec here?

And why?

I was about to come to the conclusion I'd been hit in the head by one of the protestor's signs and was having a concussion dream, but then Alec managed to speak again, and it was enough to convince me he was, in fact, real.

Real and standing in front of me.

For the first time since I'd broken up with him nine years ago.

"Dani?" He sounded as shocked as I was. Made sense. It was about the only thing that did right now.

"What are you doing here?" Jase asked. His voice had gone as stiff as the rest of him, all his warmth from a moment ago gone.

Alec's mouth moved a few times before words came out. "My insurance company is a donor for the clinic. My boss couldn't make it tonight, so he asked if I wanted to go. When I found out your restaurant was catering, I said yes. I tried calling to tell you, but you never answered."

Stephanie squeezed his hand and pointed toward the ladies' room. "I have to…"

Alec's face softened as he looked at her. "Yeah, of course." He squeezed her hand back, then released it. "I'll wait right here."

She flashed Jase and me a sympathetic smile, and if she wasn't so far along in her pregnancy, I'd wonder if she was trying to escape the avalanche of awkwardness currently burying us alive. But I had no doubt the tiny human inside her was probably jumping on her bladder like a trampoline. If it wouldn't make things a thousand times weirder, I'd escape with her.

"Why didn't you leave a message?" Jase asked.

Alec's shoulders rose to his ears. "I thought it'd be a fun

surprise. I didn't think..." He gestured to me. "I mean, how...?"

"I work at HBC," I explained. "I planned the symposium."

"Oh." He scratched the back of his neck. "I didn't know that."

"My boss was the one in contact with your boss." I'd handled the panelists directly, but Talia had been the one to manage the donors. "There was no way you would have."

The silence stretched between us, as heavy as the humidity outside, thick enough to choke on. A moment later, the bathroom door creaked, and Stephanie reemerged, sidling back beside Alec, her fingers lacing with his.

I glanced at Jace, trying to get a read on where his head was at, but his eyes were fixed on his brother.

I ached to take his face in my hands and force him to look at me. To pull him somewhere private and have the talk we'd both known was coming. The one where we laid all our cards on the table and decided together how we would move forward.

It was supposed to happen after the symposium. Not now. Certainly not here or like this.

But there wasn't time for that conversation now, either. Not with guests arriving, and paint on my dress, and speeches about to start.

I steeled myself with a breath and turned back to Alec and Stephanie. "Let's make sure you two find your table. I'll have name tags made up for you. Any food allergies for us to be aware of?"

Stephanie gave a grateful smile. "No, none. Thank you."

I extended my hand down the hallway. "Right this way."

They headed toward the ballroom, and I followed, glancing

behind me to where Jase still stood, hands clenched in fists, red paint smeared across his crisp white shirt, a different kind of storm in his eyes. One he was already lost in.

I didn't let myself focus on it. Not while I got Alec and Stephanie seated or when I officially introduced myself to her. Based on the lack of confusion on her face, I assumed she already knew who I was, but I didn't focus on that either.

I didn't focus on it while I changed out of my paint-stained dress into the simple black sheath I'd brought as a backup in case a drink spilled or I fell victim to a tray of wayward food. Paint hadn't been on my list of possibilities, but at least I'd been prepared.

I didn't focus on it the rest of the night. Not when I went into the kitchen to check on how they were doing and found Jase with his chef jacket half buttoned over his dress shirt, suit pants still on as he cooked on the line next to Zach, his eyes never once leaving his task.

Not when Director Gardner gave her speech, thanking everyone from our board to our panelists to our donors for making not only this event but also our mission possible, mentioning Talia and myself by name, and giving a special shout-out to Jillian and her incredible restaurant team.

And not when Robin came to me with an update from Geffery that the protestors had dispersed and it was safe for guests to leave out the front doors.

Somehow, the night passed, and I made it through, conversing with donors, overseeing volunteers, and sharing a hug with Talia, who whispered in my ear, "Nicely done," in a way that brought tears to my eyes. The final donation amount hadn't been totaled yet, but I knew we'd reached our goal. The donated paintings alone had gotten us nearly halfway.

In most ways, the night had been perfect. Exactly what I'd imagined it being three months ago. As the last of the guests departed, telling me how much they were looking forward to the event again next year, it didn't feel surreal like most of my successes had up to now.

Mostly, I just felt tired.

Across the lobby, I spotted Alec and Stephanie waiting for the elevator. His arm was around her shoulder, her head on his chest as she leaned against him in a picture of contentment. They really did look good together. And after seeing them tonight, it was obvious it was more than just how they looked.

They worked. Fit in that way most couples hoped to fit but so few seemed to truly manage. The way that appeared easy, but you could tell from how they talked and interacted with each other was built on years of trust, communication, and effort.

I watched them and waited, bracing for the gut punch of jealousy to slam into me. For the self-doubt to sneak up, always a hair short of regret, that had me questioning every decision I'd made since college, wondering about the trajectory of my life.

It never came.

There instead was recognition of a life that never belonged to me. Not because I wasn't worthy of it but because it never would have made me happy.

Not the way they were together.

Not the way I knew I could be.

That was the thought that dragged the sliver of unease up from where I'd buried it all night. Because for once, I knew what I wanted, straight down to my gut.

I wanted to go home with Jase and fall asleep in his arms. I wanted him to take me to his parents' house so his family could meet me—*this* me, the me I felt at home in. I wanted us to go on more dates and order entire menus and compete for which of us Baxter cuddled with more.

I wanted us to work. To fit. To bicker and argue and talk it out and make up. To always be the place we could be real, no masks.

But that future wasn't up to just me. And no matter how willing I was to navigate the storm, there was always a chance of being thrown overboard.

Chapter Thirty-Two
Jase

My brother stepped into the elevator with his wife curled against his side, Dani's eyes never once leaving them, and all I could think as I watched her from across the lobby was *What if he's the one she really wants?*

I hadn't been able to look at her after he'd shown up, afraid I'd find the answer in her eyes. See her gaze at him with the same openness and longing she'd started to direct at me, but *more*, weighed by years of want and regret.

It would break me.

More than anything my parents could ever say.

When I'd walked back into the kitchen, Aubrey had taken one look at me and stopped mid plating. "What happened?"

"My brother's here." *What if he's the one she really wants?*

I'd tugged my chef jacket on over my shirt, not bothering to change out of my dress clothes, needing a cutting board or sauté pan or sheet tray in my hands—any task to bury myself in to escape the thought of the woman I loved and my brother who she'd loved first.

Aubrey hadn't asked more questions; she just went back to work, taking the lead like she had the day before as practice for tonight. My grand idea. Let Aubrey act as head chef so I could surprise Dani with a dance.

One hell of a different surprise we'd gotten instead.

The elevator doors closed, and Dani's gaze lifted to me. It stayed there with an expression I was too far away to see clearly, the distance offering as much pain as it did relief.

Which was why when she took a step forward, I did too. And another. Until we were only a few feet apart. Too far to touch but close enough for me to make out the strain in her eyes, the beauty of their blue-green color too much for me to take.

My gaze dropped to my shoes, my right hand tightening around my chef jacket. I wanted to slip it on and wear it like a shield. Not that it would work on her—my shields never had. And it wasn't her that was hurting me now anyway. Not really.

"Will you look at me?" she asked, her words agonizingly soft. So soft they threatened to topple me.

I flicked my gaze up and caught the corner of her jaw, the long line of her neck, the shine of her hair, before it was too much.

What if he's the one she really wants?

My head didn't believe it. I didn't think my heart did, either, but neither of those were in charge right now.

I cleared my throat, emotion pinching it shut as I stared at my shoes. "I'm feeling a lot," I managed to get out. "In the way that makes me want to push away. I don't—" My throat closed again, and my chest felt like a pressure cooker, the lid about to blow off, all of it too much for me to hold on to much longer. "I don't want to do that. Push you away." God, it was the last fucking thing I wanted. "But I think maybe it's what I need. Some space to just…process this."

I kept my gaze down, stare fixed on the burgundy swirls in the carpet, too much of a coward to look at her.

"Okay," she finally said, still gentle. "I get it."

The slight quiver in her voice was what finally brought my eyes up. Tears rolled down her cheeks.

I wanted to dry them, to hold her.

To cry with her. To scream.

Most of all, I wanted to believe that the emotion in her eyes was the same I felt for her—not just desire but recognition. The certainty of being seen, and the freedom of being set alight by that knowing and of sharing in it with the one other person who's ever understood you in this way.

But I didn't trust myself this second to know what was real and what was my fear. Not while so much of it was blasting through me like gunfire, tearing into wounds I'd been living with since I was a kid. The very ones Alec had ripped open by showing up here tonight. It wasn't even his fault.

It was mine.

For avoiding this for so long, thinking it would be easier to handle if I didn't look at it head-on. The same way I'd tried not to look at her. Only now, I couldn't look away.

I was weak.

Pathetic.

Too afraid to act on what I wanted but not strong enough to walk away from it either. The opposite of the kind of person Dani deserved. The opposite of Alec.

What if he's the one she really wants?

I squeezed my eyes shut and clenched my jaw. Took one step back. Then another as I turned away.

"Jase."

I stopped.

I couldn't not stop for her.

But I didn't have the strength to look at her again either, my gaze instead clinging to the nearest light fixture lining the wall. My heart was a hammer against my ribs.

"Thank you for tonight," she said. "For yesterday. For all of it. The success of this is as much yours as it is mine. I never could have done it without you. Not like this." Her voice was strong as she said it. Definitive. "You should be proud."

Her words wrapped around me, and I wished I could reach out and catch them. Pull them to me and absorb them into my skin. Believe them as entirely as she did.

The problem was I still didn't know how.

"AND ARE YOU PROUD?" Dr. Ohara asked.

I shrugged even though he couldn't see me. I sat beside my coffee table with my back against the couch while my fingers picked at a loose strand Baxter had snagged from the rug, my phone to my ear.

Don't ask me why I wasn't sitting *on* the couch. Normally, I'd get down here to pet Baxter, maybe sit next to him while he played with a paper bag or something, but he was still curled up in the patch of morning sun on my bed where I'd left him twenty minutes ago when Dr. Ohara had called.

"I guess," I said eventually. "Not necessarily of myself, though."

"Why not?"

I bent my knees and rested an elbow on one. Then I dropped my elbow and straightened one leg.

Finally, I stood and paced between my couch and the kitchen island as I waited for this process to get easier. For the moment to hit when it no longer felt like opening the door to a creepy basement every time my therapist asked me a question and having to wade into the cold, damp dark to find the answer. Knocking into stuff I didn't realize was there, being forced to dig through it, to rummage around other shit I only had a vague sense of, never knowing which would be the thing to jump out and get me.

It hadn't been this hard in a while. Didn't that mean I was close to a breakthrough?

Maybe that was why Dr. Ohara had offered to talk on a Sunday morning after I'd messaged him last night on the brink of a panic attack minutes after walking away from Dani.

"Dani's the one who had the vision for the whole thing," I answered. "And Aubrey and the guys are the ones who ended up carrying most of the work in the kitchen. The only thing I feel like I can really take credit for is putting together a team that could take on that kind of challenge so readily. They never backed down, never once complained. It's them I'm proud of."

"Do you think they would have been as ready to take on such a challenge if you hadn't been there to teach them this past year and foster their skills?"

"If Aubrey was there to teach them, then yeah. Probably."

"What about the menu you created? Could Aubrey have come up with that?"

I shrugged as I reached the couch. Spun on my heel,

headed back toward the island. "Hers would have been different but just as good."

"Jase."

I couldn't tell if it was amusement or exasperation on the edge of his voice.

"Tell me one thing about last night's event that wouldn't have been possible without you. One thing you can own and feel good about."

I tried to think. Tried to remember the work I'd put into the symposium over the past three months. I'd never doubted it would be a success. Never questioned whether people would like my menu or whether my team was skilled enough to pull it off.

I searched for that confidence now, knowing it used to be there. But it was like reaching for a door handle that had already swung shut. All I came back with was air.

My head went dizzy. I stopped pacing and covered my eyes with my hand, then shoved it into my hair and tugged hard.

"I don't know," I said.

"One thing, Jase."

My breaths came faster. "I don't *know*."

"What if I asked Dani the same question? What do you think she would give you credit for?"

Too much. She always had. There wasn't anything I'd helped her do that she wouldn't have figured out a way to accomplish on her own.

Or maybe nothing.

What if everything she'd seen in me hadn't been me at all? What if all along, what she'd thought she'd seen in me had really been reminiscences of Alec, diminished by their time apart? What if seeing him last night had brought it all into focus, making it crystal clear in her mind who I was and who I wasn't. How little I lived up to the person she'd been missing all this time. The person she really—

"What if he's the one she really wants?" It broke from me, the words that had been taunting me all night finally out there in the world, free to come true. And with them came all the fears I'd been holding in, forcing down with my denial since the moment I'd learned Alec was her ex. "What if she'll always love him, and I'll always be her second choice? How am I even supposed to know? Am I supposed to ask her? What kind of fucked-up question is that?"

I could already imagine it. The pain that would slash across her face when I asked. What it would imply about the months we'd spent together.

They'd been real.

I knew it.

So why was there still this gaping pit inside me as if someone had cleaved through my stomach with a butcher's knife?

There was no judgment in Dr. Ohara's voice when he answered. It was part of what I liked about him. That what felt like the ugliest parts of me were just normal to him.

"The truth is there may always be a part of her that loves a part of him," he said. "And vice versa. People tend to stick with each other in small ways, and it's common for relationships formed earlier in life to hold significant meaning. That doesn't mean she's still *in* love with him, and it doesn't mean she has to love *you* any less."

I barely heard the words over the pounding in my ears. My hand was back over my eyes as I stood in the middle of my apartment, struggling to fill my lungs all the way.

"What you and I both know," he went on, "is this has never really been about whether she compares you to him. It's always been about *you* comparing you to him. A habit you no doubt picked up from your parents."

I nodded.

"But you'll never feel like you're enough if you keep telling yourself you're not. Because you *are* enough. Exactly as you are, in all the ways you are similar to your brother and in all the ways you are different."

I spit out a laugh. "Learn to love myself before anyone else can, is that it?"

"No," he said simply. "Just learn to trust her when she tells you *she* loves you."

"She hasn't told me she loves me."

"Have you told her you love her?"

He had me there. He knew it too.

"What has she said?"

I thought back to the day of the menu tasting when she'd first tried my food. What she'd told Jillian. *"You were right about Jase. He's incredibly talented."*

I remembered the way she looked at me right before the first time I kissed her, when she'd called me a liar. How she'd looked at me the same way after I'd asked her if she liked dancing with me, and she'd said, *"Yeah, I do."*

"You're the best man I've ever known."

That one.

That one had nearly wrecked me from how scared I'd been to believe it. I still was. Maybe Dr. Ohara knew that too.

"You don't have to believe you're enough to be with her, Jase," he said as if reading my mind. "What you have to believe is that *she* thinks you're enough. Trust her judgment. Trust her to know her own mind, even if you're struggling to find peace with yours. Take her at face value when she says she couldn't have done last night without you. Whether you agree or not, it's *her* truth. Honor it. Believe your staff and your boss. Believe your friends. Hell, believe your cat. The people in your life who make you feel good to be around, who make it easy to be you? Believe *them* when they say you're worth it. Let them love you. That's how you'll learn to love you too."

"What if they're wrong?" I asked, voice shaking.

For fuck's sake, my own parents thought I was a fuckup. Weren't they the ones who were supposed to love me most of all, no matter what? How was I supposed to trust what anyone else thought of me if they didn't see it?

"They're not." His words were so matter-of-fact, as if there was no question about it.

"How do you know?"

"Because, Jase," he said, and this time, I was pretty sure it was with amusement. "Everyone's enough. The ones who don't see it just aren't really looking."

Chapter Thirty-Three
Dani

"Thank you again. I'll be in touch." I shook the hand of one of the silent auction winners from last night before she walked out the hotel's main doors to her waiting taxi.

I wasn't the official farewell committee, but I'd sort of fallen into the role while carting the rest of HBC's stuff to the lobby to be packed into volunteer cars and brought back to the office.

Most of the out-of-town guests had already left, the hotel's impressive continental breakfast was winding down, and as soon as the last of these boxes were out of here, I would be too, back to my apartment and into pajamas, where I'd spend the rest of the day vegging out on my couch while watching reruns of *Project Runway*.

There would be no productivity until Tuesday since Talia insisted I take Monday off, and honestly, I wasn't sure my brain would fully work again until then anyway. Especially after I'd spent all last night poring over our final fundraiser numbers to keep from focusing on anything else that had happened.

I wanted to text him.

I wanted to text him so badly to tell him how much more we'd raised than we'd hoped, and how every single guest I spoke to raved about the food. I wanted to send him every online article and social media post I saw about the virtual panel, which I never would have had the courage to suggest doing in the first place if it weren't for him.

I wanted to ask him if he was okay. If I could come over.

I wanted to hold him. Kiss him. Curl into him and around him and meld myself to him, catch the pieces of him that so desperately needed to fall apart so they could fit themselves back together without all the rust and gunk and pain that was wedged in there now.

I just wanted to see him. Hear his voice. Read his name pop up on my phone.

It wouldn't. Not today, at least.

I didn't know for how long, but there were a lot of seasons of *Project Runway* to distract me in the meantime, and if that was what I had to do to give him the space he needed, then that was what I'd do. After everything he'd done for me, it was the least I could do.

"Oh. Hey."

I abandoned the box of branded tablecloths I'd started reorganizing and rose from my crouch, prepared to greet one of the staff volunteers. Instead, I found myself face-to-face with Alec.

He stood tall and straight, his broad shoulders filling his crisp button-down shirt, his short brown hair neatly styled, and his bright blue eyes on full display. His hands were tucked into his pants pockets, the only sign he was at all uncomfortable.

He was as handsome as I remembered. Maybe even more

so, those last boyish charms from college having matured into adulthood. If you'd have asked me my junior year what Alec would look like in ten years, this would have been it. A prince among men, assured and composed, successful in all things. As close to perfection as you could get.

His hand fidgeted in his pocket, and I wondered for the first time if his version of perfection was as calculated as mine had been. I hoped not. I wouldn't want him living with that burden.

"Hey," I said. I fiddled with the pendant of my necklace and glanced toward the elevator. "Where's Stephanie?"

"She has a few friends who live in Philly. They're out to brunch."

"Oh. That's nice."

He nodded.

I dragged the pendant along its chain and dropped my gaze to the boxes. I looked back up again. "Did you both enjoy the gala? I mean, after, um—"

"Yeah, it was great," he said, pulling a hand from his pocket to make some sort of gesture. He seemed to second-guess it halfway through, or maybe didn't know what he'd meant to do in the first place, so his hand just kind of hung there between us before he finally scratched the back of his neck. "You did a really good job. The food especially was fantastic."

I couldn't help my smile. "That was all your brother's doing."

He gave an uncomfortable laugh and peered at his shoes. "Yeah…I was actually hoping to catch him this morning before I left. Do you know if he's around? He sort of disappeared last night."

"I'm not expecting him to be here today," I said, keeping

my voice what I hoped was naturally light. "You might have better luck calling."

His mouth pulled weakly to one side. "I'm not so sure about that."

I wasn't either, but it didn't feel right to say it. Whatever was between Jase and his brother wasn't for me to get in the middle of. Yes, I saw the irony. But their rift went back a lot longer than three months, and what I knew of it only scratched the surface.

"I think he just needs some time," I offered. "It was unexpected, you know?" His gaze met mine, and I shrugged. "All of it."

It wasn't an explanation exactly, but it was the truth. About a lot of things still lingering between us.

"I hadn't expected you to end things with us," he said, the words almost cautious, like he didn't know if now was the time to say them, but also, what other time would there be? "I spent a long time wondering why you did."

"Me too," I said honestly. "For a while, I thought of you as the one who got away."

"Not anymore?"

I shook my head.

The corners of his mouth lifted. "Me neither."

I found myself smiling, and my next words came out easily. "Congratulations, by the way. About your marriage and the baby. I'm happy for you."

His grin had always been contagious, but this one could power a small country. "Thanks. I guess I owe you for breaking up with me."

I chuckled as something seemed to lift around us, the shadow of it blowing away, leaving me lighter and more hopeful than when I'd gotten here this morning.

His phone rang in his pocket. "Oh, it's Steph," he said as he pulled it out. He hurried to answer. "Hey, hon. You done?"

Marcus, one of the staff volunteers, walked through the lobby doors, and I waved him over, pointing at the boxes behind me. He grabbed one and headed out to his car. I leaned down for another.

"Wait, now?"

I paused at the shift in Alec's voice. His skin had gone pale, the fingers of his free hand clutched in his hair, making it stick up left and right.

"Are you sure? You—Okay. Okay, yeah. Which hospital?"

That had me standing, the box forgotten.

He hung up a moment later, disbelief and a little panic in his features. "Stephanie's water broke." His eyes met mine, quickly filling with tears as he burst into a smile.

My concern swept into joy, a breath of relief escaping my chest as my own smile spread.

"Her friend's taking her to Philly Memorial," he said, his hand dropping from his head as he spun, frantically searching the lobby. "I need to meet her there. I should…where—"

"My car's right out front. I'll take you," I volunteered.

"I don't know where the hospital is—"

"I do."

Marcus came back for another box, and I asked him to finish up without me, then grabbed my purse and fished out my keys. I tossed a look at Alec, who was still scanning the lobby with wide eyes.

"Let's go, soon-to-be Dad."

He froze, shoulders dropping as if those words made it sink in. A grin flooded his face, and we hurried to my car.

Ten minutes later, I pulled in front of the hospital entrance. Alec was out of the car before I'd even fully stopped, rushing for the doors. He slid to a stop just before he reached them, spun on his heel, and ran back to where I idled. I rolled down the passenger window.

"Thank you," he said, a little out of breath.

I tilted my chin. "Now you owe me twice."

He smiled and dropped his gaze, then returned it to me. "About Jase."

My heart kicked in my chest as I tightened my grip on the steering wheel, unsure of what Alec might say next.

No matter the closure it seemed we'd gotten, my dating his older brother could still be hugely awkward for him, and as lovely as Stephanie had been to me last night, I had no idea how she felt about the whole thing. She could hate it. Hate me.

I had a feeling their parents would take Alec's side over Jase's every time, and if that was the case, I didn't know what it meant for Jase and me. And that was only if Jase didn't decide to end things on his own first.

But all Alec said was, "I want you both to be happy. That's it."

My throat closed up at the sincerity of his words.

I was lucky, I realized, so lucky to have this man as my ex. To have experienced love for the first time from someone so willing to give it. There was a lot I'd built up about Alec in my mind over the years, the fantasy I'd created in my self-doubt and loneliness, but this much remained true: he was a good man. Just not the right one for me.

With that, he tapped the car's windowsill and ran inside to his growing family.

Not letting myself think too much about it, I dug my phone from my purse and typed out a text.

Me: Congrats. You're about to become an uncle.

I added the name of the hospital and hit send. Something told me Alec wouldn't remember to let everyone know right away, and Stephanie was a little busy. But Jase would want to be a part of this.

With him in mind, along with Alec's words, I put the car in drive. *Project Runway* could wait. I had another stop to make first.

Chapter Thirty-Four
Jase

SETTING foot in Ardena after three nights away was like stepping outside after a seven-hour flight and taking that first breath of fresh air. I even felt a bit jet-lagged. Everything about my world was slightly off, as if my brain hadn't quite fallen into sync. Especially after spending the past four hours in the time warp that was a hospital waiting room.

Stephanie hadn't had the baby yet, though she seemed to be doing well. Better than Alec, at least, who was a nervous wreck now that their birthing plan had gone off the rails.

Not gonna lie, I kind of enjoyed seeing him so unraveled for once. It reminded me of when we were kids and how worried he would get about whether Santa could still make it in the snow. He'd stay up as a six-year-old on Christmas Eve watching the Weather Channel until our parents forced us to go to bed.

This time, instead of the Weather Channel, he'd fixated on the nurses' station. The nurses seemed mostly amused by his constant questions and requests, but I still planned to pick them up some baked goods when I grabbed Alec's and my takeout. Right after I checked on a delivery here first.

I made my way up to the office, taking comfort in each familiar step. Things had changed last night—with my brother and Dani both, in ways I hadn't quite figured out yet—but Ardena, at least, was the same. And with each step I climbed, I remembered a little more of how it felt to be proud of something.

This restaurant was an achievement I could claim. Not mine alone, but still mine. Remembering it was like rediscovering a piece of myself, feeling it click back into place the way it first had the moment Frank put a knife in my hand.

I'd fought for those pieces of myself. Endured grunt work and burns, sometimes for no pay, often not knowing where I'd end up the next week. I'd dug deeper with each challenge, with each success, pulling myself together one chunk at a time until I finally felt whole.

Somehow, going back to my parents' house always made me forget that. Like that version of myself I had created was nothing but an act, a clever disguise I fooled the world with while the real me was the equivalent of three monkeys in a trench coat. A poor imitation of what a son, a brother, a man was supposed to be.

But this place around me I had helped build—it was real. I could reach out and touch it. See the truth of what I had accomplished in every room and during every shift.

Where was the truth in what my parents thought of me? Their words? Their assumptions? Their expectations based on their own beliefs?

Next to the concreteness of this restaurant, those didn't seem so substantial.

I walked into the office and paused at the sight of Jillian at her desk.

"I didn't expect to find you here," I said as I approached the order clipboard hanging on the wall beside her.

Her gaze stayed trained on her computer screen. "Just going over some numbers. Turns out we did very well this weekend."

"Oh yeah? Talia have good things to say?" I was more ready to hear them than I had been last night. Might even have been willing to believe some of them. Or at least accept that others believed them like Dr. Ohara had said.

"No. Dani came by earlier."

Her name shot through me like a pinball ricocheting around my chest, and I held my breath in anticipation of where it would land.

When I'd gotten the text from her earlier this morning that Stephanie was in labor, I'd still been reeling from my conversation with Dr. Ohara. It hadn't even been twenty-four hours since she and I had last spoken, but it felt like it had been weeks. I'd wanted to pick up the phone and call her, hear her voice, ask her to meet me at the hospital so I didn't have to endure my parents alone.

But it wasn't her job to shield me from my parents. I didn't want it to be. Which was why I needed to decide for myself what I wanted my relationship with my family to be before I brought Dani the rest of the way into my life.

So I'd texted her back to thank her for letting me know and headed to the hospital alone to be with my brother. It turned out my parents wouldn't make it until tomorrow, so I had a bit longer to prepare myself. Which was good because I needed every second.

I cleared my throat. "What'd she say?"

"Apparently, they nearly doubled their funding goal," Jillian said, still typing. "And then she informed me that not only did you stay within their slated food budget for the entire event but you managed to come in under it." Now she pinned her focus on me, scrutinizing me over the rim of her reading glasses. "Do you know how many catering inquiries I got last night?"

I shook my head.

"Twenty-three. Ranging from private weddings to corporate events. Am I to understand you impressed them all with food that cost pennies a plate?"

"The budget wasn't that small—"

"Did I not make it clear that the budget wasn't an issue? That I would cover any additional costs?"

I fought to keep my eyes from rolling. "I wasn't going to spend your money if I didn't have to, Jillian."

She closed her laptop and angled her body toward me, one leg crossed over the other, hands clasped in her lap in the picture of ladylike elegance. I knew enough to be terrified.

"This accessible fine-dining restaurant of yours," she said. "What kind of investment would you need for that?"

I opened my mouth to defend myself, then froze as her words registered. "What?"

"Dani seems to think I should take the money I'd been prepared to spend on food costs for the symposium and use it to fund your new restaurant idea. She said that the overwhelmingly positive response to the event's food was proof of concept, and I have to say, I don't disagree."

"Dani pitched you my restaurant idea?" I stood a little straighter as the pinball machine in my chest went off like the jackpot, sending my heart flying against my ribs as a new kind of pride seeped through me.

"She did. Did a convincing job of it too. To the point that I spent the last three hours looking over spreadsheets, considering it."

"You're serious?"

We'd talked about it before, but the plan had always been to wait at least a year after Ardena's opening to fully discuss it. And until hearing her say just now that she was seriously considering it, I don't think all of me had accepted she actually would.

"I am," she confirmed. "If you are."

Was I serious about accessible fine dining? Without question. Catering the symposium only reinforced for me that not only could it be done, but it could be celebrated. Hearing Jillian say she believed in it—in *me*—enough to back it with her money…it was the opposite of how my parents made me feel.

This was what Dr. Ohara had meant. Dani and Jillian— they were the ones who knew the real me, who saw what I was capable of, who made me feel good.

But it wasn't just that.

What I was doing here with Ardena felt good too. This thing Jillian and I were building wasn't finished yet, and what else the symposium helped me see was how much further it could grow. I wanted to be a part of that growth. Even if it looked different from what I'd originally envisioned.

Clarity settled over me, another piece of myself clicking into place. I crossed my arms and leaned back against the wall. "Here's what I propose."

"He's so little," my brother said softly, gazing at the bundle of blankets in his arms that held his newborn son.

Oliver Lawrence Beauford, six pounds, fourteen ounces, born at 11:07 p.m. after nearly twelve hours of labor. No wonder Stephanie was passed out.

It was nearly two in the morning, and Alec and I each sat in one of the two reclining chairs beside her hospital bed. Alec rocked his chair as he cradled his son, happier than I'd ever seen him. I welcomed the warmth it brought to my chest, grateful and relieved to find no jealousy there beside it.

He glanced at me. "Thanks, by the way. For being here."

My chest constricted. "Of course."

He looked down shyly, his eyes returning to his son. "I wasn't sure if you'd be too busy. Or…want to be here. With what happened at the shower and then after last night…"

I blew out a breath. "Look, about last night. I know I need to explain—"

"No, it's not that," he said. "I'm not mad that you're dating her. I mean, sure, I was surprised. But mostly I wish you'd felt comfortable talking to me about it. About anything in your life. I feel like I hardly know you anymore, you know?"

He wasn't wrong. Truthfully I'd grown to assume over the years that he didn't care whether I was around or not. He and my parents seemed to make this perfect family unit, and I'd figured he didn't need me. That he probably thought I was making an endless stream of bad decisions, slowly wasting my life.

"You always had everything so together," I said. "It didn't really seem like you needed a big brother. And then when you were older, I didn't want to get in the way."

"You wouldn't have."

I shrugged. "Felt like it sometimes." Though, to be fair, that came more from my parents than it ever had Alec. I'd just assumed he agreed with them.

"If anything, I felt like it was the other way around," he said. "You were off on these great adventures in different countries, following your dream, and it seemed like you didn't want anything to do with me anymore."

"I didn't realize you saw it that way." Now that I thought about it, I could see why he would. In trying to avoid my parents, I had shut out pretty much all of my life from back home. There were a few times I'd remembered to send Alec a postcard from abroad for his birthday or graduation, but I'd never called. Rarely texted or emailed. I hadn't thought he noticed.

"Why do you think I was so excited to surprise you at the gala?" he asked. "I was finally going to get to taste your food."

"You could have just come to the restaurant. I'd have set up a chef's table, done a tasting menu. I would have loved that."

He lifted a shoulder. "You never invited me."

"You never asked."

His mouth tipped up. "I guess we both have room for improvement, huh?"

I chuckled. "Yeah, I guess."

Oliver kicked in his swaddle, the little lumps of his arms and feet moving beneath the blanket before stilling again.

"So, Dani," Alec said, tugging Oliver's cap down where an earlobe had peeked out. "That serious?"

I shifted in my seat and took a deep breath. I guess we were doing this now.

"'Cause it looked serious," he said, sounding way too amused by my discomfort. "Steph and I were standing in the hallway for a good ten seconds before I said anything, and you had no clue."

My eyes fell shut. "Great."

"We could have twerked circles around you, and I still don't think you would have noticed."

I rested my elbows on the arms of the chair and pressed my fingers against my temples. "Point made, thank you."

He gave a quiet laugh. "So? What's the deal?"

I dropped my hands and picked at my thumb. "We haven't really talked about it yet. I don't think either of us knew how to navigate the fact that she's your ex."

His brows pulled together. "What does that matter? It was years ago. I'm married with a kid now."

I shot him a look. "It's awkward, and you know it. Just because you're apparently a saint who has no qualms with it doesn't mean that's how most people would react. Plus, Mom's all protective of you…it seemed like it could get messy."

He tilted his head. "I guess."

"And to be honest," I said, studying my palm so I didn't have to look at him while I said it, "I've always been a little insecure when it came to you. And knowing she'd been with you…a part of me worried I wouldn't be enough to live up to what you two had."

I locked my fingers together, pressing my thumb to the center of my hand, bracing for his response. There came a strange sound, and when I swung my head his way, the tension in my muscles dissolved into confusion.

He was laughing.

Head thrown back, eyes squeezed shut, lips rolled together to keep quiet, full-on laughing.

He lifted his head to catch his breath and caught my

perplexed stare. "Sorry, I'm not laughing at you, it's just—" He gave another soft chuckle. "She *dumped* me. *I* wasn't enough for her. I don't even think she knew why at the time, but as much as it hurt when it happened, she was right. We weren't right for each other long term. And her gut told her that. I would have married her, been oblivious, and never had the life I have now with Steph, and it would have been all wrong, because you can't convince me this isn't where I'm supposed to be."

Affection flooded his eyes as he cast his gaze to where Stephanie slept, then down to his son. It struck me then: this life he'd carved out for himself that so perfectly aligned with my parents' vision—it was the one he genuinely wanted. Not one he'd forced himself into to make them happy, like a part of me had always wondered. A part of me that felt like a failure for not being able to force myself to do the same. And if I couldn't, then I must be a worse son. The one not trying hard enough or not willing to sacrifice as much.

But that wasn't it. It was what he said—this was where he was supposed to be. And all I could feel was relief that his happiness was truly his.

"So as far as I'm concerned," he continued. "If Dani's gut is telling her she should be with you? I don't see any reason you shouldn't trust it too. Unless it's *your* gut telling you it's wrong."

"No," I said right away. For all my doubts and fears, my gut had only ever told me one thing when it came to Dani: not to let her go. Even in the beginning, being with her had felt like waking up and coming alive. Finally.

And what Alec said…I hadn't thought of it that way before. That our differences might mean *I* could give her something *he* lacked, something she needed but he wasn't able to give. That,

like Dr. Ohara had said, my being different from Alec didn't
have to mean I was *less*.

I met his gaze. "It's serious."

He grinned. "Glad to hear it. I really didn't want Gabby
coming to Christmas."

My stomach dropped. "Mom wouldn't."

"She was already talking about it the day after the shower."

I let my head fall against the recliner. "I don't know what
I'm going to do about her."

"It's them, right?" Alec asked.

I raised a brow.

"Mom and Dad are the reason you felt insecure
around me?"

"It's not always past tense," I admitted.

He glanced at Oliver and resumed rocking. "Sorry."

"It's not your fault."

"I saw how they treated you differently. I just didn't think
you cared."

"I tried not to. It's why I left, though. Why I never really
came back. I shouldn't have left *you* behind, though. That's
what I'm sorry for."

He watched his son for a minute, thinking. Then he nodded
and raised his arms out to me. "Want to hold him?"

My pulse sped up. "What?"

"You haven't yet, right?"

"I…are you sure?"

He laughed. "Yeah, I'm sure. You're his uncle."

I swallowed. "Okay."

He stood carefully and walked over to where I sat, then
placed the bundle that was my nephew in my arms.

He weighed almost nothing. A squished little forehead and

cheeks stuck out from the blankets, all red and splotchy. His face reminded me of a potato, to be honest, but I kept that to myself. Potato or not, he was still the greatest thing I'd ever seen.

"Hey, Oliver," I whispered, pulling him in close. "I'm your Uncle Jase."

Chapter Thirty-Five
Dani

The camera panned away from Heidi Klum's solemnly sculpted face to the designer who had just been eliminated. She nodded her acceptance as the other designer left the runway, looking more shocked than she did. The designer who'd been sent home had been *crushing* it for weeks and was a favorite to win the whole season, but this week she'd choked, and like Heidi always said, in fashion, one week you're in, and the next, you're out.

The show cut to the back room where the rest of the contestants waited, and the eliminated designer walked in to say her tearful goodbyes. A moment later, Tim Gunn showed up to escort her back to the sewing room to pack up her things…or so we thought.

"I'm using my Tim Gunn Save…"

"I knew it," I said aloud, sprawled on my couch in a tank top and sleep shorts. I'd been in practically the same position all day, only getting up to occasionally run to the bathroom or get a snack. On any other Monday, I would have been coming home from work right now, and I savored the luxury of being utterly lazy instead. Like playing hooky only better because I'd been ordered to be lazy today, which meant I didn't need to feel guilty about it.

My phone buzzed, and I snatched it off the coffee table, expecting to see a text from Robin demanding I get off my butt and meet her for a drink. I'd been messaging her a play-by-play of all the juicy *Project Runway* drama throughout the day, even though it was years old at this point and honestly not that juicy, but that was part of the fun. It was low stakes. Nothing I had to think too hard about or get too emotionally involved in. Just pretty dresses and petty designers.

But the text wasn't from Robin.

Jase: I heard you drove my brother to the hospital.

My heart lurched. I hadn't expected to hear from him this soon.

Me: I wasn't confident he'd find his way in a cab. He was pretty frazzled.

Jase: Oh, I know. Yesterday he tried to use his gym ID at a vending machine that didn't even accept cards.

I grinned, bubbles erupting in my chest like a can of seltzer that had been shaken. Not at the story itself so much as the fact that Jase was texting me about Alec like it was no big deal. Like he was just Jase's brother and not some inflated

Christmas decoration the size of a house standing between us.

Jase: He's a dad now, btw.

The next message was a picture of Jase sitting in a hospital recliner holding a baby, and I'd never been much of a baby person, but holy shit, was it the cutest thing I'd ever seen.

I asked after everyone's health and sent along my congratulations, a bit of peace settling into the space where my Alec anxiety used to reside.

Jase: I also heard you talked to Jillian. Thank you.

Me: Did she go for it?

Jase: Sort of. I'll tell you about it later.

My stomach fluttered at that last sentence. When he'd said he needed "space," I'd assumed it would look more like it had when he'd avoided me. Limited to no contact. No interaction of any kind. I hadn't expected texting and baby pictures and talking.

Jase: What are you doing?

I told him.

Jase: Not the cooking one?

My lips tugged up. I'd had Jase watch an episode of my favorite professional cooking competition with me a few weeks ago because I was curious what his reaction to it would be—what he'd think of the challenges or whether he'd agree with the judges' critiques. One episode had turned into an entire season, then two. He seemed to like it well enough, but I was pretty sure he mostly kept watching for me.

Me: I decided it wouldn't be as enjoyable without a certain running commentary accompanying it.

Because now the thought of watching it only made me think of him. Any cooking show did. Any food-related thing did, period. I couldn't pour a glass of water without remembering the fancy tap system he'd had installed at Ardena or the way he always cut a fresh lemon for me to put in my glass, and the whole point of this binge-watch had been to distract me from him, not make me ache with longing.

Jase: Want to watch one now?

My smile hurt my cheeks.

We pulled up an episode and texted for the first half until, while the chefs raced through Whole Foods to buy their ingredients for the elimination challenge, my phone rang. I grinned as I brought it to my ear.

"Sarah just screwed herself," Jase said on the other end. "Canned chickpeas instead of cooking them herself? Come on. The judges are going to crucify her."

"I'm sure she has a plan. It could turn out incredible."

"It's gonna turn out a bland pile of mush."

"So what would you have done?"

It went on like that for the rest of the episode. Easy and light. Laughing and fun. I squeezed a throw pillow to my chest the whole time, wishing it was him, grateful I was getting this moment with him anyway.

The episode ended, and neither of us said anything as the credits began to roll. I imagined him on his couch in his apartment, wearing those loose gray pants that rode low on his hips, with Baxter curled up on the cushion beside him.

"I saw my parents today," he said, voice blank, like the memory alone drained him.

"Are you okay?" I asked softly. I wanted to do more. Make it better somehow. Protect him from the pain. But I couldn't control his parents any more than I could control my own, and I'd given up trying to do that a long time ago.

"I'm getting there," he said, and though his voice was quiet, it was also strong. Steady. None of the shakiness that had been there after the baby shower. "I told them about us."

Us.

There was an *us.* I didn't care what his parents thought as long as that stayed true.

"How'd that go?" I asked, trying not to sound too eager.

He made a breathy noise that might have been a laugh. "About as well as I expected. How my mother was upset when Alec was in the same room telling her it didn't bother him will never cease to amaze me."

"What's upset? Like silent judgment or full-blown waterworks?"

"More just her run-of-the-mill 'How could you do this to

your brother? Why would you bring this up today of all days? How is Stephanie supposed to feel? What will my book club think?' Nothing I haven't heard before, really."

"So I shouldn't expect an invite home for Christmas, is what you're saying," I teased.

He let out a deep sigh. "I'm saying I don't think I want to go home for Christmas at all for a while."

I swallowed as his words landed. "Really?"

"You know I used to have panic attacks in high school?" he said. "Then I went abroad, and they stopped. I spent half my time with grown men screaming at me in French and never got so much as a hand tremor. It was only after I came back and tried to force a relationship with my parents on their terms again that I couldn't find the air to breathe. I think maybe the ones I need space from are them."

"Then I'm glad you're taking it," I told him.

"Thanks. And I'm sorry."

"What for?" I asked, my mind blanking.

"This whole needing space in general thing. It was never from *you*. I need you to know that. Just space to sort myself out."

"I do know," I promised. "And never apologize for telling me what you need. I just wish there was something I could do to help."

"You're doing it right now."

I laid my head against the pillow, tracing my finger over the sunburst pattern, and pretended it was his chest.

"Maybe you could come by the restaurant tomorrow night," he said a moment later.

My heart skipped. "Yeah?"

"I owe you a celebratory drink."

I bit my lip to contain my smile, like that might somehow keep the eagerness from my voice. It didn't. "Are you sure? If you need more time—"

"I'm sure. As long as you are."

I didn't even have to think about it.

———

He told me to dress up.

This was probably more along the lines of what I should have been wearing to the restaurant these past three months instead of the business casual attire I wore for work that leaned heavily toward casual, but no one had seemed to care, and I'd been far too comfortable to be concerned.

He'd also told me to arrive late.

I walked through the door to Ardena ten minutes before the kitchen was supposed to close. The timing made sense if I was here for a shift drink to celebrate a successful symposium with the staff—God knew they deserved it. But from the way the host Amelia smiled at me when she saw my dress and immediately gestured for me to follow her, that didn't seem like the plan.

She led me through the near-empty dining room to a table in the back, the only one still set, and pulled out a chair for me. As I sat, my eyes went to the deep pink peony blooming in a small vase before shifting to the bucket of champagne on ice and finally landing on the simple menu card on the napkin.

It was the menu card I had designed for the gala. The one with the meal I'd been dying to eat ever since the first tasting session Jase had done for me.

"I figured you probably didn't have a chance to sit down and eat during the gala."

His deep voice rolled over me, drawing my gaze up to where he stood before the table, two small plates in hand, wearing a crisp white button-down instead of his chef jacket. It was tucked into a pair of black slacks, and my pulse ramped up to a thousand miles per hour as I soaked him in.

"You were right." I hadn't eaten at all that night. Hadn't stopped moving long enough to give myself the chance to think, knowing my thoughts would only lead to Jase, and I never would have made it through the night if I'd let myself go down that winding path.

He set the plates on the table and reached for the champagne. My stare never left his face as he opened the bottle and poured two glasses. If there was ever the slightest chance this was a dream, his face was what I wanted to remember of it.

The cool blue of his eyes that so easily warmed me.

The crease along the side of his mouth that deepened when he smiled.

The furrow in his brow whenever he concentrated, and the scruff along his jaw that brought a shiver to my skin—every piece of him like coming home.

Finally, he took his seat, and we were looking at each other, the rest of the world settling into place before falling away altogether.

"Hi," he said, the flicker of the candlelight dancing in his eyes.

"Hi," I said back, my lips rising.

"You're breathtaking."

My smile deepened. "You're rather impressive yourself."

"Impressing you was the goal."

"You always have."

His lips twitched as he glanced away, and I swore I saw a blush creep into his cheeks.

He cleared his throat. "For a while, I didn't think that was possible. For me to impress you." He flicked his gaze up to mine, then down again. "Not after you'd been with Alec. Been *in love* with him."

I squeezed my napkin in my lap to keep from reaching across the table, craving that connection. For him to be able to feel straight through my skin to my soul and know how I felt about him.

"I was afraid you'd compare me to him and be disappointed," he continued. "But I'm trying this thing where I believe people when they tell me things. Trust what they say over my own self-doubts."

"I did compare you to him," I admitted.

His stare locked with mine.

I took a breath to find the right words. "At first, I mostly noticed your similarities, which was annoying since all I wanted to do was forget he existed and you made that impossible."

He swallowed but held my gaze, his chest rising and falling with deep breaths. I needed him to hear this.

"But the more time I spent with you, the more obvious it became all the ways you're different. And the more I found myself relieved. Not because I wasn't thinking about Alec anymore, but because I finally felt free to be myself."

I hadn't even realized I'd been missing that before. Hadn't noticed how empty my life had been until Jase helped me fill it.

"It was being with you that helped me understand why I broke up with Alec in the first place," I said. "Because being with you was easy in a way that being with him never was." I wouldn't have ever come to that conclusion nine years ago. Never would have classified Alec as anything other than perfect. But that didn't mean he was perfect for me.

I didn't know that Jase was perfect for me either. Perfect wasn't a standard I was aiming for anymore. But I did know all the things I loved about Jase. All the ways I appreciated him. And in all our time together, I'd never once wished any of those things was more like Alec.

"I did love your brother," I said honestly. "But I didn't love myself when I was with him. I didn't *accept* myself when I was with him."

I'd hidden. Like I'd been hiding most of my life, too afraid of the possibility of rejection from my parents or bosses, or anyone else I'd deemed important, to dare show my real self.

Until Jase.

"You make me feel seen like no one has before. You make trusting myself easy. Make being myself the most natural thing in the world." My eyes burned, and I tilted my head to blink away the tears before looking at Jase again. "I'm grateful for what I had with Alec, but never, ever, would I choose it over what I have with you."

"I love you," he said, voice low and thick, the full force of his emotion pouring into the words.

My breath shuddered, and I stood, dropping my napkin on my seat before rounding the table, his eyes soaking me in every step of the way.

He slid back his chair as I reached him, enough that I could settle onto his lap and pull his face to mine.

It was an eager, needy kiss, my mouth hungry for his, determined to make up for the days apart, to show him what no words could ever truly say. I pulled back just enough to say them anyway, my lips brushing his as I did. "I love you."

His lips quirked as they pressed to mine in a lingering kiss, neither of us closing our eyes.

"Let's eat," he whispered, grazing his nose against mine. "We have a lot to celebrate. And I still owe you a dance."

Chapter Thirty-Six
Jase

We walked back to my place. Each step I took with her beside me was lighter than the last, her hand in mine anchoring me to this moment. I took in her every smile and laugh, her flush of arousal as she caught me staring at her with desire I'd long since stopped trying to hide.

Yet we didn't rush. She'd savored every bite of the meal I cooked for her, and I'd savored watching her. Then I'd pulled her to her feet, wrapped her in my arms, and danced with her in the same spot I first kissed her. I kissed her again, and instead of a free fall into the unknown, this kiss was simply freeing. The start of a future instead of the fear of what came next.

Baxter greeted us when we reached my place, walking right up to Dani and rubbing against her legs. She picked him up, brought her forehead to his, and just like that, I was home.

I stepped behind her, running my hands around her waist as she sank against my chest. Her hips tilted ever so slightly back, pressing her ass against my stiffening cock. I grazed my lips up her neck.

"Baxter may love you," I murmured against her ear, "but I love you more."

I felt as much as saw the shiver run through her body. "Are you jealous of your cat?" she teased, tilting her head to the side.

I tugged on her earlobe with my teeth, then sucked on the skin where her neck met her jaw. "In more ways than one. But right now, I'm just greedy for you."

She opened her arms to let Baxter leap down, and my hands were on her breasts before his feet hit the floor. I teased them through the silky material of her dress, drawing a groan from her throat that set my body on fire as I tweaked her nipples to stiff points.

"Get in the bedroom," I whispered as I slipped my fingers under her low neckline, catching each nipple and tugging just hard enough to make her gasp. She took shaky steps as I followed close, my fingers never leaving her skin.

I kicked the door closed behind us to keep Baxter out, then slipped off the thin straps of her dress, letting it glide over her curves to the floor. Her lace panties were next. I wanted to see and feel all of her. Worship her body and make her tremble with pleasure. Fill her with everything I had to give.

The warmth of her skin radiated along my chest as I pressed against her, leaving open-mouthed kisses along her neck while my hands trailed in opposite directions. One found her breast and cupped it gently as the other swept between her legs.

She was soaked. A single brush of her clit had her back arching, her arms clasping behind my head as her ass ground into my aching erection.

"Get naked," she pleaded on a breath. "I want to feel you."

I sank a finger into her. "You will." Her legs buckled as she clenched around me, grip tightening in my hair. "But I want to taste you first."

I guided her to kneel on the edge of the bed and withdrew my finger, circling her clit once before clasping her wrists and lowering them to the mattress so she was on all fours. Then I kissed my way down her spine and sank to my knees on the floor.

Almost as soon as my mouth closed over her, she dropped to her elbows, head falling to clenched fists. Seeing her do it was all it took for my hands to reach for my belt.

Tongue on her clit, I tore open my pants and pushed down the waistband of my boxer briefs to fist my cock. Her breaths quickened, and I gave myself a firm stroke as I worked her with my mouth.

Her tart and musky flavor flooded my tongue, driving my hand to pump faster on my shaft.

I gripped her ass with my free hand, and she rocked back against my face, her body a wave lost in the rhythm of her pleasure, one I couldn't tear my eyes from. She was so fucking beautiful it stole the air from my lungs. I closed my lips over her clit and sucked, just the way she liked.

"Yes." Her gasp turned into a moan. "Jase, *yes*."

I hooked two fingers inside her, crooking them toward her inner walls, and her breath hitched before everything in her spasmed. Her muscles contracted around my fingers, hips rocking in a frenzy, her chest pressing into the bed as she ground herself against my mouth.

Fuck.

My grip on my cock tightened to an almost painful degree

as I held off my own orgasm. When I was sure I had everything under control, I brought both palms to her ass, cupping and squeezing it gently, trailing my fingers lightly over her skin, drawing shivers from her as she caught her breath.

"You better not still be dressed," she said, breathless, before rolling onto her side.

I wiped my bottom lip with my thumb as I rose to my feet. "I'm getting there."

Her gaze lowered to my open slacks, my cock standing at full attention, and a wicked gleam filled her eye. In one graceful move, she rose to sit on the edge of the mattress, her mouth directly in front of my swollen head.

My pulse pounded everywhere, skin growing tight.

She held my gaze as her fingers found the bottom button of my shirt, breath grazing my tip as she spoke.

"I..." She undid one button. "Want." Another button. "This." Her lips brushed in the barest whisper against my cock, sending a tremor through my body. "Off."

She reached the top button and dragged my shirt over my shoulders. Her hands traced my abs up to the hair on my chest, my muscles straining under her touch as her eyes roved my body with a hunger so intense I had to drop my head back to keep from coming.

Then her mouth wrapped around the head of my cock, and my restraint snapped.

I tossed her onto the bed, her laughter tightening my chest with an unfamiliar warmth. I tore my shirt the rest of the way off and kicked my pants and boxer briefs free, grabbing a condom from the bedside table before crawling on top of her and claiming her mouth with mine.

Our bodies connected, skin to skin, and nothing had ever felt so right.

"Now, Jase. Please," she begged, rocking her wetness along my cock.

I kissed her again, stroking her tongue with mine, then rolled the condom on and hooked her legs over my arms, spreading her wide.

In one long stroke, I sank into her, filling her completely. She let out a gasp that had me clenching my muscles, her body so fucking tight around me. This position let me go deep, and I pumped into her with full, steady thrusts, dragging my pelvis against her clit with each rock forward.

Her eyes squeezed shut as her nails dug into my shoulders, making me grunt, my hips snapping faster. My name fell from her lips. "Jase…*Oh God*, Jase."

"Look at me," I said softly.

Her eyes opened and locked with mine, pupils dilated, the whole of her in her gaze. No masks in sight.

"I love you."

I'd always imagined the words being painful to say, like ripping out a piece of me. Maybe because that was what it had always been with anyone else. Others taking pieces of me and trying to mold them into something different until all that was left was a picked-over carcass at the end of a meal.

Not with Dani. Saying it to her felt as good as showing her. Freeing in a way I hadn't known opening myself to another person could be. She wasn't taking anything from me; she was filling me. Lifting me up. Giving me as much of herself and trusting me to hold those pieces safely.

Her breath caught in her throat as her lids lowered, but she kept them open, her gaze never leaving mine as I thrust inside her and gave her every single piece of me there was.

She could have it all. I was safe in her hands.

Her legs tightened over my forearms, and her head tossed back as she tipped over, triggering my own release. I pounded into her, sparks shooting down my spine, spilling from me to her as my every muscle went taut and white heat scorched through my veins.

We stilled, our breaths coming in pants as we clung to each other, sweat beading on our foreheads. I released her legs, and they wrapped around my waist, keeping me inside her as I kissed between her breasts, her chest, her collarbone. I licked the base of her neck. Kissed beneath her jaw.

She trailed her hands up my spine, threading her fingers through my hair. Our eyes met, and a smile touched her lips.

"I love you too," she said.

My chest expanded at the simple truth in her words. Even more so at how every part of me believed them.

WE MADE our way through the hospital, Dani's hand in mine. I gave it a squeeze of encouragement, and her death grip eased slightly as she tossed me a reassuring smile.

She was okay. That was what that smile meant.

And I wanted to wrap her in my arms and kiss her for it because she was here for me.

I'd checked with Alec three times that he and Stephanie were okay with Dani joining me to say goodbye before they headed back to New York. My parents had left late last night, so it would just be the two of them with the baby, and Alec had assured me they were both fine with it. When we'd spoken on the phone earlier this morning, he actually sounded excited.

Probably because I'd never voluntarily brought a girl around before. Gabby was the only one who'd ever met my family, and that was because she'd taken it upon herself to text my mom about my birthday gift one year, and the two of them had coordinated holiday plans after that. It wouldn't have been hard for Alec to figure out I wasn't thrilled about it.

Or maybe he was just happy I was showing up at all. To be honest, I was too. The same clarity that made me realize I no longer wanted to pursue a relationship with my parents made it clear how much I wanted one with Alec. And that I could still have one, regardless of where things stood with my parents. Alec was his own person, and who we were as people and as brothers didn't have to be dictated by them. I could still be a part of his family, and he could be a part of mine.

A family that now included Dani.

More than anything, I wanted her to see there was a place for her in all of this. Not on the outskirts where it might seem less awkward or uncomfortable. Not for my sake.

When we got to Stephanie's room, I rapped my knuckles on the open door. "Knock, knock."

Alec's face lit up as I stepped inside, his baby boy rocking in his arms. "Look, Oliver. It's Uncle Jase!"

Stephanie tossed me a smile from beside the bed where she was packing a bag. "Hi, Jase," she said with a laugh.

Dani stepped in behind me, her grip on my hand tight enough to cut off circulation.

Stephanie's gaze softened, and she walked over to give Dani a hug. "I'm so glad you came. I wanted to thank you for driving Alec here."

"Oh," Dani said as Stephanie pulled away. Her wide eyes flashed to mine, and I fought my grin. "No problem."

"Hon, you can't just go up and hug people," Alec said. "We're trying *not* to scare her off, remember?"

"What? I'm happy she's here. I just gave birth. Blame the hormones."

"We, um, brought breakfast," Dani said, holding up the paper bag filled with bagels we'd grabbed on our way over. We'd gotten ourselves coffees too, but those were long gone. I'd need another before I went into work later. Last night was amazing, but we did not get much sleep.

"*Now* we're talking. Here, Uncle Jase." Alec walked over and placed Oliver in my arms, who stared up at me with wide blue eyes. "Thank you," Alec said sincerely to Dani as he grabbed the food bag from her, then headed for the recliner by the window.

She smiled back, the two seeming mostly at ease with one another, and instead of pinching insecurity, all I felt was glad.

Dani peered over my arm to get a look at the baby. "He's precious." His face was both less red and less squished, and a whisp of nearly invisible hair curled off his forehead.

"You mean he's *quiet*," Alec said as he unwrapped one of the bagels. "Don't worry, it won't last long. You want some of this, hon?"

"Heck, yeah." Stephanie zipped up the last open pocket of her bag and made her way over to sit on Alec's lap. He held up half the bagel for her to take a bite. Three months ago, the sight would have sent a pang of jealousy through me. I glanced at Dani, who was watching them too, and wondered if the same had been true for her.

She shifted her gaze to mine, and I pressed a soft kiss to her lips.

No doubt I still had plenty of jealousy toward my brother to work out, plenty of hidden wounds I'd only begun to heal. But I refused to let Dani be one of them. That was the real reason I'd wanted her here. So she could see I wouldn't let her past hurt our future.

She leaned into the kiss before we both pulled away, a knowing glint in her eye as her mouth curved into a smile.

"You look good with a baby, man," Alec said, mouth half full of bagel.

I shot him a glare. "I swear to God, if you turn into Mom, I *will* stop talking to you."

He laughed, though there was a heaviness to it.

I didn't plan on never talking to my parents again. I wasn't cutting them out of my life entirely. But it was still an end of sorts, at least for now. One that would impact Alec more than I think either of us was willing to focus on just yet.

"I just meant maybe you should consider an official role," he said.

My brows pulled together.

Stephanie smacked his arm. "That was his way of asking if you'd be Oliver's godfather."

My mouth fell open as I stared at Stephanie and Alec across the room. Alec's brows were raised as if asking, *So?* Stephanie's eyes shone with tears.

Dani's hand landed just above my elbow and gave a gentle squeeze.

I looked down at the tiny human in my arms, traces of Alec already noticeable in his chubby features. I wondered how much he'd look like Alec when he was older. How much he'd be like Alec in other ways. If life would come easy for him or if he'd feel like an outsider. If he'd struggle to find his place, to know his worth.

Maybe. But Alec would love him regardless. And so would I. As someone he could turn to when the pressure became too much. Someone he could ask the questions that were too awkward to bring up with his parents. Someone to spoil him with presents and play all the reckless games with. Someone to listen. To offer advice.

I'd get to be a part of this little man's life. Not from the outside looking in.

From right here, in the middle of it all.

Epilogue
Dani

Three Months Later

THE APARTMENT WAS STILL dark despite the sun being up. I'd kept the living room curtains closed, using only the light above the stove to guide me as I flipped a pancake, a satisfying *hiss* gurgling up as the wet batter hit the hot pan.

There was a stillness to Christmas morning that I'd always loved, a quietness before the chaos of gift opening ensued, like a deep breath before a shout, when wonder and anticipation crackled through the air like magic. Even after I'd stopped going home for the holidays, I'd still felt it, faint as it had been. Never more than I did this morning.

I glanced at the Christmas tree in the corner of Jase's apartment—*our* apartment now. It glowed from the multicolored twinkle lights strung through its branches, illuminating the eclectic mix of ornaments on display. There were the crystal icicles Jillian gave us as part holiday, part housewarming gift when I moved in at the start of the month. The blown glass orbs Jase and I had picked out at a holiday craft market. Our DIY attempts at popcorn garland (his contribution) and paper snowflakes (mine).

My graduation tassel was there too, finally the ornament I'd intended it to be.

Robin had run with the idea, setting up a DIY ornament station at the office holiday party. An office I once again worked in four days a week—Fridays, we now had the option to work remotely.

I almost always spent it at Ardena, which had quickly become my favorite spot for brainstorming new HBC fundraisers for the coming year. Nothing on the same scale as the symposium, which Talia and I were already outlining the theme of for next year, but I'd thought up some smaller events I hoped would engage the community as strongly as the virtual panel had.

Not only had we reached our fundraising goal for the clinic —the building plans were officially underway—but our regular donations had seen an uptick as well. People were excited about the work we were doing. They just needed the chance to be a part of it.

HBC still got a steady stream of enraged messages with the occasional hate mail, but not nearly to the level it had been. And Geffery was still around just in case, making plans to be ready for worse when the clinic opened in the fall. I was happy to let him be the one to worry about it.

A groan came from the hallway.

"That smells so good," Jase said as he shuffled into the

kitchen, his voice still scratchy with sleep. He stepped behind me, hands landing on my hips, and dropped a kiss to my shoulder over his long-sleeved shirt I wore.

I leaned into his warmth as I scooped the cooked pancake off the griddle and transferred it to the serving plate beside the stove. "I was going to bring them to you in bed."

"That my Christmas present?" he grumbled beside my ear in a low voice that sent a thrill up my body.

"Only part of it." He loved when I cooked for him, and I loved making him feel loved.

Before I could add more batter to the pan, he switched off the burner and threaded his fingers through mine, wrapping both our arms around my waist. "Come lie with me first."

He didn't have to ask twice.

We snuggled on the couch under a blanket, lying so we could peer at the Christmas tree together, both of us cocooned in the magic of its light. The card Rachel had sent me this year was taped alongside the window between the few others we'd gotten from Colin, Sal, and Frank.

My head rested on Jase's chest, and his hand slipped under my shirt, tracing small circles at the base of my spine above the waistband of my flannel pants. Baxter hopped up to join us, curling himself into the dip at our waists, and the whole cozy bundle was almost enough to lull me back to sleep.

The buzz of Jase's phone broke through the stillness. He shifted beneath me to reach into his pocket.

"Brace yourself," he murmured before answering, but his tone was light.

Alec's face filled the screen, a cacophony of voices, Christmas music, and baby wails coming through the speaker.

"Are you two still in bed? How is that even possible?" he asked over the noise.

I checked the time on Jase's phone. A little after ten.

"First of all, we're on the couch," Jase replied. "And it's called the beauty of not having kids."

"Trust me, Oliver would rather still be asleep too," Alec said. From the dark circles under his eyes, I guessed he felt the same. "It's Mom who had other plans."

"How many photo ops have you been subjected to so far?" Jase asked. "And at any point today, will you have to wear a Santa costume?"

"No, thank God. And not for lack of trying on her part. They were sold out of the one she liked online."

Jase laughed, the crinkles beside his eyes deepening as his head fell back, bringing my own smile to my lips. This lightness between brothers had come more and more easily over the months, and it meant almost as much to me as it did to Jase.

"Did you get our gifts?" I asked Alec. We'd mostly sent toys for Oliver. As his godfather, Jase was determined to spoil him more than anyone, a steep feat considering he was going up against two sets of first-time grandparents.

We'd also thrown in a few small things for Alec and Stephanie—artisan chocolate from a local shop, some body oil I thought Stephanie might enjoy, and gingerbread cookies Jase and I had baked together. He'd done most of the hard work; I'd just cut out the shapes.

"That's actually why I called. We thought we'd open them with you. Let you see Oliver in action."

The video went shaky as Alec walked into another room, the background noise growing louder as he did. I recognized the living room of his parents' house, the same one from the

Christmas party where I'd first laid eyes on Jase all those years ago. I snuggled closer to him, tightening my arm across his stomach. He pressed a kiss to my forehead.

A massive Christmas tree came into view, pristinely decorated with white and red ornaments, that looked like a Pinterest post come to life. Alec sat on the floor in front of it and pointed the phone to face Stephanie beside him, Oliver in her lap.

She lifted Oliver's arms, his snowflake onesie stretching across his round tummy. "Merry Christmas!"

"Is that your brother?"

Jase tensed slightly beneath me at his mother's voice, but his own was steady as he spoke. "Hey, Mom. Merry Christmas."

The video jostled again, and then Mrs. Beauford filled the screen. It was the second time I'd seen her since I'd broken up with Alec, the first being a video call over Thanksgiving. We hadn't spent that with them in person either, choosing instead to join Aubrey and Evan at Evan's dad's house. Despite their protests, he hadn't let Aubrey or Jase do any of the cooking, and it had still been delicious.

Jase's mom gave us the same sullen stare she had then, words clearly on her tongue that she was actively holding back. Jase's hand tensed on my back, and I rubbed mine in circles on his chest. It didn't bother me what his mom thought anymore. Not about me, at least.

Jase had been consistent in his boundaries with his parents, talking with them over the phone a couple of times a month, shutting down the conversation any time it took a turn into unsolicited advice or criticism territory. His parents were trying. I gave them that much. Maybe over time, they'd be able to rebuild in the way Jase had hoped.

For now, it was tense video chats over the holidays.

"Merry Christmas," she finally said. "Do you have plans for the day?"

"I think we're keeping it just the two of us," Jase said, his hand resuming its circles on my back. "Gifts this morning. Dinner later." He glanced at me and mouthed, *"Dancing in between."*

I grinned. Our dancing almost always led to something else entirely unless we were in public. And even then, Jase liked to tempt me.

"Well…that's nice."

"Here, let them see Oliver, Mom."

She handed the phone back to Alec, and we watched Stephanie open the gifts we'd sent as Oliver bobbed adorably in her lap. Sometimes he grabbed for the paper or ran his hand over the toy packaging, but mostly, he was oblivious to what was going on.

By the time they reached the last of Jase's gifts, Oliver was crying, and Stephanie excused herself to go nurse him.

"You two still planning on coming to Jillian's New Year's Eve party?" Jase asked.

The party was serving as the soft opening for Ardena's new division, Arden Catering. It had been Jase's idea in place of his accessible fine-dining restaurant. He said there was more he wanted to do with Ardena, and with Aubrey heading up the catering division, he could do that while still taking full advantage of all the interest they'd generated at the symposium.

Plus, Jillian had agreed to let him feature an accessible menu once a week at Ardena with a significantly lower price point. It would allow a wider range of customers to eat at the restaurant while giving Jase and Jillian more information to work from if they decided to invest fully in the accessible fine-dining concept.

"Yeah. Mom and Dad are going to watch Oliver."

"Will that be your first time leaving him with someone else?" I asked.

Alec sighed. "Yup. I'm both eager for it and dreading it. I think Steph feels the same."

"Your next visit, you can bring him along," Jase said. "I'll cook something just for him."

"Next thing I know, you'll be coming out with a gourmet baby food line."

Jase chuckled. "You think there's a market for that?"

"Diamond pacifiers exist, man," Alec said. "I think anything's fair game."

Jase flashed me his brows. "Should I pitch it to Jillian? Matice Munchies. Practically sells itself."

"When this goes big, I want half the profits," Alec chimed in. "Seeing as I gave you the idea."

Jase scoffed. "Ten percent, max."

My stomach rumbled, and I got up, leaving them to their banter so I could finish cooking the pancakes. A few minutes later, Baxter made his way into the kitchen, rubbing against my legs before crouching at his food bowl. I set the island with two plates and placed the maple syrup out, then mixed some hot cocoa.

Jase made his way over and set his phone on the island just as I finished with the last pancake. He wrapped his arms around me, this time from the front.

"Alec and Stephanie said bye."

I rested my chin on his chest. "Sounded like a good conversation with your brother."

He smiled. "Yeah."

"I'm glad."

"Yeah," he said again, softer, his eyes tracing over my face.

"You okay not being there?" If he'd changed his mind, we could get in my car and be at his parents' in two and a half hours.

He lowered his head and kissed me, his palm cupping the back of my neck as his lips moved tenderly against mine, stealing my breath right out of me.

"I don't want to be anywhere but here," he said as he pulled away. "Do you? We could always plan a trip to Pittsburgh."

But I was already shaking my head. We'd video chatted with my mom a few times too, and it was more than enough for me. Pittsburgh was where I'd grown up, but it wasn't my home. And after all my years of searching, I'd finally found it. We both had.

"This is exactly where I want to be," I told him.

In his arms, in our apartment, with our friends, in this city.

Building our future, whatever it may bring, together every step of the way.

Thank you for reading *Don't Remind Me*! If you enjoyed it, please consider leaving a review. Even a short line or two is a huge help!

Want more of Dani and Jase?

Join my newsletter to receive their bonus epilogue!
(Plus a bonus scene/teaser from Aubrey's POV)

laceyburke.com/dont-remind-me-bonus-epilogue

Acknowledgments

Whew! We made it! It doesn't quite feel real that I've published my first book, but you're reading this, so I guess that means I did.

I started reading the acknowledgments of books somewhere around ten years ago when I decided I wanted to become a published author. Suddenly it mattered to me who all the people were who had contributed to turning one person's idea into a reality.

It's never mattered more to me than it does now that my own book is finally out in the world, something that never would have happened if it weren't for the unflinching support of several people.

First and foremost, I'd like to thank my family as a whole for the way you bolstered me when I lost half of my first draft to my computer crashing (back up your files, y'all!) and through the trying year that followed. I can't tell you what your caring meant to me.

Thank you to my parents for how fully you've supported me since the moment I walked into the kitchen ten years ago and declared I wanted to be a full-time author. You never questioned whether I could do it or pushed me to go a more predictable route.

Thank you to my sister for being my most enthusiastic

cheerleader and the ultimate hype-woman. You remind me to celebrate even the smallest of wins, which I'm all too quick to downplay on my own.

Thank you to Steph for giving feedback on my early drafts and for being my go-to sounding board as I wrestled through edits.

A huge thanks to Andy and Meaghan for always believing this dream was legitimate, even at moments when I had doubts, and for never once in all these years making me feel embarrassed for being an aspiring (and at times struggling) writer.

Thank you also to Donnie and Matt for gifting me a whole-ass computer so I could format my books. I was serious about the baked goods.

Thank you to Hannah, John, Samantha, and Matt for being safe spaces to practice talking about my book. You nudged me outside of my comfort zone in the gentlest of ways with your genuine curiosity.

Lastly but certainly not least, thank you to Howard Rice for guiding me back to writing when I was lost, for feeding my inspiration and belief in myself, and for reminding me of the power stories have.

Here's to the first book of many.

About the Author

Lacey Burke is a contemporary romance author who's lived all over the place but finds herself most often in Vermont. She loves writing relatable characters finding their happily ever afters and all the emotional twists, turns, and climbs that come with them.

www.laceyburke.com
lacey@laceyburke.com

instagram.com/authorlaceyburke
tiktok.com/@authorlaceyburke
pinterest.com/authorlaceyburke
goodreads.com/laceyburke